MAINELY FEAR

MAINELY FEAR

A Goff Langdon Mainely Mystery

MATT COST

Encircle Publications, LLC
Farmington, Maine, U.S.A.

Mainely Fear © 2020 Matt Cost

Paperback ISBN 13: 978-1-64599-096-3
E-book ISBN 13: 978-1-64599-097-0
Kindle ISBN 13: 978-1-64599-098-7

Editor, Encircle Publications: Cynthia Brackett-Vincent
Book design and cover design by Deirdre Wait, High Pines Creative, Inc.
Cover photographs © Getty Images

Published by: Encircle Publications, LLC
PO Box 187
Farmington, ME 04938

Visit: http://encirclepub.com

Sign up for Encircle Publications newsletter and specials
http://eepurl.com/cs8taP

Printed in U.S.A.

Acknowledgments

If you are reading this, I thank you, for without readers, writers would be obsolete.

I am grateful to my mother, Penelope McAlevey, and father, Charles Cost, who have always been my first readers and critics.

Much appreciation to the various friends and relatives who have also read my work and given helpful advice.

I'd like to offer a big hand to my wife, Deborah Harper Cost, and children, Brittany, Pearson, Miranda, and Ryan, who have always had my back.

I'd like to tip my hat to my editor, Michael Sanders, who has worked with me on several novels now, and always makes my writing the best that it can be.

Thank you to Encircle Publications, and the amazing duo of Cynthia Bracket-Vincent and Eddie Vincent for giving me this opportunity to be published. Also, kudos to Deirdre Wait for the fantastic cover art.

And of course, thank you to the Coffee Dog, his namesake bookstore, and the inspiration he provided.

Dedication

*To the Ice Storm of 1998 that knocked power out
for 60% of Maine residents, many for over three weeks.
In true Maine spirit, they helped each other to their feet,
got back to business, and gave inspiration to this novel.*

Chapter 1

The ice storm had already done most of the work. Much of Maine was still without power nine days after the freezing rain had ravaged the state. The thin coating of ice, initially turning the world into a glistening fairyland, had morphed into a deadly menace as tree limbs broke and fell onto power lines, cars, and houses, and wide swathes of the state went dark.

Many people had fled their homes. Hotels were at full capacity. People moved in with family or neighbors with generators, or better yet, left the desolation behind for warmer climates. This presented opportunity for those not bound by laws.

The procedure was simple. Pick an isolated house that seemed without life and park just down the road. Stanley, because he was white, would go knock on the door. If somebody was home, Stanley would ask directions to an address down the street. If nobody proved to be home, however, then the looting could begin.

They took televisions, VCRs, stereos, jewelry—some people had even left money lying around. This night was the team's third in action, with a new element of wanton abandon added. Stanley had found several cans of spray paint and began to graffiti the walls. REDNECKS, PERVERTS, QUEERS, he scrawled, that and worse.

What started as a simple act of vandalism unleashed something in the three boys that couldn't be stopped, and they began smashing china, furniture, mirrors, anything that would break. They took no joy in their actions, rather, there was a grim tightness to their eyes and their maniacal energy was that of beings possessed.

It was in the town of Brunswick that a man came home to find his house trashed, having just missed the vandals by about two minutes. He immediately called 911 and reported having passed a maroon van with out-of-state plates. The one problem with picking isolated homes meant a lack of escape routes, and it didn't take long for the police to locate the van.

The officer flashed his lights, and Maurice stomped down on the accelerator, which, on the still icy roads, proved one mistake too many. The next thing the three boys knew, they were in a ditch, the officer, gun drawn, ordering them to exit the vehicle with their hands on their heads. Maurice was angry. Stanley was terrified. Jamal was relieved.

~ ~ ~ ~ ~

"Langdon. Coffee Dog." Rosie was frantically working the cash register. The diner had been closed for the first three days of the ice storm, but the seven since had been a gold mine. It was hard to beat hot food and heat when there was so little of either to be found anywhere but downtown.

Langdon and his dog walked casually past the line of waiting people and over to an empty booth. They were regulars. Rosie worked hard to ensure that her regulars didn't have to wait. The increased cash flow created by the ice storm was certainly welcomed, but it wouldn't last. Rosie understood the importance of taking care of the people who lived there, ate at her place—and would long after the storm was little more than a bad memory.

The last few years had been bumpy for Goff Langdon given his ongoing separation from his wife, but the one constant had been breakfast every morning at Rosie's. He'd started going there his junior year in high school when he was trying to put on weight for football and had missed very few days over the past thirteen years, though only recently gained the distinction of being a regular. That wasn't bad, given that many old-timers didn't even consider you "from Maine" unless your lineage went back at least three generations.

Langdon was a mass of contradictions. He was a private detective and a bookstore owner. He supported the environment and ate red meat and played football. He voted Independent, sometimes Democrat, and never Republican.

A police officer approached his table when he was most of the way through his bacon, eggs, home fries, and five slices of buttered toast. "You need a shave and a haircut," the cop said.

"Bart," Langdon greeted him. "Sit."

It was true in the best of times that Langdon's hair was wild and unkempt, the dark red mop sprouting in every direction atop his head with little obvious effort to contain it. Shaving, well that happened when it happened, a matter of convenience, and there just weren't that many available time slots for such a banal activity. With the recent power outage rendering even the most mundane daily task unbelievably inconvenient, he now had 12 days of bristle on his face, a patchy mix of yellow, brown, and red shot through with gray posing rather unconvincingly as a beard.

"And have that mutt of yours think I'm moving in on his food? No way, partner. I know better than to get between Coffee Dog and food."

"Suit yourself." Coffee Dog was the gentlest of souls, but if he had one true calling in life, it was to eat ravenously and whenever possible.

"I just stopped in for a cup of joe."

"No donuts?"

Bart started a curt response, thought twice, and decided that donuts might not be such a bad idea. "Thought you might be interested to know we caught those boys who were robbing and vandalizing all those houses."

"Yeah? Boys? How old were they?"

"Old enough to be tried as adults."

Langdon nodded. "How many were there?"

"Three."

"Local kids?"

"Boston."

"Damn creeping urbanization."

Bart nodded his head in agreement and ambled towards the door, or as much as a man seven inches over six feet and weighing in at over 300 pounds could amble.

Once he was gone, Rosie came over with a malicious glint in her eyes. "I need to talk to you about your dog."

"My angel?" Coffee Dog had grown bored waiting for Langdon to give him scraps and had gone in search of easier game. His chin was currently resting on a table between a young couple, his mournful brown eyes imploring them to show just a bit of generosity.

"Had a customer complaint," Rosie said.

"How could that be?" Langdon smiled sweetly. "That would be like complaining about a giggling baby." Coffee Dog had now moved on to an elderly lady who appeared to be not quite finishing all the food on her plate.

"I know, but I have to take a stand somewhere."

"I could see if it would be okay for me to bring him to McDonald's from now on?"

"Goff Langdon!" Rosie cuffed him upside the head with the palm of her hand. "You know perfectly well what I told the customer."

He did know. On more than one occasion when a customer made the mistake of lodging a complaint with Rosie about the dog, her response had never once wavered. "I'm sorry about that," she would say. "Your meal is on me. Don't ever come back."

People from away who didn't know better might start to bluster, but even they caught on when they saw the look on her face. Rosie was only about two inches over five feet tall, but probably weighed close to 200 pounds. When she moved in to stare grumbling customers in the face, they generally recognized the danger and quickly apologized. Most of them chose to stay in the company of the Coffee Dog.

The phone at Langdon's hip vibrated, and he answered the call. It was Jonathan Starling, his bookstore clerk, telling him he had a client waiting for him. Langdon slapped a twenty on the ten-dollar meal and whistled for Coffee Dog. They passed Danny T. on the way out, and Langdon, excited to have a client waiting for him, begged off the sports banter they usually engaged in.

It took Langdon just five minutes to get to the Coffee Dog Bookstore. The shelves were stocked with the best collection of whodunits in the entire state. Langdon was the owner, and under the bookstore name, there was also the inscription: GOFF LANGDON— PRIVATE DETECTIVE. Langdon had split his overriding passion for mystery into these two distinct businesses. The latter one in particular had significantly contributed to his marital difficulties, and had almost cost him his life, yet he refused to step away from being a gumshoe.

"Good morning, boss," the man at the counter said with a grin. He was only about forty years old but looked sixty.

"Star," Langdon said. "How's business?"

"With the electricity out and all, it's like people have discovered reading all over again." There was indeed a crowd of people milling throughout the store. "If you're going to come sauntering in at any time of the day that suits you, then we might have to consider hiring somebody else."

"Or maybe just hire somebody with a little more energy than you," Langdon replied.

"Where else are you going to find somebody with my education to work for next to nothing?" Jonathan Starling had been a successful lawyer before running from his problems and hiding in a bottle of bourbon. Langdon was helping him get back on his feet, and in turn, the man had truly been a godsend in filling the need when Langdon had been laid up.

It was Chabal Daniels, with the help of Jonathan Starling, who'd taken over running the bookstore when Langdon had been in a coma almost two years earlier. Both the bookstore and the private detective business had been booming since Langdon had been shot in the head. He wondered why he hadn't tried it before. Being shot in the head, that is. It was, by far, the best advertisement he'd ever had, and it had cost him nothing except a hole in the head and a slight increase in his insurance rates.

"Is the potential client back in the office?" Langdon asked.

"Yep. Says she had to see you immediately. I told her you were on your way."

"What does she want?"

"Didn't say."

"She local?"

"Don't think so."

"What, then?"

"Nothing, boss. Just go on back and see her, she's been waiting long enough."

Langdon continued on to the back of the bookstore where a door led to his office. Not much more than a hole in the wall, the room had no windows and very little space. That was fine with him, because he could imagine Sam Spade in the same sort of dimly lit office.

As he opened the door, a woman stood and turned to face him. He noticed that she was very attractive, but it was the anguish on her face that grabbed his attention. "Good morning, ma'am."

"Mr. Langdon?" Her eyes carried a palpable distress.

"The very same."

"Mr. Langdon, I have a problem and was hoping you might be able to help me out."

"I'm sorry, but I haven't even gotten your name yet?"

"Latricia. Latricia Jones."

"Would you like a cup of coffee, Ms. Jones?" He was trying to slow down the conversation, as he liked to get a sense of potential clients before making any commitments, a lesson he'd learned the hard way.

"Yes, yes I would." She took a deep breath, and then exhaled. "That would be great. Thank you."

Langdon casually went back into the bookstore and grabbed two cups of coffee from one of the dispensers they kept filled all day long, the beans coming from the Lenin Stop Coffee Shop right across the street. Once back in his office, he handed her a cup and moved around her to his chair behind the desk and motioned that she should sit.

"Now, what seems to be the problem, Ms. Jones?"

"My son was arrested last night for theft, vandalism, and may possibly be charged with hate crimes."

No wonder the lady was jittery. "This happened in Brunswick?"

"Yes."

"How old is your son?"

"Jamal is eighteen, almost nineteen." Tears began to stream down her face. She made no effort to wipe them away or even to acknowledge their existence.

"Did he do it?" This was the moment when most clients got the chance to proclaim their innocence.

With difficulty, she nodded her head. "Yes."

Langdon tried to sort this out. What was he needed for if the crime had been done? It sounded like she needed a lawyer, and not a private detective. "Where are you from, Ms. Jones?"

She leaned forward in her chair. "Massachusetts. We live in Roxbury."

Langdon knew that most people within a thirty-mile radius of Boston would have replied that they were from Boston, especially if they were from Roxbury. Instead, Latricia Jones seemed almost defiantly proud to be from a rougher section of town. "And your son lives with you?"

"My son is doing a postgraduate year at the Molly Esther Chester

Institute in Skowhegan." Latricia Jones stood up, unable to remain in the confines of a chair any longer, and began pacing the small space. "Jamal is boarding there for the year, but he's been home since the second day of the ice storm."

"Your son is an athlete, Ms. Jones?" Langdon knew that MECI, which served as the public school for Skowhegan, took private students from around the state, and boasted that it was one of the best postgraduate programs in the country for students looking to raise their prospects of getting into D1 athletics at four-year colleges.

"He is a basketball player, Mr. Langdon. A very good one."

"Just Langdon will do," he said with a smile. "Where does he want to go to college?"

"He was told by the basketball coach at Boston College that if he could bring up his SAT score by 100 points and strengthen his math skills that he'd get a full scholarship." Latricia spoke as a mother proud of her son for his achievements, and not as the mother of a boy who'd recently been arrested on multiple charges.

"And where is his father?"

"He's out of the picture."

Langdon decided not to follow up on what that meant. "So, you think that your son is guilty of the charges?"

"I think he was put up to the whole business by somebody else. I think another person is using my son, and that Jamal will take the fall for that person. I won't have it. Jamal isn't a bad kid. His actions, what he did… that's just not normal for him." This single Black mother of a star athlete from Roxbury with an iron will and the love only a mother could know stood in the dingy office of a PI in a small coastal Maine town, a single tear running down her right cheek. "Why?"

"Can't you just ask him?" Langdon already knew the reply.

"He would never *rat* on somebody else, not even to save himself. But it's more than that, something deeper, something I can't quite get to with him."

"What?"

"Since before Christmas vacation he's been withdrawn, brooding. That's not like him."

"Isn't that normal teenage boy behavior?"

"We have a very tight relationship, Mr. Langdon." She stopped pacing and fixed her intense dark eyes on his. "It is not an easy thing to bring up a boy all by yourself in Roxbury, and I couldn't have done it without us working together, my son and me. He's always been honest with me."

"Until recently." Langdon clarified.

"Just a few weeks ago he was home for break, and I knew something was up. I wish I'd dragged whatever it was out of him. But now this? Of all times? When he has the world by the tail?"

"The world by the tail?"

"My boy was on the verge of leaving Roxbury behind for a better life. He was going to get a college education and have a shot at playing in the NBA. After eighteen years of steering clear of trouble on the sidewalks of Roxbury, he goes and does this? It doesn't make sense." More tears ran in rivulets down her cheeks, but she made no move to wipe them away.

"What do you want from me, Ms. Jones?"

"I want you to find out who is responsible for ruining his life, and I want them to pay for it."

Chapter 2

For twenty minutes after Latricia Jones had left, Langdon did nothing but stare absently into space. He tipped back in his chair and put his feet up on the desk. This was how he organized his cases, with a period of deep thought followed by stubborn and relentless action. Of course, this usually entailed figuring out how best to get pictures of so-and-so stepping out with his or her illicit lover, as adultery was the mainstay of his business.

After a bit, he sat up and scribbled something on a piece of paper. Then he went back to reflecting. Finally, he wrote down several more things, ripped the paper from the pad and stuffed it in his pocket. He wouldn't refer to what he'd written again, and as a matter of fact, most likely wouldn't see it again until one day he'd reach into his pocket and pull out wadded up mass that had cycled through the washing machine and dryer several times.

He made two calls. The first was to page his friend, Bart, the Brunswick cop he'd seen at the diner earlier. The second call was to Jimmy 4 by Four, his lawyer and good friend.

"Jimmy, if you got a minute, I need to stop by and see you about a case I just picked up."

"I got nothing but time," 4 by Four replied in a careful monotone. He'd had his jaw broken the same time Langdon had been shot in the head. "When works for you?"

Langdon checked the clock on his desk, not quite sure if it was fifteen minutes fast or slow, but fairly certain it was one of those two.

"How does noon sound?"

"Perfect. Lunchtime. You can buy me a meal. How about the Wretched Lobster?"

Langdon emerged from his office to find both Chabal and Starling staring at him with ill-concealed curiosity. Langdon was supposed to be working out with Chabal right then, as a matter of fact, but had called to delay their normal exercise routine to meet the new client. It was obvious that Starling had been filling Chabal in, that there was something different about Latricia Jones, her case more interesting than the normal philandering. Perhaps it was her calm dignity that had piqued his interest—and now Chabal's.

"Spill it, Langdon," Chabal said.

"She's the mother of one of the boys picked up last night for theft and vandalism," Langdon replied, thinking, so much for client confidentiality.

"She thinks her baby prince is innocent?" Starling asked.

"No, she admits he's guilty, but wants to know why he did it."

"Because he's a juvenile delinquent, is my guess," Starling said.

"She claims he's a good boy, and there must be somebody or something behind this out-of-character incident."

A customer came to the counter with a pile of books, what appeared to be the entire John Dunning series, and Langdon observed that *The Bookman's Wake* was one of his favorite mysteries of all time. The woman nodded impatiently, obviously not interested in reviews, small-talk, or conversation. People might be buying more books, but many certainly weren't in a jovial mood.

Once the customer had moved on, Langdon continued, "Her son, Jamal, is doing a post-graduate year and playing basketball at the Molly Esther Chester Institute."

Starling nodded with recognition. He'd spent fifteen years of his life in Madison, the town next to Skowhegan, where MECI was located. "I know the school well."

"Tell me about it," Langdon said.

Starling delved painfully into his clouded memory to pick the right words. His first seven years in Madison had been as a lawyer, while the last eight had been as a broken-down drunk. "It's a wonderful school. It brings a level of education to Skowhegan that the students would never receive in a regular public school, not off the coast anyway."

"What do you mean?" Chabal asked.

"In Brunswick, we're living in the suburbs of civilization. You go to most inland towns and education isn't taken all that seriously. Oh, sure, there are a few college-bound students, but for the most part kids are looking to get a mill job, or maybe at the shoe factory. I guess you'd say most people here aren't so convinced that college is the be-all end-all."

"And MECI has changed that perception?" Langdon asked. He remembered playing the Indians in football, but other than their ability on the gridiron, he hadn't given much thought to the school or the town.

"Oh, completely. Their college program blows other inland towns out of the water. Back when I had my practice, I went in once a year on career day to talk about being a lawyer. They had tons of programs like that." Starling had been an environmental lawyer who'd become radicalized into passive-aggressive protest. And when his actions had led to the death of an innocent man, he dove into the bottle to escape the guilt.

"But?" Langdon asked.

"But what?"

"There are always two sides to the coin. What's the downside?"

Starling rubbed his jaw. "I suppose the negative would be the pressure. Classes are much more intense than, say, Madison. In Madison the teachers aren't trying to change a kid bound for the mill into a kid headed to college. You stay out of trouble and you get your degree. In Skowhegan, there is no free pass."

"I think that's great," Chabal said. "Kids need to learn there are no free rides in life."

"Yeah, I guess," Starling replied. "It's certainly great for the motivated student wanting to better prepare for college, and those that are interested in learning, but awful tough for those who don't give a damn about ancient Roman history, Henry James, calculus, or the sex life of a flower."

"Not much need for Henry James in the mill," Langdon said.

"You got it," Starling said. "Working in the mill is a legacy. If your father works there, then you can most likely get a job there. It's like winning the golden ticket. The pay is good enough so you can buy your toys."

"Toys?" Chabal asked.

"Snowmobile, motorcycle, three-wheeler, guns, whatever floats your boat, including a boat," Starling said.

"So, what you're saying is that on one hand MECI provides a superior education and sends a ton of kids to college…" Langdon began.

"And on the other hand, it creates a bunch of failures," Starling finished for him.

"And what about the post-graduates?" Langdon asked.

Chabal had moved away from the two men to wait on a customer who had been patiently standing at the register.

"The post-grads are mainly athletes looking to strengthen their grades, test scores, or fulfill a credit for a class they failed, maybe more than one, so as to get into college and be allowed to play sports. Generally speaking, there's an athletic scholarship waiting for them. The football and baseball programs are fair, but the basketball team is incredible," Starling said.

"Define incredible." Langdon said.

"It might be the best post-grad program in the country. If you go to MECI to play basketball, well then, there's a good chance you're headed for a top-twenty college, and possibly on to the NBA."

"The best post-graduate basketball program in the United States of America is in central Maine?" Langdon was openly skeptical.

Starling reeled off a list of names Langdon knew, all of them professional basketball players. "All of them went to MECI. Believe me, when you spend as much time in bars as I did up in Madison where high school sports are more like a religion than an activity, well then, you get this stuff drilled into you."

"Okay, okay." Langdon raised his hands in mock surrender. "Tell me more about the downside. How do these post-graduates affect the school?"

Starling drummed his fingers on the counter. "They create tension."

"Tension?"

"Where the downside of the educational aspect is pressure, the downside of the athletic programs overall is tension. What you have in Skowhegan is a population that is ninety-nine percent white. The few ethnic families are assimilated into the cultural norms of the society. All of a sudden you throw in some Black boarding students from the city, places like Boston and New York, and they stick out like a sore thumb."

"And this is a problem in Skowhegan?" Brunswick, with the Naval Air Station and Bowdoin College, was one of the most diverse towns in Maine, which is to say, given the whiteness of the state overall, barely tipping the scale of diversity at all.

"It might be fine if they kept a low profile. It's not like it was twenty years ago. These kids come in with all the attitude it takes to be on the fast track to the NBA, and they're taller, more muscular, and more fit than any of the other students."

"Yeah, I guess that could be a problem," Langdon said.

"Most of these post-grads are male, so who do you think they date?" Starling raised an eyebrow.

"The local white girls?"

"Bingo."

"Educational pressure, athletic, ethnic, *and* sexual tension?" Langdon spoke in a barely audible tone as he processed the information. "Skowhegan must be a boiling cauldron of teenage stress."

"So, where do we begin?" Chabal asked as she rejoined them.

"It would be great, Star, if you could take advantage of any lulls in business to do some research. Find out anything you can about MECI," Langdon said.

"Like, what do you want to know?" Starling asked.

"How about the name of the headmaster, the athletic director, and the basketball coach for starters," Langdon replied. "And whoever is in charge of admissions, heck, get me the name of the janitor."

"Is that all?"

"No, I need to know what qualifications you need to get into the school, how hard it is to get through it, and what it costs to go there."

"What's his name?" Chabal asked.

"Who?"

"The Ringmaster of Barnum and Bailey's circus," Chabal said. "Ah, no, I meant the name of our client."

Langdon barely registered the sarcasm. "Jamal Jones."

"And he's a post-grad basketball player at MECI?" Starling asked. "Where's he from?"

"Roxbury," Langdon replied.

"Okay, I'll see what I can find? Where are you off to?" Starling asked.

"Me and Chabal are going to knock down a quick workout, and then we'll be back to help you with the store and whatnot," Langdon replied.

Langdon, Chabal, and Coffee Dog went down the stairs into the basement of the building that housed the bookshop and rang a buzzer. The Coffee Dog Bookstore was located in a building that had once been a thriving department store along with various other businesses—that is, until Sam Walton had come along to put it *out* of business. A tunnel ran under an alleyway to a building out back. This was once a warehouse for the department store but was now "The Cellar of Fitness." The underpass connecting the two buildings had initially been used to bring product into the department store, but now it allowed Langdon and Chabal to access their health club without going outside.

Chabal had not only taken over the responsibility of running the bookshop while Langdon had recovered from being shot, she had also become his personal trainer on his road to recovery. These workouts had become a part of their daily routine. Now that Langdon was mostly recovered, these sessions acted as therapy for each of them. Among other things, Langdon's marriage was barely clinging to life by a thread, and Chabal's was dissipating at an alarming clip. With the loss of power caused by the ice storm, the gym, being downtown where the power had first been restored, had the added benefit of a hot shower afterwards.

They were buzzed through the door and went off to their respective locker rooms. Once changed, Langdon traversed the tunnel to the workout area, and barked a quick hello to the woman at the counter, a young lady by the name of Jacqueline who everybody called Jax. Coffee Dog ran around the counter in search of food, somehow forgetting he'd already eaten twice that day, and it was not yet ten o'clock. The best Jax could come up with was a rice cake, which the dog ferociously gobbled down.

Chabal was already on a treadmill, having worn her workout gear from home. "About time you got changed," she said. "I've been working out for twenty minutes already."

Langdon started the treadmill next to her and grinned. "No offense, but you could probably use an extra twenty minutes."

"Just because you're a guy doesn't mean you don't have some serious love handles developing there," Chabal retorted.

"Love handles are one thing, but when you get an extra set of cushions on your butt?"

The banter between the two of them was brutal, but all in good humor. Truth be told, there was minimal fat on either one of them. Chabal had been Langdon's workout partner for the past nine months, ever since the start of his rehab program. Recovering from being shot in the head after spending three weeks in a coma hadn't proven easy. It had been slow going at first, and Chabal was the spark that kept him at it.

"Bart had already told me the police arrested three boys robbing a house last night. He figures they're the same ones that did all the other places," Langdon said as they moved from the treadmill over to the free weights.

"How old are they?" Chabal's oldest, Jack, was now twelve and on the verge of rebelling, as all children must. She was terrified she wouldn't know how to deal with it.

"Old enough to know better," he said. They had set up two bench press stations with different weights and were taking turns spotting each other. "Latricia said Jamal is almost nineteen."

"It can be pretty screwy being a kid these days."

"We're not talking about petty mischief here. These boys smashed everything they didn't steal and left nasty graffiti all over the walls to boot."

"Sounds like a lot of anger to me. I wonder why?"

Chapter 3

It was 12:05, making Langdon late for his meeting with Jimmy 4 by Four, but luckily, the Wretched Lobster was only a few doors down. The day was a real corker, the baby blue sky crisp and cold, and the sun glittered fiercely off the ice that coated everything. It was hard to believe that the entire region was in the grip of a deadly crisis, but three-fourths of the state was without power, and days like this only magnified the problems, the melting ice cracking more limbs, toppling trees, and sending already-damaged light poles crashing down to block streets. Add a stiff breeze, and electricity was being lost faster than the crews could restore it.

At the door to the restaurant, Langdon threatened Coffee Dog with an empty bluff to leash him if he wasn't good. He, of course, had no leash with him. Langdon had seen dogs who trotted dutifully alongside their owners and never strayed, but Coffee Dog was not cast from that mold. When Langdon opened the door, the dog went through it like a bullet through a gun barrel. There was a high probability of food scraps lying around just waiting to be gobbled up, and he wasn't going to give some busboy a chance to beat him to the punch.

The hostess, a pretty girl of about twenty-two, smiled weakly at him. "Goff Langdon, you've got to put your dog on a leash if you're going to bring him in here, and even then, he shouldn't be allowed, but if you at least tried?"

Langdon wondered why women always seemed exasperated with

him, including his wife—so much so that she'd left him. It seemed that he was supposed to care about inconsequential things like a leash on a dog, changing a light bulb that had burned out, or taking out the trash when it was overflowing. It wasn't that he was lazy, or didn't care, but rather, he more often than not just did not notice. In the background there was suddenly a crash, most certainly related to Coffee Dog.

"Here I am bringing my dog to clean up your floors—for no charge I might add—and you have the gall to complain?" Langdon shook his head in consternation and walked past her, having spotted 4 by Four at a table.

Coffee Dog had also spotted the man and came zipping across the floor like a brown cannonball. From about five feet away, the Chocolate Labrador went airborne and launched himself into the lawyer, knocking him backwards in the chair and pulling the table over as well.

"Hi, Coffee Dog," 4 by Four said from the floor as his face was being eagerly licked. "I hope you have a good lawyer."

Langdon was picking up the table when the manager came rushing over. He was a thin, nervous man with a tight pinched face. "I thought I told you not to bring that mutt in here ever again."

"Sorry about the ruckus." Langdon raised his hands apologetically. "I just wanted to get some lunch."

"Take that mongrel out of here," the man said.

"I didn't want to have to play this card, Marcel, but you leave me little choice. Must I remind you that you don't own the place?" Langdon raised his eyebrows and cocked his head to the side. "Henry has said that Coffee Dog is welcome anytime." Langdon had done some investigative work for the owner several years earlier, exposing a former manager who had been embezzling money. Ever since, Henry had been eager to show his appreciation of Langdon.

"But I'm the one who *runs* the place." Marcel looked like he might cry he was so mad.

"Don't make me go over your head on this one," Langdon said. He laid his hand on the anxious man's shoulder.

Once the manager had left, cursing under his breath, Langdon helped 4 by Four back to his seat. The waitress came and took their order, and Coffee Dog sat quietly under the table on his best behavior, most likely because Langdon kept dropping soup crackers down to him. Both men were drinking water, neither of them having had a drink of booze since the "Shoot-Out at Fort Andross," as they'd come to call it, when Langdon had been shot in the head and 4 by Four had had his jaw broken by a woman to whome he'd just made love.

4 by Four once had another name, back when he was a big-shot lawyer in New York City. One day the stress got to him, and he packed his belongings and moved to Maine to become a hippie, smoking pot and living off the land. Eventually he had opened a small practice in Brunswick where he worked just enough to make a meager living.

"What's the deal?" 4 by Four asked once order had been restored.

"You know the rash of thefts and vandalism that have been occurring since the power went?" Langdon asked.

"Sure."

"Well, the police have been thinking it's all the same person or persons, you know, because the MO is the same, empty house, broken windows, hardware stolen, and whatnot."

"Yeah, I got all that," 4 by Four said.

"They caught three boys from Massachusetts last night."

"Red-handed?"

"Close enough."

"Where does Goff Langdon, private dick, come into play?" 4 by Four had joined the game of idly dropping soup crackers under the table, which quickly disappeared.

"I was hired by the mother of one of the boys," Langdon said.

"To do what?"

"My client says her son is a good boy. She thinks somebody put him up to this."

"So what? He still did the crime."

"It might go easier on him if we locate a bigger fish for the police to sink their teeth into."

"And your client's son? He won't give up a name?"

"She doubts that he would rat somebody out, you know, the code of the hood," Langdon said.

4 by Four nodded. "I can see that. If you can track down whoever put them up to it, we can probably plea bargain for a lighter sentence."

"That's what I was thinking. And that's where you come into play."

"What's his name?"

"Jamal. Jamal Jones."

The food came, interrupting their conversation. Langdon had ordered a steak bomb and a coffee milk shake while Jimmy had chicken soup.

"You want me to show up and get Jamal out on bail?" 4 by Four asked.

"Yeah, Ms. Jones gave me a retainer that should cover it."

"How about the other two?"

"We're only paying for the one," Langdon said around a mouthful of steak sandwich.

"Good enough," 4 by Four replied. "How are Amanda and Missouri doing?" Amanda was Langdon's wife from whom he'd been separated for the past couple of years, and Missouri was their five-year-old daughter.

"They're down in Atlanta staying with Amanda's parents."

"How are you two doing?" 4 by Four pried into the privacy of Langdon's life with the ease of one who had seen him through all manners of trials and tribulations.

"Peachy." Langdon and Amanda had been working towards repairing their badly damaged marriage, but it was a tough process. Cheating and lying were obvious issues, but the temperature may have been the real crux of the problem.

"Even though she's a thousand miles away?"

"Amanda said she was willing to give Maine winters another chance, but that didn't include ice storms. She said to let her know when it was over, plus she got herself a small gig in a gallery with some of her work down there."

"So, are you two thinking of moving back in together?"

Langdon eyed the lawyer carefully, measuring his reply. "We're both still a little bit worried that living together doesn't give us the room we need. We seem to do better if we create a little breathing space."

"So, you're saying you're happiest together when you're apart?"

Langdon began an angry retort that was meant to include an insult, but paused, reflected, and said, "Yeah, that sounds about right." He didn't mention that it was hard to just call it quits when there was a daughter in the middle.

"Why don't you pay for the bill so we can get over to the police station and see what the deal is." 4 by Four dropped his napkin over his half-finished bowl of soup.

Langdon pulled a twenty to drop down on the twelve-dollar meal. With the last bite of his steak sandwich in hand, he lured Coffee Dog out of the restaurant without further incident. He decided to not give it up until they'd passed over the wide Maine Street, the only one of its kind spelled just like the state. The police station was just across this street and through the municipal parking lot. While 4 by Four checked in with the officer on duty, Langdon slipped into the interior of the station in search of Bart. He found the man in the break room stuffing donuts into his mouth.

"Got a second?" Langdon asked.

Bart chewed steadily without attempting a reply. He did, however, break off a piece of donut and toss it to Coffee Dog.

"You know that arrest you told me about this morning? The three kids? Well, one of them, Jamal Jones, is my latest client."

"The problem with lawyers and private dicks is you get stuck representing scum. You do it long enough, and you're going to become a bottom feeder," Bart said through a mouthful.

"Scum? The poor kid is eighteen."

"Yeah, and he was preying on folks in the middle of a natural disaster. It don't get much lower than that. They're not just stealing, they're sucker-punching people when they're already down."

4 by Four entered the room, hovering by the door. He and Bart had had a running dispute ever since the events at Fort Andross. Bart blamed the lawyer for leading the enemy right into their midst, one Jordan Fitzpatrick. 4 by Four had been unable to defend his actions for almost six months, as his jaw was wired shut, and the verbal abuse heaped upon him by the surly police officer continued to rankle.

"They transferred all three of them down to Cumberland County. I'll have to make an appointment to see him. They're tougher on that sort of thing in Portland."

"Give me a couple of hours," Langdon said. "Bart is going to take me out to the house that got burglarized and vandalized last night."

"The hell I am," Bart retorted. "I'm on duty, and that don't make me your damn personal chauffeur."

"You want to besmirch my client without backing it up? Plus, yes, as an employee of the state, paid with my taxes, in a way, you do work for me."

Bart was still rolling the word 'besmirch' through his head along with several choice curses as they pulled into Kimberly Circle twenty minutes later. It was a quiet middle-class neighborhood close to the ocean, if not on it, but also just minutes from the shopping center known as Cook's Corner. Each house had at least an acre of land and trees separated the dwellings from each other for privacy.

"Nice homes," Langdon said as Bart zigzagged the cruiser around the latest batch of trees and limbs that littered the road. "It looks like most of the people out here have generators." The steady hum of the small engines permeated the air, as did their rank exhaust, and there were some lights on in many of the homes. There were even kids playing in the yards, as if belying the recent natural disaster.

"Too much money out here for these people to be out of power like the rest of us. They probably all got built-in generators and barely noticed the lights flicker," Bart replied.

"You can get a portable generator for a few hundred bucks," Langdon said, not that he had one, but that was mostly because he was too lazy to maintain the damn thing.

Bart pulled carefully into a driveway cordoned off with yellow police ribbon. From the outside it looked like any of the other homes in the neighborhood. "The first four days of the ice storm, I had a total of nine hours off from work. I chose to use that time to sleep. By the time I got done saving people's lives, you couldn't find a generator within a million miles."

Langdon refrained from telling his surly friend that maybe he should have planned ahead. "Why didn't these people have a generator?" He nodded towards the house.

"They did."

"I thought the burglars were only hitting homes that were out of power?"

"He just wasn't home. Name is Bill Martinson. Sent his wife and kids off to visit the grandparents in Connecticut, and had the house to himself. Not much to do, so he went out. Gave the generator a break and went down to Goldilocks Pub to have a few pints. He was probably hoping to score with the missus out of town and all."

"And comes home to find his house in shambles?" Langdon asked.

"Poor guy strikes out at the bar, drives home drunk, and then finds a mess to pick up."

"Tough night." The two of them sat in silence, not yet ready to enter the wreckage that waited within.

"Speaking of wife and kids out of town," Bart said, keeping his eyes pinned on the house. "Are Amanda and Missouri still down south at that art show or whatever it is?"

"Yeah. I need to call her and let her know she can come back. Her house got power back yesterday."

"You must miss them something awful."

"For sure. I'm used to hearing E's little giggle all day. Now I turn around, and she's not there." He called his daughter E instead of Missouri most of the time, probably in reaction to his wife calling her Missy. Langdon looked around. "They park the van right here in the driveway?"

"Probably."

"Did any of the neighbors report seeing or hearing anything?" Langdon opened the car door and got out.

"Nope. It was night and everybody was huddled inside trying to stay warm. Plus, you can't hear anything over the noise of those generators," Bart replied, leading the way up the front door of the house.

"Fingerprints?"

"Don't know yet, but I doubt it. They all had gloves on when they got picked up, and they haven't left any at the previous places."

"So, all you have is circumstantial evidence?" Langdon asked. "You can't even place them in the house. The best you can do is say they were pulled over with stolen property in their possession."

"It was just around the corner from here." Bart wrenched the door open. "They sure enough done it."

"Holy cow," Langdon said. The destruction was terrible. Artwork torn down from walls sprayed with graffiti, lamps smashed, books ripped apart, and cushions shredded. "Why do you think they were so angry?" he asked.

"I don't know, and I don't care." Bart scowled. "Ya know, once you get Jamal off, maybe you should have him over to redecorate your house for you."

"He does have an eye for color, but I don't know if I'm quite into the casual messy look." Langdon knew Bart was outraged and looking to pick a fight, so he decided to float this flippant attitude to put Bart off his game. "Where's Mr. Martinson now?"

"We put him up at the Wayfarer Inn. It'll probably be a few days before we're done in here so that he can come back and start putting things back together." The refrigerator had been emptied of its contents, which were currently splattered all over the walls of the home.

"Seems a little bit angrier than just a bunch of kids messing around," Langdon said.

"That's what I'm telling you. These three are bad apples. Your client was part of this carnage." Bart swept his massive arms around the shocking scene.

Chabal's question from earlier spilled from Langdon's lips. "You could be right. There certainly seems to be a lot of anger tied up in this. I wonder why?"

Chapter 4

"How can you do this?" Latricia Jones asked her only son with all the anguish of a mother at her wits' end. "You have a gift that people see and value so much that they give you a college education, and you just let it go?"

Jamal stared defiantly at his accusers: Langdon, Jimmy 4 by Four, and his mother. They were in a small conference room at the Cumberland County Jail. He didn't so much as blink, his face as impassive as an Easter Island statue. Perhaps, without the two strange men present, he would have shown more compassion to his mom.

"Well, I'm telling you that you now have a tiger by the tail, and it's only going to be a matter of time before it turns around and eats you," Latricia added.

Jamal rolled his eyes.

Latricia went to slap him but pulled her arm back. "You have to help yourself, Jamal, don't you see? Who put you up to this?"

"I told you already," Jamal said patiently. "We came up to Brunswick to see a basketball game at Bowdoin. After the game, we were out walking around and saw a van on the side of the street with the keys in the ignition. On a lark, we jumped in and drove off. We weren't really stealing it, just taking it for a ride. We were going to bring it back, but next thing we knew, there were blue lights flashing behind us and we panicked."

"Who won the game?" Langdon spoke for the first time. It was his intention to befriend the youth, not attack him. Latricia had introduced him, of course, but he'd merely nodded, letting 4 by Four cover some of the legal stuff, and Latricia the mother stuff, knowing the boy must be wondering what Langdon's purpose was.

"What?"

"Who won the game?"

"We, um, left before it was over."

"Who were they playing?"

"Uh, Bates."

"What'd you think of that kid Williams?"

"He, uh, wasn't bad."

He stared at his new client-by-proxy, letting him squirm with what Langdon was sure had been a lie. Jamal was probably six or seven inches over six feet tall. The jail scrubs that had been provided for him were too small, making the pants look almost like Bermuda shorts. His legs and arms were thin. Only in his chest and shoulders had he begun to develop some of the size that his mature frame would eventually carry. Langdon had noticed his awkward grace immediately when he'd entered the room, almost as if he'd be more comfortable running down a basketball court than walking. There was a pencil-thin sketch of a mustache on his upper lip. His eyes were scared.

4 by Four excused himself to begin the process of bailing the young man out.

As the silence deepened, Jamal began to fidget. "You gonna tell me who you are?"

"My name is Goff Langdon."

"I got that already. Don't tell me you're my mother's new boyfriend?"

"I'm a private investigator."

"That don't tell me what you're doing here."

"Your mother hired me to help out."

"What do you mean… help out? You mean break me out? My momma hired some redneck to break me out of jail? I don't think that's necessary. We was just messing around."

Latricia Jones stood up angrily. "That's it. I've had enough of your smart mouth. You want to throw it all away? Go ahead. Find someone else to take care of your sorry ass." She stormed out, leaving behind a deafening silence.

Langdon sat quietly.

Jamal stared at him, begging for a chance to release his stormy emotions in anger.

Langdon gave him no reason to do so. After a few minutes, Jamal's expression turned to fear, confusion, and deep sorrow.

Then, and only then, did Langdon speak, "I'm not going to press you to tell me anything. That, you have to decide for yourself. Your mother hired me to find out who put you up to robbing houses. You want to talk to me about anything, anything at all, here's my card." Langdon stood up just as a guard entered the room and placed handcuffs on Jamal Jones to bring him back to his cell. "And Jamal?" The guard and prisoner stopped at the door. "Bowdoin played Colby on Saturday. I was there. And neither team has a player named Williams."

"Do you have a place to stay?" Langdon asked Latricia when he found her standing forlornly in a corner of the lobby.

She shook her head no.

"I'm sure we can figure something out. First, let's find 4 by Four and see what's going on with getting Jamal out."

Latricia allowed herself to be eased down the hall with Langdon gently holding her elbow. "I'm not so sure we should get him out," she said.

"Jail is no place for a young man," Langdon replied.

"He talks and acts like he needs a whooping. I don't think I can do that no more. Maybe some time behind bars will do that for me."

"Jail doesn't teach you the sorts of things you're talking about. Unless you are hoping that your boy becomes hard and cynical?"

"I don't know what to do with him," Latricia said. "I can't control him. What he needs right now is a father."

4 by Four was waiting for them at the front door. "They haven't set bail yet, won't do that until the day after tomorrow at the earliest. He's going to be charged with breaking and entering, burglary, running from the police, and hate crimes."

Langdon whistled. "The whole nine yards."

"I think they're throwing the whole book at him as an example because the ice storm has everybody a little bit on edge."

"Well, let's get out of here," Langdon said. "Did you manage to get off work?" he asked Latricia.

"My boss at the bank told me to take whatever time I need. She knows about raising a boy in Roxbury, not that she lives there anymore." Latricia spoke quickly in a tone that hinted that she was feeling guilty for having let her son down. "I wish I could have gotten us out of there. I was so close."

"Is there somebody you can call to come up and stay with you? Give you some moral support?" Langdon had little interest in spending his time consoling a bereft mother.

"No."

They managed to get Latricia a room that was fifteen minutes from the jail. Once they helped her carry her one small bag to her room, they went up to the bar on the top floor of the hotel and ordered drinks. 4 by Four had raised his eyebrows when Langdon ordered a rum and Coke, but after a year of abstinence, the sheer uncomfortable nature of the situation suggested that it was a good time to break the ban. After a few seconds of thought, 4 by Four had shrugged and followed suit.

"Is there anything else we can do for you right now?" Langdon asked Latricia.

"Just stay with me for a few minutes, if it's not too much trouble? I know you both have lives to get back to, families, friends, work—whatever," Latricia replied. She was most of the way through the first drink of hard liquor she'd had in eleven years.

"I have nowhere to be," Langdon said. He should have checked in with Starling and Chabal at the store, but it was too late for that now. "My wife and daughter are down south, and my house is dark and cold."

"There's nowhere I'd rather be," 4 by Four added.

Langdon shot him a back-off glance that was soundly ignored. "Is it okay if I ask some questions about Jamal?"

"What do you want to know?" Latricia was staring blankly out the dark window overlooking the city of Portland.

"Just tell me some things about him. What makes him tick?"

"Jamal was eight years old when his father died."

"How did he die?" Langdon asked.

"Sledding."

"Sledding?" 4 by Four blurted out.

"Yeah, go figure, right? We'd taken Jamal out to a hill in the suburbs…"

"Yes, you have to wear your hat," Latricia said to her young son. She was twenty-five, healthy, fit, and beautiful with bright dancing eyes. "It's cold out here, don't you have any sense?"

"If he wants to freeze his ears off, then let him." Devan Jones smiled as he ruffled his son's hair.

"Let's just go, already, the mountain is waiting." Jamal pulled his hat on and started up the hill.

Devan Jones smiled at his wife, a look that lit up his entire face. His face was full of who he was, a happy, fun-loving, and confidant man with a touch of the devil in him. It was this image of him that would remain imprinted on Latricia's mind for the rest of her life.

"One," Devan said.

"Two," Latricia said.

"Three," Jamal said.

"Go," they all yelled. The race was on.

Latricia was content to fall behind and watch her two men vie for the lead. The snow was packed down taking on an icy coating and she dragged her feet to stay in control. Jamal and his dad were neck and neck when a young girl walked out in front of them. Devan Jones swerved to miss her, but never saw the tree until it was too late.

"Jamal didn't see any of it. He kept right on going to the bottom of the hill. By the time… we didn't talk about what happened, not then, not ever. That was the end and the beginning," Latricia said.

The three teetotalers had pounded their second drinks and now ordered a third.

"Sledding," 4 by Four finally said.

"So, you raised Jamal by yourself?" Langdon asked.

"I worked as a clerk in a convenience store for a while, taking classes at night. I kept mornings as our special time. We had breakfast together every single morning until he came up here to MECI."

"And then you got a job with the bank?"

"Yes."

"What would Jamal do after school?" Langdon asked.

"At first he stayed with his Uncle Eddie." Latricia was now staring intently into her glass, as if the mystery of life might lie within. "Eddie was my husband's younger brother and was no account. At first, I thought he was harmless, just another lazy brother hanging out on the streets with no direction."

"But?"

"Gradually I realized he had too much money to be just a loafer. So, when Jamal was eleven, I had it out with Eddie. I told him to stay away from my boy."

"How'd that go down with Jamal?" Langdon asked.

"Not well," Latricia admitted. "It caused our first fight since his daddy died. He told me he didn't have to listen to me, and I told him fine, move out. He blustered a bit, but I made it clear it was my way or the highway." As a tear leaked from her left eye, she excused herself to go to the powder room, swaying slightly under the effect of the alcohol.

Langdon was riding the high that a few drinks gave him, a sense of energy, enthusiasm, and clear thinking. Many more would first dull those edges and then leave him mumbling incoherently, but at the moment he was feeling pretty good.

Latricia's purse was open and a card had fallen to the bar top. Landon went to put it back in, glancing at it as he did, and then paused as he read the front: QUEEN LATRICIA, 15 WARREN STREET, ROXBURY, MA. It would probably be good to have her address, after all, so he slipped the card into his pocket.

"What do you think of her?" he asked.

"I think she's fine," 4 by Four answered. The alcohol was burning in him with intensity.

"I don't mean as a potential mate for you," Langdon retorted.

"My first impression is, she is one tough lady."

"I think I need to get down to Roxbury and look around some, maybe check into this Uncle Eddie character. He sounds like a dude who might know something about boys ripping off houses." Langdon was now chewing the ice cubes that were all that was left of his drink.

"Jamal hasn't spoken with the man since he was eleven."

"Did you always listen to your mother when you were eleven?"

Before 4 by Four could reply, Latricia returned to the table and continued her monologue as if there'd been no interruption. "I knew I couldn't just take a piece of my son's life away without filling the empty spot, so I sent him to a basketball camp. I'd saved some money, thought I might buy a television with it, but this was a better use of the money. Best decision I ever made in my life."

"Is that when he began playing ball?" Langdon asked.

"Oh, he'd been going to the courts down the street and messing around, but this changed him. He was at that crossroads in life, you know, where you can go bad or stay true. It saved him from a life on the streets, or so I thought. If I was going to lose him, I thought it would have been then," Latricia said.

"Did Jamal have a job?"

"He's never worked a day in his life," Latricia said. "I worked so that he could play basketball. It was his ticket out of the ghetto."

"Some of that stuff can be pretty expensive," 4 by Four said.

"His school team was always doing fundraisers, you know, where the boys would get sponsors and get paid for every foul shot made out of 200 or something like that. At first, people in the neighborhood were shocked when he'd make 180 or more, but they never stopped helping, bless their souls."

"You must have sacrificed a lot," Langdon said.

"My purpose was to live for my son."

"How did Jamal take to you dating?" 4 by Four asked.

"I had a date planned with a man from my office for next Friday. It would've been my first time out with a man since Devan died," Latricia replied.

"Eleven years?" 4 by Four widened his eyes.

"Did you and Jamal go out? Take vacations?" Langdon asked.

"Every penny I had went for Jamal to attend basketball camps in the summer. He didn't just go for a week, but for the whole summer. I gambled everything I had, and it worked. He was going to Boston College in the fall. Full scholarship."

"That's the real deal," Langdon said.

"Now it's all gone to shit." A tear slid down her cheek.

"We'll see what we can do." Langdon put down a fifty on the bar tab and stood up.

"Thank you." Latricia looked at him with large sad eyes.

"We should let you get some sleep, Latricia." The rum was starting to push Langdon more towards murky than brilliant. "I'll call you in the morning. If you could put together a list of people for me to talk to, that would be great."

"A list of people?" Latricia asked.

"Yeah, anybody that might have some insight into Jamal. Teachers, coaches, friends, relatives, teammates. I'm going to pay a visit to MECI and then head down to Roxbury once I get a chance and poke around," Langdon said.

"Roxbury?"

"If somebody put Jamal up to this, they are most likely from either where he goes to school or where he lives. I'll be looking into both places."

"Okay, sure. Whatever I can do."

"I might go ahead and stay here, get myself a room," 4 by Four said. "I'm pretty bushed, and I should probably be down at the courthouse first thing in the morning."

It wasn't a bad line, but Langdon knew him too well. "Didn't you say there was nothing to be done until the day after tomorrow?"

"I, uh, think there is a chance of getting him out early," 4 by Four said.

"You're coming with me," Langdon said. "We have places to go and people to see."

4 by Four looked to Latricia Jones to come to his defense, but she merely bid them farewell and went back to staring into her glass. Langdon grasped him by the elbow and guided him over to the elevator.

"Dang it, Langdon, I just wanted a good night's sleep so I could get a bright start on tomorrow," 4 by Four said.

"And I didn't want poor Ms. Jones to get any more of your slobber on her," Langdon replied.

"One of these days I'm going to sock you one."

Langdon laughed. "The last fight you got into, the lady broke your jaw, so excuse me for not exactly quaking in my boots."

They were both quiet as they walked to the car. The night had come in cold and hard. The rawness was enough to take your breath away. The car had not yet warmed up when Langdon pulled into Cumberland Farms. He hopped out and soon returned carrying two large coffees.

"I'll never get to sleep if I drink this," 4 by Four said. They were standing outside letting Coffee Dog stretch his legs and pee in the bushes.

"We've got a long night ahead of us still," Langdon replied.

"What's that supposed to mean?"

"We need to go up to Skowhegan."

"Tonight?" It was a bit less than a two-hour ride in the winter, bypassing Brunswick on the way.

"I was gonna go up first thing in the morning and visit with the headmaster and the basketball coach, and I started thinking it made sense to go up tonight and poke around a bit."

"So how does 'I' turn into 'we'?" 4 by Four asked. "I'm needed down here tomorrow first thing."

"The bail hearing is set for Friday. There's nothing to be done until then. Latricia Jones doesn't need you consoling her. Must I remind you again of the last time you mixed business with pleasure?"

"Yeah," 4 by Four said. "And I think it was worth the broken jaw."

"Whatever, but if you go messing around with Latricia, well then, Jamal won't be all that happy with us, and we do need to gain his trust."

Langdon whistled for Coffee Dog, and they all clambered back into the car. Once on the highway, he opened the convertible up to a steady seventy-five, one hand draped casually on the wheel.

"You want me to drop you at your home on the way by?" Langdon asked.

"Nah, I got nothing better to do than hang out in Hicksville with you. I think I'll live life in the fast lane for a change, although it would be nice if we were working one of those adultery cases of yours where we get to take pictures of cheating spouses."

"Most times I wish I could look away."

"Yeah, but I bet there are some choice ones as well."

"What do you say we grab a few beers for the ride?" Langdon asked as he finished his coffee.

"Sounds good, maybe a couple stogies, too." 4 by Four leaned back and promptly had his hat plucked from his head by the Coffee Dog. "Give that back, you worthless mutt."

Coffee Dog, happily chewing, didn't deign to reply.

Chapter 5

Two beers and one cigar later they came rolling into Skowhegan. "What's the game plan?" 4 by Four asked.

"There's a bar in the center of the town called The Indian. I thought we'd check that out." They crossed over the river and passed a group of young adults stumbling along the sidewalk, indicating the bar was close.

"What for?"

"I was just hoping we could get a handle on what the locals think of MECI."

Wednesday nights turned out to be ladies' night, and The Indian was packed. Heavy metal music blared from the stereo system. Smoke filled the air so densely that it was hard to breathe. Flashing lights illuminated the dance floor, and a writhing mass of flesh gyrated to the thudding music as partners ground their bodies together.

Groups of women sat at isolated tables and were eyed by hungry men working up the alcohol-fueled nerve to approach them for a dance. Men who didn't care to dance sat and smoked and drank while they eyed the women dancing. Some were too scared to speak to a member of the opposite sex, some were waiting for the end of the night to cast their net, while others were there just to fight.

As Langdon and 4 by Four entered the bar, one such man whose girlfriend was apparently dancing a little too intimately with another man, strode out on the dance floor. Without a word of warning he struck the offender in the side of the head and knocked him to the floor. A scuffle ensued, but was quickly broken up by several bouncers, huge beer-bellied men with arms the size of small trees. The girl seemed conflicted as whether to stay and dance with the bleeding man or follow her boyfriend out the door. She chose to follow, whether due to fear of repercussion, to reward him for his warrior manliness, or out of love, it was tough to tell.

4 by Four offered to get them drinks while Langdon secured a table in the far corner of the room. Something about the way Langdon moved made people clear out of his way. It was not an aggressive edge so much as a laid-back confidence in himself.

"You want to dance?" A drunken girl of no more than twenty-one leaned against him as he passed, rubbing her breasts on his arm.

Langdon smiled and shook his head no.

She followed his progress with her eyes, as did the three girls she was with. He was a new face in an all-too-familiar place. When 4 by Four finally made it to the table some minutes later, all four ladies were sitting with Langdon and the waitress had already delivered them all drinks.

"This is my friend Jimmy," Langdon said. "Pam. Jodi. Lisa. Jill." He pointed at each of the young women in turn. "We were talking about MECI. I was just about to ask if any of these young ladies were basketball fans."

"Ooohhh," Jodi said. "I never liked basketball much, but I do love to go to those games and watch those Black boys in those tight clothes. I sit back and let my imagination go wild."

"You are such a naughty girl," Lisa said. "I like my men a bit more mature." She winked at Langdon.

"And white," Pam said.

"That's not true," Lisa said. "I just don't like little boys."

"From what I hear, there isn't anything little about any of those boys," Jodi said. All four women laughed loudly.

"I don't think I could handle something that big," Pam said.

It was all Langdon could do to keep his mouth shut. This, after all, was what he was trying to get a handle on. What was the public perception of Black star athletes in Skowhegan? These young women were giving him an inkling.

"I sure would like to try," Jodi said to more laughter. "I think those Black boys are mighty fine."

"Jodi has always liked dark meat." The speaker was a burly man wavering over the table. He was three inches under six feet, and probably ten pounds over 200. His eyes were cloudy from beer.

"Shut up Ralph," Jill said.

"You probably wouldn't mind some of that soul food either, would you, Jill honey?"

"You're a pig," Pam piped in.

"I'm not the one drooling over some darkie running half-naked up and down a basketball court." Ralph usually ended his nights at the Indian with a fistfight after he struck out with the women.

"There's no need talking like that," 4 by Four said, providing the opportunity. There was a bit of the Lancelot in him, always ready to fight for truth, justice, and chivalry. Unfortunately, he didn't have much to back up his best intentions, so perhaps he was more of a Don Quixote.

"What, you have a thing for those dark boys, too?" Ralph asked.

"Maybe you should just walk away," 4 by Four said.

"How about you make me?"

4 by Four stood up.

Langdon sighed.

Ralph slammed 4 by Four in the jaw. His knees buckled, and he sank back into the chair with a blank look on his face.

"You want some of what your boyfriend just got?" Ralph was staring at Langdon, disappointed that the fight had been so short in duration, but there was something about the careless disregard of Langdon that was concerning him.

"You seem to have some hang-ups over skin color and sexuality," Langdon said.

"What? What's that? I don't got no hang-ups."

"Come on Ralph, let's just go." Jill stood and grabbed him by the arm. Ralph allowed himself to be pulled away from the table. He really wanted no part of Langdon and was happy to have an excuse to walk away.

"I don't know what she sees in him," Jodi said.

"He sucker-punched me." 4 by Four rubbed his jaw.

"He insults you—you stand up—what did you expect? A hug?" Langdon asked.

"I didn't see you being a whole lot of help," 4 by Four said.

Langdon shrugged. "I didn't see much sense in getting in a fight with a drunk guy who doesn't know any better."

"I thought you did just wonderful," Pam said to 4 by Four. She didn't really believe that, but she was lonely, the night was getting late, and this fellow was pretty cute, if not tough. "Come on, let's go dance." Jodi followed the two of them out and began dancing with a man weaving back and forth with a beer bottle.

"We're not really like that, you know," Lisa said to Langdon.

"Like what?" he asked.

"Racist," she said. "The girls have a few drinks and make some jokes. They don't mean anything by it."

"Did you go to MECI?"

"Yep. Graduated almost three years ago. Tried a year of community college but it didn't really take."

"How'd you like the school?"

"Everybody was real nice. A couple of teachers were dicks, you know, but I suppose that's always going to be the case."

"What'd you think of Jerry Peccance?"

"The headmaster?" She wrinkled her nose. "Only the problem students and the real good students had anything to do with him. Jill? She hated him. Of course, she was in trouble just about every week. Me? I was somewhere in the middle and had nothing to do with the dude."

"Did you know any of the athletes? Particularly the Black ones?"

"What's this about?" Lisa went from flirting to wary in a split-second.

Langdon looked her in the eye. "I'm going to level with you. I came up here specifically to find out what it is like for the Black athletes in Skowhegan and at MECI. I got a buddy who lives in Detroit and is thinking of sending his son here to play basketball. He's a bit worried that it's a little too white-bread up here."

"Does that mean too white?" she asked.

Langdon laughed. "Yeah, I think so. I imagine he thinks I'm too white-bread as well. Anyway, I told him I'd swing up and check it out." He shrugged. "I gotta admit that I didn't get a great first impression."

"That's just the booze talking. Ralph might be a racist asshole but most everybody else up here has embraced the program, Black or white."

"That's good to know. I'll pass it along."

"His son will be well protected. He won't be hanging out in a place like this. All those prep school kids get tutors and life coaches. Every move they make is micromanaged. There's no chance any of them will get into trouble."

As far as you know, Langdon thought. The waitress came by and Langdon gave her $50 to cover the drinks. "I need to go and get some shut-eye. Been a long day."

"Staying here in town?"

"I'm going to hit up the motel out on the main drag."

"Want some company?"

He did not need another entanglement in life. After all, he was married, and had a sneaking suspicion that he'd fallen in love with his employee and exercise partner. That, coupled with his precious five-year-old daughter, seemed to be enough women in his life.

"Not tonight," he said. "Can I get you a cab?"

"No need," Lisa replied. She watched as the large red-haired man slid through the dance floor, whispered something in his friend's ear, and then headed out the door.

Chapter 6

Langdon woke with a head that felt like it was about to explode. It wasn't the amount of alcohol consumed, he reasoned, but rather his lack of practice as of late. Like anything else, drinking required a bit of training or else one was faced with unpleasant side effects. What he needed now was water to rehydrate his body. The problem with that plan was that he knew any more than a small sip would make him nauseous.

He'd stayed in a motel on Route 201, just north of Skowhegan. It was three hours past his normal waking time of five a.m. when he stepped into the shower, gradually making it colder until it was almost spitting ice. This partially cleared the cobwebs from his head, and at the same time, reminded him why he'd quit drinking.

From the store across the street he got a donut for himself and five for Coffee Dog, a large cup of coffee, and a quart of orange juice. So much for breakfast being the most important meal of the day. He missed Rosie's Diner. After donuts, the man and dog went for a brisk walk to stretch their legs, but then returned to the room so Langdon could make phone calls.

The first was to catch Chabal at the Cellar of Fitness. "Hi, Jax. Is Chabal still there?" She was. "Hey Chabal, it's Langdon. I'm going to miss our workout this morning." He was already almost an hour late.

"I've been sitting here on my duff waiting for you," Chabal said. "Any special reason? You forgot you had your knitting group this morning?"

"I'm in Skowhegan sort of unexpectedly. Can you tell me what you and Jonathan found out yesterday?" Langdon was alternating between sips of orange juice and coffee, but both were making his stomach queasy. Any progress he'd made on his headache was fast disappearing.

"Why didn't you call me at home?" she asked. "I could have looked at my notes. Now they're down in the locker room."

"I'm afraid of your husband," Langdon said. "He seems to think we are more than just co-workers."

"He likes you just fine."

"Last time we spoke he told me he wished the bullet had killed me."

"That was just a joke."

"Some joke."

"Yeah, you might be right, I don't think he cares for you much."

"Let's not test the waters quite yet." He smiled, Chabal's gentle banter easing the pain in his head.

"Okay, fair enough, where should I start?"

"Did you find out anything about the headmaster?"

"Yeah, his name is Jerry Peccance. He's been there for fourteen years if I remember correctly, and he doesn't look to be leaving any time soon. No police record, but you wouldn't expect the headmaster of a school to have one. That's about all we got on him."

"What about the basketball coach?" Langdon was scribbling notes on the motel stationary. He probably wouldn't refer to them again, but it somehow helped cement the knowledge in his brain to write it down.

"His name is Rick Pious."

"Rick Pious? I know that name. He used to coach college basketball, didn't he? Kentucky or Las Vegas or something like that?"

"We didn't have much time to dig into his past. The store was pretty busy yesterday. We were buried making you money, thank you very much."

"Can you see what you can pull up today? I should be back a little later."

"Sure thing, boss," Chabal said. "But you might check in with Star. He was still at the computer when I went home so my husband and I could ignore each other."

"Okay, I'll do that," Langdon said. He was sorely tempted to ask about her marital difficulties, but he figured it was none of his business and kept quiet.

"You doing okay? You sound a little... froggy this morning."

"4 by Four and I had a few drinks last night."

"Oh." The single word held a question, an accusation, and concern. "Is Jimmy still with you?"

"He went home with some young lass barely out of high school. I have to track him down soon or leave him up here in Skowhegan."

There was a long pause on the line. "And how about you? Do you have some young chick lying in your lap right now?"

"No," Langdon said. "I had to drop her off at school by eight."

Chabal swore at him and hung up the phone.

Langdon laughed. He could curse and banter with Chabal, and it was just as natural as the earth spinning. At the same time, since being shot and with everything that had led up to that, he was completely unable to joke with his own wife. They walked on eggshells around each other. Of course, she had slept with one man and run off to Florida with another before deciding she wanted to return and give it a go with Langdon. He wasn't completely sure that he could forgive her, but he did still love her.

Chabal's husband, John, had been convinced that something was going on between her and Langdon, and at one point, took the kids and moved out, albeit temporarily. A short time later, he'd returned home to try and work things out, and that is where things stood.

As a matter of fact, most people who knew them assumed something was going on between Langdon and Chabal. There was not. At least not physically. Their emotional connection, however, was intense. Was that cheating, Langdon wondered? What actually constituted being unfaithful? A wandering mind? A wandering heart? Or wandering genitals?

Langdon dialed the bookstore. "Star? Langdon. Chabal says you got to digging into some of those MECI names. Whatcha got for me?"

"I've been here all night. I think I've found some pretty interesting stuff." Starling was excited, a hint of youthfulness in his voice masking his exhaustion. "You know how I told you that MECI is a seething bed of tension?"

"Yeah, sure, between the superior Black athletes and the more rigorous academics."

"Nine students over the past ten years have died by suicide," Starling said enthusiastically, not thinking of the young deaths behind the words.

"Nine suicides in Skowhegan?" Langdon asked.

"Nine suicides of students at MECI that were successful."

"That's like one a year. Wow."

"Kids try to kill themselves all the time," Starling said. "But usually they're just trying to garner some attention and not serious about dying. These nine seemed pretty intent on wanting to escape this life."

"How many attempts were there?"

"Don't know."

"Fascinating information," Langdon said, processing what had been said. "Anything else?"

"Only thing of interest is where the name came from. Molly Esther Chester donated some huge sum of money back in 1972 to get the school started. Her husband was some big shot in the mill business. When he died, she spread a lot of money around town."

"Okay. You say you were up all night?"

"I might have put my head down on the counter for a quick nap."

"Why don't you go home and grab some shut-eye when Chabal comes in?"

"I might just do that," Starling said. "Where are you?"

"Me and 4 by Four are up in Skowhegan. He discovered firsthand some of the seething racial tension in town."

"How's that?"

"Oh, some guy made disparaging remarks about Black people, Jimmy took offense, and promptly got punched in the head."

"Seems to be pretty standard for him."

"Sure enough," Langdon said. "After you get some sleep, see if you can find out anything about failed suicides and accidental deaths, would you?"

"Will do, boss. I gotta open the store now."

Langdon hung up and paged 4 by Four with his room phone. He had a cell phone, but it was in the car plugged in. He supposed he should go see if he had any messages on the thing. If he was going to make the trip to the car, well, then, he might as well check out and head over to the school to see what he could dig up.

It was the eleventh day of the ice storm, and the school, a cluster of nine edifices, still had no power. The buildings were dark, cold, and forbidding. Langdon parked behind what he took to be the main office and began to walk around to the front. The Coffee Dog circled him in ever-widening loops, not in a protective fashion, but scrounging for food. Four of the buildings appeared to be dormitories, while the others were for classrooms, and a larger one that must have been the gymnasium.

There was absolutely no sign of life in any of the brick structures. Langdon was about to give it up, when a man emerged from one of the buildings. His head was down, and he was taking short, nervous steps across the iced-over walkway. He wore no hat, leaving his partially bald dome exposed to the freezing morning temperatures.

"Excuse me," Langdon said, stepping in the man's path.

The man jerked his head up, and he slipped and almost fell. "What?"

"Didn't mean to startle you," Langdon said.

"What do you want?" The man was short, no more than five-six, and thin, almost frail.

Langdon's friendly grin faded as he surveyed the bird-like creature in front of him. "I'm looking for the headmaster, Jerry Peccance."

"What for?"

"Are you screening his visitors?"

"He should be in his office," the man said. "I saw him headed that way about fifteen minutes ago."

"And his office would be?" Langdon smiled wholesomely at the tiny man who reminded him of Rumpelstiltskin.

The man waved at the building behind them and then continued on his way.

"Thank you so much for your help," Langdon called after him.

The third door he tried proved to be unlocked. Coffee Dog was happily sniffing in some bushes and most likely wouldn't get in too much trouble outside, so Langdon went in and called out a cautious hello. There was no answer, so he walked down a dark hallway and came to reception desk that was unoccupied. Behind it was a heavy oak door that was slightly ajar with artificial light seeping out.

"Hello," he said louder as he knocked.

"Yes? Come in." The voice was strong and confident.

Langdon pushed open the door and stepped in. A man sat at a desk by the light of a battery-powered lantern. He had papers spread out in front of him and a pen poised in the air above them. He was immaculately dressed, obviously not a person to let something so trivial as an ice storm and its concomitant emergencies affect his lifestyle. He wore a gray suit with a starched-white shirt. The one contradiction to his sober presentation was his tie with Disney characters on it. His head was clean-shaven, but unlike the man earlier, he presented an aura of power that made Langdon think of Kojak, from the old television series.

"Mr. Peccance?"

"The very same. What can I do for you?" Jerry Peccance had well-defined features. His nose was sharp, thin, and pointed. His angular cheeks came to an acute point at his chin, but it was perhaps his eyes that were the most keen-edged.

"I was wondering if I might speak with you about one of your students?"

"Who?"

"Jamal Jones."

"Aha, so that's who you are. What did you say your name was?" Peccance visibly relaxed.

"Langdon. Goff Langdon."

"What school are you a scout for?"

"I'm not a scout, Mr. Peccance."

"Are you a coach?" Suspicion began to leak back into his eyes.

"I'm a private detective, Mr. Peccance."

"Maybe you should be talking to the school lawyer?" Peccance stood up and went over and shoved the door wide open. "I've nothing to say. You are trespassing. I'd like you to leave now."

"What does your lawyer know about Jamal?" Langdon ambled over and sat down on the overstuffed sofa.

"What?" Peccance asked. "I'm sorry, Mr. Langdon, but you've taken me by surprise. Who do you work for?"

"His mother, Latricia Jones, hired me."

"What for?"

"He was arrested yesterday morning in Brunswick for robbing and vandalizing houses." Langdon looked for what reaction this might provoke.

"Did he do it?"

"It looks that way."

"Then what did she hire you for?"

"She thinks somebody else is behind this whole thing, a mystery man who put them up to it, and she thinks it might go easier on Jamal if that person is identified."

"Them?" Peccance asked.

Langdon sighed. Instead of asking questions he seemed to be doing most of the answering. He felt like he was back in high school and had been called into the principal's office for any one of the myriad of offenses he'd so often committed.

"Maurice Jackson and Stanley Krachit were also arrested," Langdon said.

Peccance licked his lips. "I am sorry, Mr. Langdon, but I am sure you know that I am not at liberty to discuss any of my students with you."

"Can you tell me how Jamal was doing in school?" Latricia had not seen his second quarter grades, but his first ones had been excellent.

"I can have his most recent report sent to his mother," Peccance replied.

"Who were his friends?"

"That, I do not know. But I wouldn't say even if I did." Peccance rose to his feet.

"I am trying to help Jamal stay out of jail. We're on the same side, or at least I think we are."

"Don't make me call the police." Peccance motioned to the open doorway next to him. "We don't like private detectives poking into our business here in Skowhegan."

Langdon's cell phone rang. He was happy to have the interruption to buy some time. It was 4 by Four. "Where are you?" Langdon asked as a greeting.

"I've no idea. Did somebody kick me in the head last night?" His voice was bleary and discordant.

"I'll fill you in later. I might need you now. I've just been threatened with arrest for being from away," Langdon said.

"Is that illegal up here?"

"Good thinking," Langdon said, choosing to ignore the unintelligible thought process of his hung-over lawyer. "I will come pick you up, and we'll go file a complaint with the police department." It was, largely, an empty threat.

MAINELY FEAR   51

"I'll go ask the girl in the bedroom where I am. How about I call you back in five minutes? Can you keep from getting arrested for that long?"

Langdon hung up and looked up at Peccance. "I have to leave now and pick up my lawyer. He thinks that there are several legal actions we could pursue, and then there's always the media."

"Perhaps I could be more helpful if Mrs. Jones and Jamal were present? Or at least if I get some sort of consent to speak with you?" His face had turned pasty, and what passed for a smile struggled onto his features.

"Jamal is currently in a jail cell."

"I will contact his parents as soon as service is returned."

"His father is dead, Mr. Peccance. I will have his mother contact you."

"You must understand that I cannot discuss the private affairs of any of my students with a complete stranger." Peccance stretched his hands out to his sides.

"What surprises me is that you have expressed no concern or interest in the welfare of three of your students," Langdon said.

"I am not the boys' father," Peccance said. "My job is to see that they receive a quality education."

"That might prove difficult from prison. Will you be personally tutoring them?"

"There are 979 students at MECI. What is it that you want from me?"

"976," Langdon said under his breath.

"What's that?"

"Tell me, do you wash your hands and move on this quickly every time a student is in serious trouble, like after, say, when one of them dies by suicide?"

There was a long silence, the two men staring at each other without expression. It was Langdon who finally retreated, deciding to leave his last question as an invitation to battle. Peccance knew that he would be back.

When Langdon reached the outside door, Coffee Dog was sitting there waiting, almost as if he'd sensed the tension and come to be of service. Or, perhaps, he was just hoping for another donut.

The phone rang as Langdon climbed into the car. It was 4 by Four with garbled directions to a small house on the outskirts of Skowhegan. He was standing outside waiting when Langdon arrived.

"I think I overstayed my welcome," he said. "She wasn't too happy to find me using her toothbrush."

"Spare me the gory details," Langdon said, jealous of 4 by Four for having brushed his teeth. A workout and a real breakfast would be nice as well. Routines were generally not appreciated until they were interrupted. "I just had an interesting talk with the headmaster of MECI. He seemed fairly antagonistic." Langdon described the conversation to the lawyer in detail.

"He really can't say anything about any of his students to a stranger," 4 by Four pointed out.

"Yeah, I know, but it felt like he was hiding something. Plus, there was a certain lack of any sort of empathy that was disconcerting."

"You can be pretty abrasive at times," 4 by Four said. "He probably felt like you were coming at him. I mean, he's responsible for those kids, even if the school is closed down."

"That's exactly the problem. He didn't ask for any details. He didn't ask if they were okay, or where they were, or even what had happened."

"Yeah, I have to say that's pretty odd."

"Hold on a second." Langdon pulled into a Rite Aid parking lot that had lights shining from inside, its power back on likely due to its location right next to the police station. He came out brushing his teeth with a new Power Ranger toothbrush, went into a phone booth, flipped through the phone book, and then returned, rinsing with bottled water.

"What's up now?" 4 by Four asked once Langdon was settled back in the car.

"I thought we might pay the basketball coach, Rick Pious, a visit. There's only one Pious in the phone book, so it must be him on St. John Street."

"You know where that is?"

"I think I saw it back over by the school."

"What did you say his name was?"

"Rick Pious."

"That's right. Sometime in the middle of the night I woke up and remembered who he is," 4 by Four said. "He used to be the coach at Las Vegas. He had some pretty good teams."

"Las Vegas? Aren't they D1?

"Yep."

"Why would a Division 1 major college basketball coach come to a prep school in the middle-of-nowhere Maine?" Langdon asked.

"I don't know." 4 by Four shrugged. "Maybe he just wanted to get out of the fast lane?"

"Yeah, well he's all the way over in the break down lane now."

"There's St. John Street." 4 by Four pointed to the right.

"We're looking for number nine," Langdon said as he swung the car onto the short neighborhood street. There were only about fifteen houses, all small Cape Cods. There were no signs of life from any of them, the power outage still gripping this street in its icy claws.

They rang the bell of number nine. Langdon thought he saw a shadow flit by one of the windows, but there was no answer. 4 by Four knocked to no avail, and then went over to a window and peered in.

A car pulled in, and a burly man wearing a black wig jumped out. "Hey, get away from there."

"We're just looking for the owner, Mr. Pious," Langdon said. "Is that you?"

"I'm Ed Helot." The burly man with the rug weave on his head stared hard at both of them. "Maybe you should try the door?"

Langdon noticed the man didn't ask who they were, meaning that

Peccance must have told him they were nosing around and sent him over. The front door suddenly opened to reveal a tall, athletic—and very bald—man of about fifty. Langdon idly wondered why so many of the males at MECI were bald, but assumed it most likely resulted from a lifetime of dealing with teenagers.

"I'm Rick Pious. What can I do for you?" This wasn't so much of a question as it was an invitation to rumble.

4 by Four rubbed his jaw nervously where he'd been punched the night before. Sober, he wasn't nearly so brave.

"Hi, I'm Goff Langdon and this is my associate, Jimmy 4 by Four."

"I don't care who you are. I asked what you wanted." Pious made no move to take Langdon's proffered hand.

Langdon felt Ed Helot take a step closer behind him. This was not shaping up to be a very warm welcome. "I've been hired by Latricia Jones, the mother of Jamal Jones, to help her son, who was recently arrested for theft and vandalism."

"Jerry said to tell you we have no comment," Helot said.

"I'm merely trying to help," Langdon said.

"What's to investigate?" Pious asked.

"Jamal was arrested along with Maurice Jackson and Stanley Krachit. They all play basketball for you, don't they, Coach Pious?"

"I have no comment at this time," Pious said. "Let me confer with Ed, here, and Jerry, and I will get back to you."

"If you could just give me ten minutes?" Langdon stepped to the side so that Helot was not directly behind him. "Actually, I'm glad to have both of you here. You're the assistant coach, correct?" he asked turning towards Helot.

"Yep, and I don't like private dicks poking around my neighborhood. Why don't you shove off?"

Langdon assumed the man read mystery novels, or he wouldn't have been using phrases like "private dick" and "shove off." "Coach Helot, these boys are in serious trouble. This is really happening, and the quicker we can get a jump-start on figuring out what's going on, the better for them. The boys are in trouble and need help, and that's all I'm trying to do."

"If we have to, we'll get a warrant," 4 by Four said, demonstrating his natural gift for saying the wrong thing at the wrong time.

"You do that," Helot said.

Langdon's cell phone suddenly rang, making all of them jump. "Langdon here," he said into the phone with an apologetic shrug of his shoulders to the others. He squinted his eyes as he listened. "Are you sure?" He bit his lip. "Okay. Thanks for the information. I'll call you back in a little bit."

"Please leave my porch," Pious said.

"You can tell Mr. Peccance that the number is now ten." Langdon's face was grave.

"What are you talking about? Ten? Ten what?" Pious asked.

"The Molly Esther Chester Institute has now had ten suicides in ten years," Langdon replied. "Stanley Krachit just died by suicide in the Cumberland County Jail."

Chapter 7

Langdon went home expecting the pipes to be broken. He'd been gone for thirty-six hours and that was more than enough time at this temperature to rupture the copper tubing circulating water through his house. The woodstove would do the job for about twelve hours and by hour twenty, freezing and cracking could be expected. He had not expected to be gone so long, nor thought to call anybody to check on the house.

Instead of ruptured piping, he found the lights on and the furnace heating his digs to a cozy seventy degrees. His first thought was joy at the restoration of electricity. His second was that somebody must have turned his furnace on for him once power had returned.

He wondered who that somebody might be, but this curiosity dimmed when the idea of a warm bath came to mind. Langdon had just eased into the steaming water when he heard the front door open and pitter-patter of tiny feet running up the stairs. The door burst open, and his daughter came hurtling through the opening yelling "Daddy" and dived on top of him, oblivious to the fact that she was dressed—and that he was naked.

This was followed by a sharp 'woof' from the bedroom as Coffee Dog became aware that there was a commotion taking place that he was not in the middle of. He came barking loudly into the bathroom. Once he realized that his Missouri was home, and in the tub, he attempted to follow her in, but Langdon fended him off with his foot.

Missouri was five years old, and the best description of her was that she was a firecracker. She ran on adrenalin, was whip-smart and athletic to boot. She had a way of summarizing thoughts in the most efficient manner possible. Langdon believed that certain intelligence is born and not taught, and his daughter had somehow arrived with this gift inherent in her.

When Missouri had been just two, Langdon had taken her to see *Beauty and the Beast* on Broadway. Halfway through the show, the lights came on, and the curtain came down. Missouri had asked if it was all over, and Langdon had stumbled through the explanation that no, it was not over, but a short break for people to stretch their legs, get a snack, and so on. Missouri let him finish his labored spiel, and said, "Oh, you mean intermission."

"Missouri Langdon, get out of the tub this instant." His wife, Amanda, had appeared in the doorway. She was unable to comprehend the thought process that would lead anybody, even a five-year-old, to jump fully clothed into a bathtub. That trait had come from Langdon.

"I missed you, Daddy," Missouri said. She strained her arms to hold him as Amanda plucked her from his grasp. "But I got to go swimming every day, and we went shopping, and I got a new jacket and three new dresses and a Mulan backpack, and we went out to eat every meal."

She was still gabbing away as Langdon climbed out of the tub, feeling uncomfortable standing naked in front of his wife and daughter. He hastily wrapped a towel around his waist without taking time to dry off first, which turned out to be fortuitous, as Coffee Dog shook himself off, soaking Amanda.

"Why don't you slow down and tell me everything while you come help me pick out some clothes to wear," Langdon said, scooping Missouri up in his arms. As an afterthought, he leaned over and kissed his wife.

"Where should I start?" Missouri asked.

"When did you get back?"

Missouri giggled as she ran her teeny fingers through the soapy bubbles in his red chest hair.

"Last night," Amanda said. "Jewell called yesterday morning and told me the power was back at my house."

"I'm sorry," Langdon replied. "I meant to go check on your place yesterday, but I got a new client and got thrown off balance."

"Don't worry about it," Amanda said. "We got in last night and came over to surprise you, but you weren't here. We turned your furnace on. Did you just get home?"

"Yeah. I was down in Portland yesterday afternoon and then headed straight up to Skowhegan on this new case I picked up. You should have called my cell phone." Langdon wondered what happened to 'I missed you and good to see you.'

"I called all night, but there was no answer. And I paged you. Twice," Amanda said, following Langdon and Missouri into the bedroom.

Langdon slid into a pair of boxers, eying his pager where he'd left it on the top of the bureau two days earlier. He figured there were probably a series of missed calls on the cell phone whose messages he always forgot to check. For being a private detective, he wasn't very observant, he thought, and not for the first time. Missouri brought him a pair of jeans from the closet, and he pulled these on, feeling more comfortable now that he was partially dressed.

"The reception in Skowhegan stinks," he said.

"Where are all your shirts?" Missouri asked.

Langdon couldn't but help let his gaze skip to the huge pile of laundry in the center of the bedroom floor. Amanda gave an exasperated sigh and left the room.

"There's been no power," Langdon said, but the only one listening was Missouri.

"This one looks good," Missouri said, picking a random shirt from the pile.

Langdon picked her up in a huge bear hug. "Tell me all about your trip."

Missouri was still chattering away a mile a minute when they descended the stairs with Langdon freshly shaved. They both carried an armload of dirty clothes, Missouri's bundle almost as big as she was. Langdon took them and wedged them into the washing machine, paying no attention to whether they were whites or darks.

"Can Missouri spend the day with you?" Amanda asked as they emerged from the laundry room.

"Of course," Langdon replied.

"Yay," Missouri yelled.

"Come over to my place around six, and I'll make us some dinner," Amanda said.

"Sounds great," Langdon said.

"Okay, then. I've got to run. Bye, honey." Amanda pecked Missouri on the cheek and gave Langdon a quick kiss on the lips. "Don't forget, dinner at six."

"Should we go visit Uncle Star and Chabal at the bookstore?" Langdon asked of his daughter once her mother had left.

Langdon, Missouri, and Coffee Dog climbed into the convertible for the three-minute drive into town. He had recently bought his own home in Park View, a development that abutted the Town Commons. This forty-acre tract of land gave Coffee Dog and Missouri plenty of room to play and explore. For the past couple of years, he'd been living separately from his wife as they tried to reconcile their differences.

Amanda had been waiting for him in the hospital when he came out of the coma almost two years ago and had been quite attentive until he got back on his feet. Langdon couldn't help but think that she might like him better when he needed to be nurtured. As a general rule, being emotionally or physically needy was not a trait that he wanted or needed. Well, perhaps some would think he needed it, Langdon thought, visions of the laundry pile in his bedroom, the luck in no busted pipes, and the previous evening's excessive drinking sliding through his mind.

As Langdon's health had improved, Amanda's mothering seemed more like nagging, and they realized they had very few similar interests. She enjoyed art, opera, wine parties, and long, drawn out dinners. Langdon liked sports, books, 80's rock, beers at happy hour, and pizza. They managed to have sex once a week, but that too had become a chore to be checked off the reconciliation list, rather than a source of intimate pleasure. When did one give up on a marriage, say enough is enough and move on, Langdon wondered?

They passed Bowdoin College, and downtown Brunswick opened up in front of them. Maine Street led from the college to the river and the Green Bridge to Topsham on the far side, the half-mile or so in between filled with small shops and restaurants. On their right was the Mall, a grassy park that now held a skating rink, and in the summer was filled with food vendors and live music. While much of the nation had opted for strip malls and chain stores, Brunswick had managed to retain its character and small-town flavor. The population appreciated this and made efforts to support these businesses, patronizing the locally-owned video store and coffee shops, instead of one of the mega-stores or the Starbucks on the outskirts of town.

The Coffee Dog Bookstore was a product of this environment. While the bookstore did service a niche by carrying the most extensive mystery collection in the state, including backlist titles by excellent but obscure writers, the bulk of its daily revenue came from new titles written by mainstream authors such as John Grisham, James Lee Burke, Walter Mosley, and Dick Francis.

Langdon did not discount these new hardcovers, whereas Barnes and Nobles would be selling them from twenty-five to forty percent off. What his customers lost in cost, he made up to them in personal service. He knew them by name, what they did for work, how old their kids were, and what type of books they liked, offering recommendations. Plus, they got to say hi to the Coffee Dog himself.

"Morning, Chabal," Langdon said as they walked into the store.

"Missouri Langdon," Chabal said, holding her arms out for the girl to spring into. "When'd you get home?"

"I got a new dress," Missouri said.

"I see that," Chabal replied. "It's a beautiful blue."

"It's pink," Missouri said. "Not blue."

"That's funny," Chabal said. "Don't you have nineteen other pink dresses?"

"Why is that funny?" Missouri asked.

"This will be known as her pink phase when she's rich and famous," Langdon said as he went over to a customer standing at the counter. "Hi, Bill. What can I help you with?"

"Hey, Langdon. How you doing today?" Bill asked. He owned a novelty shop across the street.

"Peachy keen. My daughter just got home from a trip."

"I see that," Bill replied. "Hey, I read a mystery a few years ago about a guy named Reckwitz or something like that, and I was wondering if you could help me track down another one in that series?"

"Resnick, Charlie Resnick," Langdon replied.

"Yeah, that's the one. Who is the author?"

"John Harvey. Excellent writer. Which one did you read?"

Langdon led Bill over to the shelf on which the entire John Harvey collection was displayed. He browsed through and settled upon *Cutting Edge*. It was for this reason that Bill would willingly pay the full price for the new Stephen Greenleaf hardcover when it came out. As well, Bill knew that Langdon would shop for Christmas presents in his novelty shop.

Langdon grabbed the store phone and called Bart, idly wondering what he'd done with his cell phone.

"What?" Bart hated to be bothered as a general rule, but especially by the phone, which he saw not as one of the great inventions, but rather as an intrusion into the privacy of his sanctuary. It was a very sorry telemarketer indeed who caught Bart at home.

"It's Langdon."

"I'm busy. What do you want?"

"Busy napping?"

"Tell me what you want before I hang up on you." Bart was sitting at the desk in his apartment with a writing journal in front of him. Not even Langdon knew that this huge, gruff man dabbled with poetry in his spare time.

"Did you hear one of those boys robbing and vandalizing homes killed himself in Cumberland County Jail last night?"

"Serves him right. Punk-ass kid."

"Can you find out the details for me?" Langdon knew that Bart didn't really mean his crass retort, but rather covered up his emotions with crustiness.

"I'll see what I can do. Where are you?"

"Call my cell phone." Langdon figured he'd best find the dang thing. He hung up just in time to see Missouri throw a tennis ball down an aisle with Coffee Dog in hot pursuit. As he leaped to snatch the ball out of mid-air a woman rounded the corner and an ugly collision occurred.

Langdon hurried over with Missouri and Chabal right behind him as the Coffee Dog trotted off proudly with the ball clutched in his mouth.

"What was that?" Latricia Jones asked, flat on her back and puffing.

"That was the Coffee Dog. I'm sorry," Langdon said.

"The namesake himself?"

"The very same."

"And who is this beautiful little girl?" Latricia did not seem to be taking the collision personally as she allowed herself to be helped to her feet.

"My name is Missouri Langdon, and I'm very sorry you got runned over," Missouri said with wide eyes.

"Missouri? What a pretty name. This, then, must be your father?" She was still leaning against Langdon after being helped up.

"Yep."

"You are indeed a very lucky girl," Latricia said, and then turned to Langdon and whispered in his ear. "Can I talk to you in private?"

"Sure," he said. "Missouri, you help out Chabal at the counter. I'll be in back if either of you need me. No more ball in the store."

"Whatever you say, boss," Chabal said with her lips pressed tight together.

"I'm very sorry about my daughter and dog," Langdon said once he'd led Latricia into the back room.

"They were just having fun," she replied. "I need to pay better attention. Actually, it was all pretty funny, especially the look on your little girl's face." Latricia giggled behind her hand. "And where is Mrs. Langdon today?"

"She had some errands to do, but I'm going over to her house tonight for dinner."

"To her house?"

"We're, uh, separated at the moment, but we're trying to work things out."

"That must be tough. How long have you been separated?"

"Um, I guess it's about two years now." As usual, Langdon did not want to talk about himself. "What'd you need to talk to me about?"

"My boss called and desperately needs me to come back and handle a project. I'm the only one who knows what's going on with it."

"You're going back to Roxbury?"

"I should be able to get back here by Saturday at some point."

"What about Jamal?"

"I spoke with Mr. 4 by Four, and he seems to think that it would be appropriate for Jamal to be released into your custody." Latricia stared intently at Langdon. "He said he believes the bail will be set at $1,000." She reached into her purse and pulled out a stack of bills and counted ten one-hundred-dollar bills onto his desk. "And here's another $500 for expenses. Food, maybe some clothes, whatever he needs. I will be back Saturday."

Langdon took the $1,000 and slid it into a drawer on his desk. "Keep the rest. Can we talk about this over lunch? My daughter needs to eat, and I need to ask you a few things before taking custody of your son."

"Sure."

Langdon held open the office door for his client as they stepped back into the bookstore. "Missouri, grab your jacket, let's go get some lunch."

"I'm not hungry." She was busy dusting books with a feather duster.

"You can get an ice cream sundae for dessert if you eat your whole lunch." Langdon was fairly certain she hadn't eaten since breakfast. She dropped the duster where she was and ran to get her coat. Coffee Dog was already leaping excitedly around, for he well knew the word "lunch."

Chabal was looking cross. "I need to speak with you," she said. "I dug up a few things about the school. Plus, Star left a note for you before he headed home to get some sleep."

"I'll stop back after lunch," Langdon said.

In what used to be the old department store, now, along with the bookstore, gym, and connecting tunnels, there was also a small gift shop, a camera store, a massage studio, and several other family-owned practices. Latricia held the front door open for Missouri and Coffee Dog to bound through, she holding his leash, as Langdon called for them to stay away from Maine Street. It was a beautiful day outside, the sun having finally warmed the air above the freezing mark, a brief respite from Maine's harsh winter.

Coffee Dog suddenly froze and whined down deep in his throat, and then bolted pulling the young girl forward and flat on her face as dog and girl skidded across the icy sidewalk. Langdon heeded the warning and stepped forward while at the same time pushing Latricia back into the building.

And then Langdon realized he was on his knees, his head throbbing like he'd been hit with a baseball bat. Coffee Dog was barking now, and this pushed the darkness away as his concern for his daughter's safety lifted. He stumbled forward and found his leg clutched, and looking down, he saw Missouri staring up at him in fear. He picked her up, fiercely holding her tight, as his head swiveled around looking for the danger. Latricia came up behind and gently pushed him further away from the building.

"It was falling ice." Latricia spoke, her words seeming as if from far away, echoing in a cavern.

"Daddy, you're bleeding," Missouri said in a tiny voice.

"It's okay, honey. I'm okay. Just a boo-boo." Langdon put his hand to the back of his head, and it came back sticky with blood.

"I've been saying for a week that that ice up on the roof was an accident just waiting to happen," an elderly woman said. "Does anybody listen to me? No."

They all looked up at the solid sheet of ice on the roof, except for one clear spot just above their heads, the missing chunk—about the size of a five-gallon bucket—now residing on the sidewalk just outside the door.

"Everything is fine," Langdon said. "But I should probably step back inside to get cleaned up."

"They finally got fed up with your dog at the Wretched Lobster?" Chabal asked as they re-entered the store, just as quickly sucking in her breath when she saw the back of his head.

"And I only asked for more ice," Langdon joked.

He went back to his office and stripped off his shirt. There was a small bathroom, and he cleaned the clotting blood from his hair as best he could, which was to say, not very well. Chabal came in and gently cleaned him up with a washcloth.

"Do you have a winter hat?" she asked.

"By the coat hook," he replied.

"Hold this," Chabal said, pressing a wad of paper towel against his head. She retrieved the hat and pulled it over the wound and makeshift bandage, holding it in place. "You probably need stitches."

"'Tis but a scratch," Langdon said in his best Monty Python voice.

"A scratch? Your arm's off," Chabal replied as King Arthur.

"I've had worse," Langdon continued.

"Look, you stupid bastard, you've got no arms left."

Langdon laughed. Chabal always made him feel better. "Come on, let's go see what's going on." He draped his arm around her shoulders, and suddenly felt light-headed again, but in a good way.

Two men were at the counter speaking with Latricia Jones. One was Billy, the maintenance man for the building, and the other was Goldilocks, who owned the pub across the street and was a father figure to Langdon.

"I'm so sorry. Are you okay?" Billy asked.

"I'm fine. But if you get a chance, you might push the rest of the ice off the edge up there, now that it has warmed up." Langdon reluctantly removed his arm from Chabal.

"I'll stay late and do that tonight," Billy said.

"It doesn't look like it made you any uglier," Goldilocks said. "But then again, that would be hard to do."

"What are you doing here?" Langdon asked. "Can you even read?"

Goldilocks shrugged. "One of my middle-of-the-day drinkers came in and said you'd been knocked on your ass by a bit of falling snow. I thought I'd check and make sure you were okay."

"Good as gold," Langdon said.

"How about those stitches?" Chabal asked.

"We'll see about them after lunch," Langdon said.

"So, Jamal should post bail tomorrow, but won't be able to leave the state?" Langdon asked once they'd ordered sandwiches with a grilled cheese for Missouri.

"That's what Mr. 4 by Four says," Latricia replied.

Langdon thought it odd that Latricia was going to leave her only son in the care of a complete stranger and go back to work. But at the same time, he kicked himself, for he was thinking from a place of white privilege, two parents, and money in the bank. He realized that she couldn't take the chance of losing her job over this, because that wouldn't help Jamal out in any way.

"Please, Langdon." Latricia implored him with her large, sad eyes.

"Okay, but what if he doesn't want to stay with me? I have no legal authority to force him to abide by my rules."

"He will do what you say," Latricia said. "Trust me."

"What's the position of MECI?"

"What do you mean?"

"Have they contacted you? Have you let them know what is going on?"

"It hadn't crossed my mind."

"You didn't get a call from the headmaster or basketball coach yesterday or today?" Langdon thought this very odd indeed.

"No." Latricia looked oddly at Langdon. "I expect they haven't heard yet. Why?"

Langdon looked into her dark eyes that were no longer sad, but now shone in anger and determination. "Tell me about Uncle Eddie?"

"There's nothing to tell. He watched Jamal when he was young. I realized he was not the best role model. I ended it."

"Humor me," Langdon said. "He's about my only lead at this point." Langdon had not yet shared with her the strange visit he'd had with the administration and coaches at MECI. He wanted to turn that rotisserie a few more times to try to understand what was behind the stonewalling and closing of ranks.

"I told you Eddie was no-account for most of his childhood. At some point, he must have come into some money because he opened up a nightclub right in the middle of Roxbury that has done pretty well over the past ten years."

"Where'd he get the money?"

"Couldn't tell you."

"But you have some guesses. That's why you won't let Jamal see him."

Latricia put down her napkin, indicating she was done and ready to go.

"I need to speak with Eddie," Langdon said.

She reached into her purse and handed him a business card. One side said "The Glitter Club" with an address underneath, while the other had the name Edward Jones and a phone number. "That is his private number," she said. "Give him a call if you must."

There were just a few odds and ends to tie up, and then Latricia Jones was on her way to Roxbury, leaving Langdon in charge of her son. He'd fought against this responsibility, but she was insistent. Langdon was also left the bill, which was not the way that private detective/client luncheons were supposed to be taken care of, but whatever.

"How about we go see Uncle Bart?" Langdon asked Missouri as they emerged onto the sidewalk.

"I just want to play," she replied.

"How about we get a new Barbie doll to take with us?"

Twenty minutes later, Langdon, Coffee Dog, Missouri, and Flower Blossom Barbie rolled into Bart's driveway. He lived on the second floor of an in-town apartment just off of Maine Street.

Langdon rang the door and settled back to wait patiently. He'd never seen Bart answer the door in less than two minutes. The man didn't like to be bothered, and this was how he weeded out the casual population from the people who really wanted to see him. Finally, the door cracked open, and Bart stuck his head out.

"What do you want?"

"We've come for your women and children," Langdon replied.

"We're monster dragons here to eat you," Missouri said.

"Monster dragons, huh?" Bart curled his lip. "Well, come right in, but look out for the monster dragon traps." If the man had any softness at all, it was for Missouri.

"I'm not scared," Missouri said and pushed the door open with a mighty roar.

She tackled Bart's leg with all the impact of a mosquito against the windshield of a race car. Bart picked her up with one hand and held her against the ceiling while she squealed with laughter. With

Missouri, Bart had even been known to crack the thinnest of smiles.

Langdon and Coffee Dog slid through the opening that Missouri had created and entered into the kitchen. They both got a drink of water. Langdon picked up the afternoon newspaper and found it open to an article about the suicide in the Cumberland County Jail, skimming it in vain for new information. He flipped through to the sports pages where he found a story about the Minnesota Vikings new standout receiver, Randy Moss. He was engrossed in reading this when Bart went to the fridge, pulled out a beer, and finished half of it in one gulp.

"What do you need?" Bart asked.

"Are you and monster dragon done playing?" Langdon was hoping to finish the article on Moss.

"I've been deserted for some girl who calls herself Flower Blossom," Bart said. "I've got to say, though, that Flower Blossom is smoking hot. Where do you go about getting one?"

"You help me out, and I'll get one for you. Hey, maybe we can even do a double date?"

"Ahh, you already got yourself one?"

Langdon laughed. "What'd you find out about the suicide?"

"The kid knew what he was doing. Got up in the middle of the night and went into the bathroom area in the corner of the cell. Tied a sheet up around a pipe, stood on the toilet, then placed a plastic band over his head held in place by a rubber band, and put the noose around his neck."

"He wasn't messing around," Langdon said, shaking his head. "Then he just stepped off?"

"Then he just stepped off."

"Nobody heard anything?"

"They think he'd been dead for about an hour when one of his cellmates went to take a crap and found him dangling by the toilet."

"Whew. That'll give you nightmares."

"What I want to know is, did the guy take a crap first and then raise the alarm, or did he raise the alarm and then realize he had to hold it?" Bart asked.

"Are you keeping a better eye on the other two?" Langdon asked. "We don't need any repeat performances."

"What's this 'you' stuff?"

"You know, the brotherhood of law enforcement, and all that."

"Those guards down at Cumberland ain't exactly real cops," Bart said.

"I just want to be sure that Jamal and Maurice are safe."

"Place is overcrowded, anyway. One or two less won't barely be noticed."

"That's why I'm going to do my part and help out," Langdon said.

"How so?"

"Goff Langdon's boarding home for wayward souls."

Bart stared at him. "You're not going to take those two hoodlums into your home, are you? Tell me no."

"Just Jamal."

"Why the fuck would you do that?"

Langdon shrugged. "Mom has to work."

"And you don't think it odd that she can't get a couple days off when her reason for living is in the middle of a shit storm?"

"I imagine she can't lose her job, being a single mother and the only breadwinner in the household," Langdon said.

"Okay, okay, let's move on. What happened to your face?"

"Falling ice."

"Yeah, whatever," Bart replied. "Usually people use the line that they fell in the shower or down the stairs. Give me the real skinny. Is Amanda beating you?"

"You gotta admit it was a unique cover." Langdon grinned. "But it's the truth. I was coming out of the bookshop a few hours ago, and a big chunk of ice slid off the roof and landed on my head. You mind if I make a quick call?"

Bart nodded him towards the phone, but Langdon pulled his cell from the clip on his belt and dialed the bookstore. "Hey, we need to get together and talk about what you know," he said abruptly, interrupting Chabal's greeting.

"I know bunches," she replied. "Including the lascivious thoughts tumbling around in my head right now."

Over the past year their flirtations and crude sexual innuendos had steadily increased. Langdon compared it to those growth years approaching teenagerhood when sexual impulses start to control the body, but the mind has no way of knowing how to act on these raging hormones, and instead, replaces it with something else.

"I was thinking about the Jamal Jones case, but I can take a few moments to hear your dirty thoughts. How about over dinner?" Langdon had the fleeting thought that he was missing something. "You want to meet me, Missouri, Star, and Bart at Goldilocks after you close up? Say, six o'clock?" Langdon raised an eyebrow at Bart, knowing the man would be in, because the golden word—*food*—had been included.

"Sounds good," Chabal replied.

"Maybe just a preview first? Does it include whipped cream?"

Chabal hung up the phone.

"You're going to get sued for sexual harassment talking to your employees like that," Bart said.

"Me?" Langdon widened his eyes in disbelief. "You should hear the mouth on that lady. Enough to make even you blush, I bet."

Chapter 8

At six on the dot, Langdon, Missouri, Bart, and Coffee Dog walked down the stairs and into Goldilocks Bar. The pub-style food wasn't bad, the ambience wasn't too preppy, the drinks were cold, and the owner was a friend. Coffee Dog got right to work cleaning up food scraps and spilled popcorn while Missouri dropped her jacket and headed for the pool table. Langdon secured a table in the corner, and Bart got himself a pitcher of beer. As far as he knew, Langdon hadn't had a drink in a year, Starling was a recovering alcoholic, and Chabal wasn't much of a drinker to begin with, which all just meant more for Bart.

"I need balls," Missouri yelled.

Goldilocks, the proprietor for whom the bar was named, went over with the key and released the pool balls for her to play with. "Don't you be scuffing the table with that cue," he said.

It was a useless request, as Missouri, playing with the short stick used for tight corners, played an aggressive game, more like hockey than billiards.

"Can we get a menu and some service?" Langdon called from the table.

Goldilocks yelled a curse over at him, but then immediately apologized for doing so in front of Missouri. He walked over to the table. "Excuse me, sir, but this is a bar. There are no dogs or children allowed in here."

"What? Why's that?" Langdon chuckled. "My dog is better

behaved than most of these guys." He waved his hand in the general direction of the five or six people at the bar, several of whom nodded their agreement. "And my daughter is the best pool player here."

"Okay, okay, the kid and the dog can stay. But how about the big, ugly guy?" Goldilocks nodded his head at Bart, who merely growled at him.

"Tequila, two of them, straight up," Chabal said, as she and Starling entered the pub, along with Billy the maintenance man in tow.

"So, two iced teas with lemon? Anything for you, Billy?" Goldilocks asked.

Billy shook his head no.

"Billy can't stay, said he had to get home to his wife, but he's got something to tell Langdon," Chabal said.

"Yeah? What's that?" Langdon asked.

Billy cleared his throat and nervously shifted his feet. "I went up on the roof to see what it was gonna take to clean the ice off, you know, like I told you I would?"

Langdon nodded, his mind wandering to what news Chabal and Starling might have for him, and what he should be ordering Missouri for dinner.

"And I noticed that somebody had already been up there," Billy said.

"What?" Langdon brought his attention back to the maintenance man.

"There was a set of footprints from the fire escape over to the edge," Billy said. "Right above the front door. It was all mashed down there, like maybe the person was there for a bit, waiting."

"What are you saying?" Langdon asked.

"Somebody tried to kill you." Chabal's eyes were tight, hard and angry.

Bart snorted. "Yeah, right. Murder by having snow pushed on your head."

"Look at him," Chabal said, pointing at Langdon's forehead where scratches streaked down from his hairline.

"I try not to," Bart replied.

"It was a warning," Langdon said. "A not so gentle recommendation to back off."

"Back off what?" Starling asked.

"It could have been a threat from one of my bookstore competitors, but I think it more likely that it must have to do with the case I'm working on, the *only* case I'm working on," Langdon said.

"Imagine if that ice had landed on Missouri," Chabal said.

"Yeah, Coffee Dog is the real hero here." Langdon bent over to ruffle the dog's head.

"It could be somebody with revenge on their mind," Bart said. "Some housewife you took photos of doing the nasty with the mailman?"

"This was pretty cold-blooded for a jilted spouse," Starling said. "I mean, think about it. Somebody sat up there in the cold waiting, and what's more, they must have had somebody across the street signaling that you were coming out the door."

"Of course, somebody could have been on the roof for some other purpose, not even necessarily today. The sun warms the ice, and it slides off the roof and lands on Langdon. Nothing more than bad luck," Bart said.

"Yeah, I've had plenty of that lately," Langdon said. "Don't run into anybody," he said to Missouri, who was running around the bar with a handful of popcorn, dropping a piece every few feet. Coffee Dog was in hot pursuit, unable to catch up as he had to keep stopping to snatch the treat from the floor. This leveled the playing field and kept the game exciting.

The rest of Langdon's merry band placed orders without having to look at the menu. Jimmy 4 by Four and Richam had shown up together, and suddenly it was like old times, back before the fallout from the sheer violence that had ended the nuclear power case which had splintered the solidarity of their friendships, with no small amount of blame falling on certain heads for endangering others' children. Richam was the bartender at the Wretched Lobster and father to Missouri's best friend.

Chabal was catching Richam up on what had happened most recently and the latest theory from the maintenance man. Billy had stayed for a cocktail and was now at the bar telling Goldilocks how he'd single-handedly uncovered a plot by terrorists to kill Langdon. 4 by Four and Bart seemed to be rekindling a friendship that had been on ice for some time.

This group hadn't been all together since that shoot-out at Fort Andross. The eco-terrorist's escape, the deaths, the traumatized children, Langdon's coma and the subsequent trial—all this had stretched the boundaries of their friendship to the breaking point, and all of them had spent the past year doing some sort of soul searching. Now, another case of Langdon's seemed to be pulling them back together, melding them again into a cohesive unit. The food came out, and there was a moment of silence as they dove into the meal.

Goldilocks, along with the rest of the downtown area, had only lost power for a couple of days. According to the television, almost all of Brunswick had now gotten power back. The last holdouts were the more rural areas. It seemed that they all had survived the crisis, and now the people and the state were busy putting their lives, homes, roads, and businesses back together.

Richam suddenly looked up at Langdon, who was sitting back in his chair surveying his friends with a smile on his bloodied face. "I thought my wife said you were supposed to have dinner with Amanda tonight?"

All conversation stopped, forks pausing in midair as all heads swiveled to stare at Langdon.

"Shoot," Langdon replied, his grin supplanted by a scowl. "You're right. I forgot all about that."

"I'll gather Missouri and get her to eat something," Chabal said.

"Good luck with that." Langdon pulled his cell phone from the holster at his belt and punched in the numbers.

Missouri, hands empty of popcorn, came over to the table. "Chabal, can I sit with you while I eat?"

"Somebody's about to get an ass chewing," Bart said.

"And in person," 4 by Four said, nodding to the bottom of the stairs from which Amanda was emerging.

"Hi," Langdon said as she approached, hanging up and setting his phone down on the table.

"Hi," Amanda said, surveying the collection of friends. "Calling anybody in particular?"

"Mommy, you made it," Missouri said around a mouthful of chicken fingers.

"Hi, little Missy," Amanda said, casting a quick smile at her daughter.

"Funny you should ask," Langdon said. "I was just calling to see if you wanted to meet us here for dinner?"

Amanda eyed the half-eaten food littering the table. "Seems like I'm a bit late?"

"I, uh, I'm sorry, but there was an incident today, and I called in the village elders to consult me on my latest case. One thing led to another, and then all of a sudden we were eating."

Everybody had become rather intent upon their food.

"Incident?" Amanda asked.

"Somebody tried to kill me." Langdon thought this might buy him some leniency.

"They failed?" Amanda asked.

"They didn't take into account my thick skull," Langdon said. "But it might have caused a brief memory loss, you know, about our dinner plans and all."

Amanda looked at his scratched face. "Did somebody throw a cat at you?"

"No, it was falling ice." Langdon was not sure which one sounded more far-fetched as a murder plan.

"And where was Missouri?"

Langdon pursed his lips. "I'm sorry I forgot about our dinner plans until just now."

"That's okay. We'll just have it as leftovers tomorrow. Same time?"

"Sure," Langdon said.

"How about I bring Missouri home with me and put her to bed?" There was only one possible answer to this question, posed as it was.

"I don't want to go to bed," Missouri said. "I want to stay here." Her blue eyes blazed defiantly at her mother.

It took ten minutes for Amanda to drag the rebellious five-year-old from the bar with a grilled cheese clutched in her hand. Goldilocks noted that of all the many people who had been thrown out over the years, Missouri had put up the greatest fight.

Everybody was still attentive to the food in front of them until the door closed at the top of the stairs. "Goff was a bad boy," a barely audible voice said.

Langdon swung his eyes from the stairs to the table but couldn't tell who had spoken. "Okay, enough of the troubled domestic life of one Goff Langdon. Who wants to help out with the new case?" he asked over the snickers.

"I should be getting home to my wife," Billy said.

Once he was gone, Langdon looked around the table. "Anybody else?"

Nobody answered.

"Let me put it another way," Langdon said. "Anybody who wants out should leave now, because from here on, I'm pretty sure we're going to get our hands dirty."

Nobody moved.

"Richam? Are you willing to face the wrath of Jewell?" Langdon asked.

"My wife doesn't run me," Richam replied. Everybody knew this was not true.

"How about you, 4 by Four? Is your broken jaw up to a new test? How about your pride?" Langdon asked.

"The jaw is fine, but the pride needs a do-over," 4 by Four said.

"Bart?" Langdon looked at the surly cop. "Didn't you just get off probation for the last time you helped me out?"

"They can take their red tape and shove it up their…" Bart looked sideways at Chabal and didn't finish.

"How about you, Chabal? Can your marriage take it?" Langdon asked.

"It'll give us something to talk about at our weekly counseling sessions," she replied. "I do have a question, though. Will we get paid this time?"

Langdon looked shocked. "You're getting an opportunity to live a life outside of the routine, and you ask for money? Hell, you should be paying me. I'm providing a service, an adventure club if you will, and you should consider yourself lucky to be invited."

"As long as nobody gets killed," Goldilocks said ominously. He was a part of the group as much as any of them.

"It's just a case investigating why a young man committed vandalism," Langdon said. He was happy to have the group together again. "Not a mysterious death at a nuclear power plant."

"Sounds harmless enough," Goldilocks agreed. "Either way, I'm in."

"Okay, then." Langdon clapped his hands twice. "Let's get down to business."

"What do you got so far?" Richam asked.

"As you all know, I have been hired to find out who may have put Jamal Jones up to robbing houses, and why that theft turned into vandalism along the way," Langdon said. "It seems to me that if the boys were actually put up to this whole fiasco, then it had to originate in one of two places."

"You said the kid was from Roxbury?" Goldilocks asked.

MAINELY FEAR   79

"Yep. That would be place number one. I'm thinking of going down there tonight," Langdon replied. "It seems Jamal's mom banned him from seeing or even communicating with a certain uncle a few years back. A bad influence. I thought I'd look him up."

"You got his address?" Bart asked.

"I've got the address of his bar. Latricia Jones tells me I can find him there every night of the week."

"You won't get down there until after ten," Richam said looking at his watch.

"The man owns a nightclub. Sometime around midnight should be the perfect time to find him there and ask a few questions."

"So, the lady, what's her name—Latricia—suggested you speak with him?" Starling asked.

"No. As a matter of fact, she tried to dissuade me, which I thought odd." Langdon thought about ordering a drink, but that seemed a bad idea before driving over two hours to go to a nightclub and then back home afterwards.

"I'll go down with you," Bart said. "I'm not in tomorrow until late afternoon."

"Okay," Langdon agreed. "The second place of interest is Jamal's school."

"MECI, right?" Richam asked.

"Yeah, up in Skowhegan. 4 by Four and I went up last night and had a bit of run-in with the headmaster and the basketball coach. They seemed pretty slippery and definitely had something to hide." Langdon chewed the last ice cube in his glass of water.

"They were not helpful?" Goldilocks asked.

"They stonewalled the shit out of us," Langdon said. "I thought we were going to throw down, but my partner makes his living as a punching bag."

"At least I stood up to that redneck and his racist bullshit," 4 by four said.

"Seems to me you stood up and sat down all in the same motion,"

Langdon said.

"How do you want to go about investigating the school?" Chabal asked.

"You working tomorrow Richam?" Langdon asked.

"Six to close," he replied.

"You think you can handle the store by yourself tomorrow, Star?" Langdon asked.

"As long as I'm allowed to hang up on sales calls," he replied.

"I was thinking that Chabal and Richam might take a ride up to Skowhegan and do some digging. I had an idea they could pose as parents of a hotshot prospect."

"I guess that might work," Chabal said. "Sometimes height skips a generation."

Chapter 9

Langdon walked out the door with Bart. "So, you suppose we can take the Caddie?" he asked.

"Wouldn't be a road trip without the Caddie," Bart replied.

They took Bart's cruiser to his house, where they traded it out for the wreck of a car in the garage. There were numerous dents, but all rust had been carefully scraped away and painted over with whatever color available over the years. Langdon was certain that if Bart called for a tow truck to come tote the automobile to a junkyard, the driver wouldn't think twice.

Unless, of course, he noticed the brand-new, expensive tires or the quality leather upholstery of the interior, in which case he might think to turn the engine over and would be surprised as it rumbled to life with a powerful purr. The Caddie was the only car Bart had ever felt totally comfortable in. Secretly, he likened the car to himself; rough on the outside, but smooth and polished on the inside. He saved the car for road trips only, and not short ones either, not wanting to taint the pleasure he took in driving it.

"4 by Four said you shared a few drinks with him last night," Bart said as he settled his immense bulk into the driver's seat.

"Enough to give me a headache this morning," Langdon replied.

"What prompted that?" Bart eased the Caddie out onto the street.

Langdon was silent as he rolled the question around in his head. "Probably the same reason everybody showed up at Goldilocks tonight ready to sign on for the latest case."

"And why is that?"

"Ah, after a bit of trying your hardest to be good in life, you get fed up with the whole thing," Langdon said. "You're not supposed to drink, smoke cigars, or play cards. Rather, you have to keep your nose to the grindstone and go to work, do the laundry, shovel the walk, take care of the kids, do the dishes, go to bed, and get up and do it all over again."

"What are you saying?"

Langdon shrugged. "Drinking is fun, relaxing, and allows you to hit the pause button."

Bart nodded and pulled into Cumberland Farms. "Why don't you run in and buy us a twelve pack of Bud."

Langdon chuckled and did mostly as he was told. He got a six of Bud for Bart, and a six of Gritty's for himself. Whereas 4 by Four was a lightweight, Langdon had personally seen Bart drink a case of beer without showing any signs of inebriation. He'd only seen Bart visibly drunk once, and that was the day they'd become friends. Bart had come into Goldilocks to roust some drug dealers from away who'd taken up residence in Brunswick, and Langdon had become involved in the melee that followed. This had gained Langdon the grudging admiration of the huge bear of a cop.

Once back on the road with open beers in hand, Bart turned his head to look at Langdon. "So, you think everybody is back together again because they're bored?"

"Don't get me wrong, I appreciate everybody kicking in and lending a hand." Langdon took a long swig of the beer. "But, let's face it. Richam works the night shift most days, gets up at the crack of dawn to help get his kids ready for school, does some chores around the house, picks the kids up, trades with Jewell over a quick dinner, and then it's back to work to do it all over again."

"He'll get a kick out of going up to Skowhegan and pretending to be the father of a phenom," Bart agreed. "And I guess Chabal's floating a bunch of responsibilities these days, too."

"We all need a bit of vice in our lives," Langdon said.

"Does that include adultery?" Bart asked.

"What's that supposed to mean?"

"Nothing. Forget I said anything. How about 4 by Four? That man is a walking vice."

"Yeah, but even smoking, drinking, and womanizing can get boring if you do too much of it."

"Yeah, I imagine never working out, smoking pot, drinking too much, and chasing women 24/7 gets old after a bit," Bart said. "Although, I'd like to give it a go sometime and see how long that takes."

"I'm not so sure on the pot thing. That shit knocks me out," Langdon said. "That would get old real quick for me."

"How about me?" Bart asked. "I mean, I am the police. I work cases all day, every day. A little theft and vandalism are nothing new or particularly exciting for me."

Langdon looked uncomfortably out the window, but when the silence became too loud and didn't appear to be easing anytime soon, sucked in his breath, and turned to look squarely at his friend. "We're all you got," he said.

They didn't have to stop for more beer until Portsmouth, even though Langdon had only drunk three Gritty's. Bart had been out for ten minutes when they spotted an easy-off/easy-on, exit. The Caddie flowed along at a steady 80, although it felt more like 50, unless you paid attention to the other cars they were flashing past.

"Just to be clear," Bart resumed their current conversation once back on the road. "You think you're some kind of messiah figure surrounded by a flock of misfits—a mix of goody-two shoes, hopeless sinners, and lonely people?"

"I'd never thought of it that way, but yeah, I guess you're right," Langdon said, and then regretted his flippancy. His friend did carry a gun, and though the possibility was distinctly dim, he might shoot him.

Bart merely cursed, which was much better than blasting Langdon with his pistol. "Just be careful you don't end up nailed to a cross," he added once his face had regained most of its normal color.

"Know that I am with you, yes, to the end of time," Langdon said, earning him another round of obscenities.

"Okay, enough of that," Bart said. "Give me the skinny on this Eddie guy."

"Sounds like he was raised a hoodlum, small-time street punk, but then something turned for him, and he now owns some fancy nightclub. Latricia didn't say, but it was about then that she forbade Jamal to have anything to do with the man."

"So, he's either backed by some big fish or he had a major score. Either way, Latricia knows enough about it to keep her baby away."

"That's about it," Langdon said.

"Why we going to see him, then?"

"You were brought up by a single mom. You always do everything she told you?"

"Pretty much," Bart said.

Langdon looked at him. It was probably true. Bart had adored his mother and vice versa. "Okay, maybe you're the exception, but believe it or not, that's not the norm. Most kids rebel against their parents, but boys with single moms discover they can get away with anything. Their mothers treat them like princes who can do no wrong."

"You're saying Jamal continued to see his Uncle Eddie?"

"I'd bet my last beer on it," Langdon said.

It was almost midnight when the Caddie rolled into the parking lot of The Glitter Club. Langdon had worked the map and only given two wrong directions, both earning him Bart's colorful castigation.

"Let's split up," Langdon said. "I'll ask around about Eddie and see if I can get an audience with him, and you watch my back. Try to blend in."

"What makes you think this Eddie Jones character isn't going to just throw your ass out to the curb?"

"I guess I'm hoping he has a soft spot for his nephew."

"The kid he hasn't seen in eight years?" Bart looked skeptical.

"I'm banking on that not being true, but even if it is, wouldn't you be curious? Wouldn't you want to know what was going on with your brother's son?"

"I hope you're right," Bart said. "Because if you're wrong, we might never walk out of this place."

"Try to blend in," Langdon repeated.

"Yeah, good luck with that. We might be the only white people here."

"Not to mention you're twice the size of a normal human being."

"At least I'm not sporting red hair."

Langdon finished his beer and dropped the empty bottle in the back. "Here goes nothing. Give it a couple of minutes, and follow me in." Langdon stepped out of the car and was met with a head-rush. The beer, coupled with the rocking motion of the car, threw him off balance, plus he had to pee. They were parked in a shadowy corner, so he stepped to the rear of the car and let some of the beer loose.

There were two huge bouncers at the door collecting an exorbitant cover charge, but then Langdon had never been to a nightclub before, so perhaps it was normal. He asked where he could find Eddie Jones, but they merely stared at him. Maybe they didn't speak English, Langdon wondered, but thought it more likely they just didn't like him.

Inside, dance music reverberated through the air, the bass making the walls seem to vibrate and the ceiling shudder. Flashing lights of all types, shapes, and colors made the room look like a crime scene, or maybe even a disaster zone. A mass of humanity surged in rhythmic movements across the immense dance floor. The bar was four deep and the tables were all full.

Suspended above the crowd were four different cages holding

female dancers with skimpy attire gyrating energetically to the music. The far-end of the room held a stage upon which a gorgeous woman wearing a glittering evening dress moved with a more subtle grace to The Notorious B.I.G. belting out his hit "Mo Money Mo Problems."

Langdon only knew who the artist was because he'd followed the assassination of the rap star in the newspaper the previous year. I guess the lyrics—recounting that money did truly seem to come with its own host of problems—could be correct, Langdon thought as he fought his way through the crowd to the bar,

"Rum and coke," he yelled to be heard. When the drink arrived, he leaned forward with a twenty-dollar bill in his hand. "Where would I find Eddie Jones?"

The bartender clipped the bill from his hand. "Who are you?"

"I need to talk with Eddie about his nephew, Jamal." Langdon understood that who he was was not important, but that blood should carry some clout.

The bartender went over to a phone and made a call. Langdon took the opportunity to look around, instantly picking out Bart in the wave of humanity. After a bit, the bartender brought over a second rum and coke and told him somebody would be down to get him. Forty-five minutes and three drinks later, a short, stocky man wearing an expensive suit jacket over a white t-shirt with several gold chains dangling from his neck came through the crowd and gathered Langdon in, people parting before them like receding waves.

The man guided him around the dance floor, which had taken on, if possible, an even more frenzied exuberance, and then up some stairs. The office to which Langdon was led was like something straight out of the movies. There was a gigantic plate glass window that Langdon guessed was mirrored on the other side overlooking the dance floor. The room must have been soundproofed, for none of the feverish activity from the bar below produced any noise, giving the spectacle a classy, silent-flick appearance. The room itself was long and thin, with a desk, several easy chairs, and two couches, all in expensive leather. A few men lounged on the furniture. As Langdon and his guide entered the room, all eyes locked on him.

"Mr. Jones?" Langdon directed the question at the only man not flashing gold bling of one kind or another.

The man smiled and nodded. Langdon realized he'd passed some sort of test. Eddie Jones was short, thin, and built like a whip. His eyes were friendly, although guarded. He stood and offered his hand.

"Langdon, Goff Langdon," he said, taking and shaking the proffered hand. "I'm trying to help out your nephew, Jamal Jones."

"What help does the boy need that I can't give him?"

"Jamal has been arrested for breaking and entering, burglary, vandalism, and hate crimes." Langdon watched Eddie's face as he spoke.

"Jamal?" The surprised tone was not very convincing.

"He was arrested in Brunswick, Maine, early Wednesday morning." Langdon decided to play along with the game.

"Yesterday?"

Langdon looked at his watch. It was now past one in the morning. "About this time two days ago."

"Are the police sure they have right boy? I know those Maine police ain't too used to seeing Black folks, and to them, we all look alike." Eddie walked over to his one-way window and clasped his hands behind his back.

"They caught him driving away from the scene of a burgled house with a van full of stolen merchandise. There is no doubt he did it."

"Damn fool boy."

Langdon said nothing. He thought that the anger and frustration seemed genuine.

"What is he playing at?" Eddie asked. "I'd give him anything he needed. That boy has a future in front of him."

"That's what I'm hoping you can help out with, Mr. Jones."

"Call me Eddie." He turned around and faced Langdon. "But, why do you think I can help? And how exactly are you involved, again?"

Langdon smiled. If Eddie didn't know what Langdon's part was, he would have asked earlier in the conversation. Therefore, he could assume that Eddie knew everything about him. "I'm a private detective in Brunswick. Latricia Jones hired me because she thinks somebody must have put Jamal up to this stupid escapade. She thinks if we can find out who was behind this thing, well then, it might make things easier on Jamal, legally." He could play the game for as long as Eddie chose.

"She told you it was me, didn't she?" Eddie strode across the room to just in front of Langdon. "That woman never liked me much."

"Actually, she told me that she didn't think there was any reason to speak with you."

Eddie laughed, a deep rumble starting in his belly and barking out like a seal. "So, the first thing you did was drive down to Roxbury to see why she didn't want you talking to me?"

"Yeah, pretty much."

"You want a drink? I got a mighty fine bourbon. You up for a nip?"

When Langdon assented, Eddie snapped his fingers. One of the other men rose from his chair and went to the end of the room where a small bar held a few bottles and glasses. Langdon knew he should be moving to coffee, but he couldn't pass up sharing a drink with the man, not unless the intent was to offend him. The nip consisted of about six ounces of Maker's Mark.

"Pretty nice set up you got here," Langdon said. "You own the place?"

"The Glitter Club? Sure."

"How long you owned it?"

"Few years now." Eddie sat back down on one of the couches and patted the seat next to him. "Why don't you all go and give Mr. Langdon and me a chance to powwow."

"My friends just call me Langdon," he said as he sat and the other men exited the room.

"I'm not sure we're friends." Eddie took a tiny sip of his bourbon and set the glass down carefully on the table. He seemed to be a very careful man. It was almost two in the morning, and he sat coiled on the edge of the couch without a wrinkle in his clothes and no sign of strain in his eyes.

"My enemies also call me Langdon."

"I don't believe I'm your enemy."

"Everybody calls me Langdon, whether they like me or not."

Eddie laughed, a short, sharp bark. "Langdon it is. Tell me about Jamal's arrest."

Langdon filled him in on the break-ins, the flight, and the capture. "One of the other boys hung himself in jail."

"White boys don't know how to deal with troubles like us Black folks," Eddie said.

Langdon had not told him Stanley was white. "You might be right," he said.

Eddie glanced at his watch. "What can I do to be of help? My brother's boy is very important to me. Devan is probably turning in his grave right now, so we best set things straight."

"I guess I agree with Latricia that it's a bit odd for three boys from away to decide to start robbing and looting houses in Maine. This makes me think the plan wasn't theirs. What were they going to do with the stolen goods? Where'd they get the van? The police are still tracking that down, but I'm willing to bet none of them own it. So, who does?" Langdon realized he'd just about finished the triple bourbon that had been poured for him.

"You think I'm the man behind it all?" The question was silent and deadly.

"I don't know."

"You're right, Langdon. I do skirt the edges of the law. I'm not an upstanding citizen. But I do give money to the community. I do want Roxbury to be a safer place for our children. And I have not been paying for Jamal's education just so he can throw his future away."

"You paid for Jamal to go to MECI?" Of course, Langdon thought, where else had the money come from?

"Latricia didn't mention that?" Eddie smiled without humor. "She forbids Jamal to have anything to do with me, but I've been giving her money ever since my brother died, first for food and clothes, and later for basketball camps and shoes, and lately for his education." Eddie's eyes burned with anger. "All so he didn't have to work, run scams on the streets, deal drugs, or whatever. I gave the money willingly, not for Latricia, but for Jamal. For the son of my dead brother."

"How much money are we talking?"

"More every year." Eddie Jones had a look that suggested it was none of Langdon's damn business.

"That's mighty nice of you."

"Yes, yes, it is," Eddie said. "So, if you are going to come in here and accuse me of ruining that boy's future for a couple of bucks, I will kill you. Do you understand? Langdon?"

"Absolutely," Langdon said. "I'm just trying to get to the nitty-gritty of the thing."

"I can ask around. If somebody from down here was behind it, I will take care of the problem."

Langdon shook his head. "No."

"What the hell you mean, no?"

"Best to contact me if you find them, and I'll take care of it—legally."

"There are certain things I can do that you can't do."

"You can't kill them. We need them alive. We need to have them arrested and charged with the crime, and then maybe we can plea Jamal down to lesser charges, or even make a case that he was forced into the deeds committed by this other person. You can't kill them. Not if you truly care for your nephew."

Fast Eddie stared through Langdon without answering.

Chapter 10

Chabal had insisted that she and Richam leave early the next morning so she could be back at the bookstore by the afternoon. Fridays were usually busy, and she wasn't comfortable leaving Starling alone all day. Richam had also given in to her request to drive, as she'd recently traded her old VW bug for a brand new one that was bright Tweety Bird yellow. She was still excited at the car's zippiness.

Richam was dressed in a gray Brooks Brothers suit with a starched white shirt and a Three Stooges tie, which had been a gift from his kids. It was blue with small squares as background for Moe, Curly, and Larry. He had a tan wool overcoat and shoes that sparkled a lustrous black. Chabal had never seen him dressed in anything other than impeccable fashion. He was rake-thin and had the bearing of a military officer even though he'd never served. He also had a broad smile of gleaming white teeth.

"What'd you tell your wife?" Chabal asked once they were underway.

"Why do you think I had to tell her anything?" Richam asked.

"Jewell is still pissed off about Fort Andross. I don't think she's talked to any of the gang since, so I'm pretty sure she's not too excited about you getting back in."

"What'd you tell your husband?" Richam asked. "I think he's angrier with the group than Jewell."

"I told him I had some errands to run this morning and was working this afternoon." Chabal grinned wickedly. "So, I didn't lie."

"Yeah, that's pretty much what I said." Richam grinned sheepishly. "Okay, let's create our backstory. Why are we visiting MECI?"

"Ooohh, backstory! Somebody thinks they're a novelist. Well, we heard good things about their curriculum and basketball program and are interested in sending our son there. He's in the middle of his senior year and just found out he didn't get into…"

"Duke," Richam said. "They have great teams there."

"And it's extremely hard to get into. We need something a little easier. How about Florida State."

"Okay, that's in Tallahassee, right?"

"Yeah, I think so. How about we live in Jacksonville. Say, he's been doing camps there for a few years now and the coaches know him and want him, but he tanked his SATs."

"What's his name?"

"Bert?" Chabal asked.

"Heck no," Richam said. "A Black basketball player named Bert?"

"See, that's good right there. If we fight enough, they'll definitely believe we're married."

It was about an hour and a half to Skowhegan, and they bickered and laughed and planned the entire way.

~ ~ ~ ~ ~

Langdon had rolled in at five in the morning and set the alarm for seven, but somehow the two hours disappeared, the buzzer going off seemingly as soon as he'd closed his eyes. In attempting to swing his legs to the floor he fell out of bed and thumped himself pretty hard, jarring what little wits he had. He almost fell back asleep on the floor, but Coffee Dog began licking his face, reminding him that it was breakfast time.

Half an hour, and one very cold shower later, Langdon greeted the cashier at the diner with a happy smile and hiked his way past the line to the table saved for him.

"Coffee, lots of it, Alison, please," he told the waitress. "On second thought, bring me two cups."

The coffee arrived at the same time as Jimmy 4 by Four, who gratefully latched onto one of the mugs and took a gulp of the steaming liquid. "Thanks," he said.

"You look like hell," Langdon said.

"I was busy most of the night doing some undercover work."

"Yeah? With who?"

"Lisa or Mary or something like that," 4 by Four said. "I'm really pretty terrible at remembering names."

"You going to be able to take care of business today?"

"It should be all set up already. Judge Reinhold has always proven friendly."

"Judge Reinhold? The actor?"

"No, shit, something like that, though. Judge Reinhardt, that's what his name is."

"Good thing to work out beforehand," Langdon said. "Go on."

"Yeah, yeah, whatever. Judge Reinhardt is on today. He's a big believer in second chances and not keeping young people in jail a moment longer than necessary. The DA, Marge Driscoll, is going to come after these kids, make scapegoats out of them, bring them to trial, and rake them over the coals. But for the time being, Marge will be content to release Jamal to your custody."

"Driscoll has always been a little keen on putting people away," Langdon said. "Plus, I don't think she much cares for me."

"Yeah, well, she downright hates me; must've been something I said."

Langdon's breakfast arrived, three breakfast sandwiches and a large plate of hash browns with extra bacon on the side. 4 by Four had a bagel with cream cheese. Coffee Dog was relegated to sniffing the air around the table.

"Did you find Jamal's uncle last night?" 4 by Four asked once they were in the car heading towards Portland.

"Yep."

"Tell me about it."

"He's a very intense man, but likeable, even if a tad bit scary."

"Why's that?"

"Scary? Well, he did threaten to kill me."

"Sounds like a suspect for the mastermind of the crime."

"Ah, I don't know. To tell you the truth, I think we'd best find out who the person in the background is before Fast Eddie does, if we want them alive, that is."

Langdon drove carefully as a mixture of rain and snow was falling from the sky and turning to ice when it hit the road. He looked apprehensively at the fragile tree branches on the sides of the roads and hoped they wouldn't begin snapping and send Maine back into the dark ages once again.

"You smell like booze," 4 by Four said.

"I had a few."

"Might be a good idea to scarf down a breath mint or two before you go into court and attempt to take custody of a criminal, and a minor at that."

Langdon nodded his agreement, although he suspected the odor was seeping through his pores rather than on his breath. "*Suspected* criminal," he said.

"Yeah, right, innocent until proven guilty. How'd I ever become a lawyer?" 4 by Four asked.

"Well, as you *are* a lawyer, I'd guess you lied your way to the bar."

"What time did you get in?"

"About five."

4 by Four shook his head in wonderment. As far as he could tell, Langdon didn't need sleep. As far as food, it seemed he ate a bundle every couple of days and then not at all in between. "Did you talk to Amanda?"

"Nah, not yet. I'm kind of scared to call her after blowing her off last night."

"She does appear menacing when angry," 4 by Four said, as they pulled into the parking lot.

An hour later they emerged onto the sidewalk from the courthouse. Langdon was struggling to keep pace with the angry young man now in his charge. Jamal was back in his street clothes: jeans, a gray hoodie that said Boston College, and untied expensive-looking basketball sneakers. Langdon wondered if Fast Eddie had bought them for him. 4 by Four stopped to exchange pleasantries with a young female clerk on the sidewalk, realizing that Langdon and Jamal probably needed a minute to get on the same page.

"Jamal, would you just take a breath? I'm trying to help you. I'm on your side."

"I don't need your help, chump."

"You have been released to my custody. That means you have to go with me."

"I don't have to go anywhere with you, man, what do you think this is? This is 1998 and slavery has been long gone."

Langdon walked silently along, letting the young man blow off some steam. He had, after all, just gotten out of jail on bail with serious charges pending against him to find, not his mother, but a stranger waiting for him. On top of that, his good friend had just died by suicide.

"Where is my mother, anyway?" Jamal stopped and faced Langdon, pulling his hood up over his head to protect against the chill.

"She had to go back to work."

"What the hell for?" The anger in Jamal now mixed with a trace of fear.

"I don't know. All I know is that she said she was the only one who knew how to do something."

Jamal punched a stop sign and cursed. "I have to get down there."

"To Roxbury?"

"No, to Oz." Jamal crossed the street as if intent on walking all the way.

"You're not allowed to leave the state unless you want to violate your bail, which lands you right back in jail," Langdon said.

"I need to see my mom."

"She said she'd be up tomorrow afternoon. Until then, you're stuck with me."

"Tomorrow will be too late."

"'Too late for what?"

"What makes you think I'm going to stick with you? You're not here to help me. You don't give a shit about me. You just want to take my momma's money. You probably want to bang her, don't you? You have some sick fantasy about my mom?"

"I have to confess that you're making it awful tough to want to help you," Langdon said. "And I've got at least one too many women in my life already."

"What do you want from me, then?" Jamal stopped again, a tear forming in his left eye.

"I have been hired to help you."

"Then give me a ride to Roxbury."

"I can't do that."

Jamal cursed and started walking again.

"How much money do you have on you, Jamal?"

There was no answer.

"What are you going to do? Hitchhike down? Because, I'll tell you how it's going to go down. If you take off on me, I *will* go right back in that courthouse and tell them you jumped bail. How far do you think you'll make it?"

"I thought you was supposed to be helping me out?"

"On my terms."

"How can I trust you?"

"I don't know. I'm being paid to help you out. What do I have to gain by screwing you over?"

"Everybody is always saying they're trying to help me out, but I don't know you, so how do I know if that's really the case now?" Tears were now streaming down Jamal's face.

"Do you want to talk about that?" Langdon asked.

"I just need to understand your angle, is all. Nobody does nothing for free."

"How about we go get some lunch and talk about it?"

"I don't really have a choice, do I?"

Chapter 11

Chabal pulled the yellow Volkswagen into the parking lot at the Molly Esther Chester Institute in Skowhegan. The bright shiny color against the dreary background of a central Maine winter caught more than one eye. When Richam and Chabal stepped out of the car, and he took her arm to help her over the slippery spots, people stopped what they were doing and stared. It was not every day that these people saw a Black man with a white woman, or any day at all for that matter. This would make good gossip over the dinner table later tonight.

Power had also been restored at MECI in Skowhegan and the previously darkened buildings and desolate grounds now buzzed with activity like a beehive on a summer day. The temperature was still below freezing, so the students and faculty were bundled up, and everybody was scurrying from class to class or upon some other undetermined errand. Laughter rang through the air along with voices ranging from the shrill to the booming bass.

"Is everybody staring at us?" Chabal asked.

"They sure are," Richam replied. He was doing his best to return the stares of all those watching them, but he guessed it merely made him look shifty.

"I always wanted to have everybody staring at me," Chabal said. "But I always pictured it more as a Hollywood Oscar night kind of thing."

"They might give you an award right after they lynch me," Richam said dryly.

"Should I flash some cleavage?"

"Better not."

"You sure?"

"You wouldn't want to take all those jackets and sweaters off to find out that you left your cleavage at home, now, would you?"

"That is domestic abuse! I want a divorce."

They went into the main office building, which was a fairly recent brick structure that lay in the center of campus. And, what a campus it was. It could have been a prestigious New England college with its sprawling building encompassing various common areas that the students rarely got to see uncovered by snow and ice. There was a prosperous newness to it all, but a foreboding eked its way through, perhaps the result of the ice storm, or maybe something else?

It was a relief to leave the stares behind, but inside was almost oppressively quiet. Large, dark portraits adorned the walls on either side of a long hallway. A receptionist with horn-rimmed glasses sat at the far end behind a thick, oak desk. Her cheeks were rosy, and she had a twinkle in her eyes.

"We have an appointment with Jerry Peccance," Richam said when they reached her desk.

"You're Mr. and Mrs. Jordan?" Her voice echoed warmly in their ears.

"That's us," Richam said.

"Mr. Peccance will be right with you. Please have a seat."

Chabal had insisted on the name Jordan, which Richam had argued against, until she suggested Abdul-Jabbar as an alternative. "And what is your name?" she asked the receptionist.

The lady looked up in surprise. Nobody ever cared what her name was. She didn't even bother putting her little placard with her name on it upon her desk, like most people did. "I am Mrs. Peach," she said. Her rotund features melted into a warm smile.

"How long have you worked here, Mrs. Peach?" Chabal asked.

"Thirteen years next month," Mrs. Peach said.

"My! That's a long time," Chabal said. "You must know everything about everybody and everything. Has anybody been here longer than you?"

Mrs. Peach giggled. "Actually, Jerry, I mean, Mr. Peccance, has been here for fourteen years."

"Jerry Peccance is the only one who has been here longer than you?" Richam interrupted with disbelief. Most of his kids' teachers had been at their school for at least twenty years, if not longer.

Mrs. Peach directed her answer at Chabal, ignoring Richam. "Mr. Peccance has been responsible for hiring everybody throughout the school." She glanced over her shoulder at the door. "He started housecleaning as soon as he was hired. The first to go was his receptionist, but over the next few years every single teacher, coach, and support staff followed suit. The last holdout from the original faculty left five years ago."

The door behind Mrs. Peach burst open. "Mr. and Mrs. Jordan! Hello. I'm Jerry Peccance. Sorry to keep you waiting." He held out his hand to Richam, and then took Chabal's. Peccance was immaculately dressed in a tweed jacket and narrow tie. He was a very thin man with jerky movements that he seemed unable to control.

"Please, call me Richam, and my wife is Chabal."

"Come in Richam and Chabal." The Headmaster waved them into his lair with a friendly grin.

When he shut the door behind them, Chabal cringed, somehow feeling trapped.

"Did you get a chance to look around the school?" Peccance asked.

"Not yet," Richam replied. "We landed in Portland about two hours ago and drove straight here."

"I'll personally give you a tour after we're done here," Peccance said. "I told the basketball coach that we'd stop by. You did say your son is a basketball player?"

"He's not just a player, he's a star," Chabal said.

Peccance nodded. He appeared unimpressed, probably having

heard many similar claims over the years from many parents.

"He has several scholarship offers sitting on the table," Richam said.

"What schools are we talking?"

"We are leaning towards the University of Florida," Richam said.

"It's close to home," Chabal added.

Peccance smiled broadly and then grew serious. "But?"

"His SAT scores need a little work," Richam admitted with a weary shrug.

"We can certainly help with that," Peccance said. "The average postgraduate student at MECI," but he pronounced it Meesie, "raises their scores a total of over a hundred points."

"He doesn't test well," Chabal said. "He is a very bright boy. He got excellent marks in school and all, but he freezes up when testing."

"It was math that really did him in," Richam said. "If he doesn't bring that up, he can kiss college goodbye. Not to worry, he's got a construction job waiting for him."

"Richam owns the company," Chabal said. "He doesn't swing a hammer or anything like that."

"But Robert will," Richam said. "Got to start at the bottom."

"So, what I'm hearing is that Robert needs to bring up the math portion of his SAT? We should probably pop in and give you a chance to talk to the head of the math department as well," Peccance said.

"That would be great," Chabal said.

"But first the basketball coach," Richam said.

"Great, let's go then." Peccance stood and grabbed an overcoat.

They passed by Mrs. Peach on the way, and Chabal gave her a smile and a wave. Peccance gave them a tour of the school along the way. There were several dormitories, in one of which the basketball team roomed together, reminding Chabal of a fraternity house. The sports complex sat slightly apart from the main cluster of buildings, next to the fields. It consisted of a basketball court, weight room, two squash courts, and locker rooms. Chabal found herself intrigued by the school. It was the kind of place she might consider sending her own kids when they were a little older, especially if it were closer to home.

"We're hoping to add a swimming pool in the next two years," Peccance said. "Raising money to fund it has already begun."

"That's quite a basketball court," Richam said.

"Do you fill all those stands?" Chabal asked.

"We usually turn people away when we play some of the college teams," Peccance said.

"College teams?" Richam asked.

"We struggle to find competition with other postgraduate programs and high schools," Peccance said. "So, we mostly play a collegiate schedule. Colby, Bates, Bowdoin, Husson, and the University of Maine to name a few."

"Wow, so Robert will be playing against college players?" Chabal asked.

"Yes," Peccance said. "The coach is waiting for us in his office."

They passed by the trophy case dominated by basketball awards. It was quite an impressive collection of hardware. The office was expansive, as it had to be, to accommodate the numerous photos of basketball stars personally autographed to Coach Pious, thanking him for his part in their success.

Peccance made the introductions and then left them to talk. Rick Pious was in a rumpled suit. When he moved, it was with a graceful and fluid motion. His wide forehead and bushy eyebrows dominated his face. Pious had stood and shook their hands when they entered, but then sat back down behind his desk and gestured at the two chairs in front for them to sit.

"Your son is interested in playing ball here, is that correct?" Pious asked.

"Yes."

"Why didn't you bring him along?"

"He has an important travel tournament this weekend," Richam said.

"And this is the only time Rich was able to get away from work," Chabal added.

"Jerry said that Billy Donovan is interested in him," Pious said.

"Billy?" Chabal asked.

"Coach Donovan? At the University of Florida?" The wild eyebrows bounced around in a jumble.

"Ah, yes, Coach Donovan. We've only talked to him twice, and always just refer to him as Coach," Richam said. "Yes, they have a solid offer on the table, if we can raise some scores."

"Any other programs looking at him?"

"There has been interest from several others but no offers," Chabal said.

"Did you bring a tape?"

There was a long few seconds before Chabal interpreted the question. "That's my fault. I thought it was in my purse, but I must have set it down somewhere. I'm terribly sorry."

"We'll FedEx it to you as soon as we get home," Richam said.

"I'm surprised I haven't heard of him. You say he plays in Jacksonville?"

Richam nodded.

"Which school?"

There's more than one high school in Jacksonville? Chabal thought with chagrin. Of course there is. There are probably multiple schools. Not to mention that Coach Pious probably knew all the top talent in the nation, and Robert Jordan was not on his radar.

"What *we* need to know is why would our son want to come to the middle of nowhere? Why is this the best place for him?" Richam half-stood and leaned across the desk.

"I'll tell you why." Pious leaned back in his chair. "We are directly connected to every major basketball program in the country. Your son will be playing on a team of some of the most elite players in the nation. Seven members of this year's class have already signed letters of intent. Georgetown, Kentucky, Princeton, Rhode Island, UConn, UMass, and VCU." He rattled off the schools in alphabetic order indicating he'd made the same pitch multiple times.

"So, you get scouts up here in Maine?"

"We sure do. Both here in Skowhegan and at the college games, but we also make a Christmas holiday trip to North Carolina every year to compete in a postgraduate tournament held there. We have won that the last three years in a row. Every major college in the land will have scouts there."

"You must have a pretty impressive scouting system yourself?" Richam asked.

"I only have one scout who travels the country looking for talent. But after the season is over, I try to visit as many players and parents as I can. It helps that our record stands for itself, and we are contacted by many families in situations like yours."

"What's next year's pool look like?" Chabal asked.

"We have most of our pieces in place including Kevin Wills."

"How many players do you roster?" Richam asked, before his ignorance of not knowing who Kevin Wills could be exposed.

"Fourteen."

"What about the seven that haven't signed letters of intent? What's their deal?" Chabal asked.

"Two of them are still hoping to retake the SATs and bring up their scores to a satisfactory level. The other five have the academic qualifications but didn't get enough playing time to get a scholarship. Two of those might be able to play D2."

"How do the basketball players fit into the school and the community?" Richam asked.

"The town loves them. It's a sports town, and they truly appreciate the level of play, so they pretty much take the players under their wing."

"And the school?"

"It's just like any other school, I suppose. The boys stick together as a team, but this is part of what makes the program so successful. They eat, sleep, practice, and study together. This brings cohesion."

"Could we talk to some of the players?"

"Uh, no, I'm sorry, but that's against Meesie policy. We try to protect the privacy of our students, especially the sports stars. They are just kids, after all, and we don't want anybody to feel pressured, whether they are currently enrolled, or considering enrollment."

There was a knock at the door and a square plug of a man stuck his head in. Pious waved him in. "This is Ed Helot, my assistant coach. Ed, this is Richam and Chabal Jordan. Ed is going to deliver you to John Danvers, the head of our math department. Do you have any more questions?"

"No, I think that pretty much covers things." Richam had to bite his tongue to not follow up on the mention of pressure on the students.

"Thank you for your time," Chabal said.

"Don't forget to send the highlight tape," Pious said.

After a brief, uninformative meeting with Mr. Danvers of the math department, Chabal and Richam found themselves walking back to the car feeling as if nothing of importance had been accomplished.

"Look, there goes Mrs. Peach." Chabal pointed across to the other side of the parking lot.

"Yeah? So what?" Richam asked.

"Let's see where she's going. I bet if we can talk to her away from campus, she might give us some good gossip. Don't forget, she's been here longer than anyone else."

"Might as well."

They followed her down the street into the center of town. She pulled into a small lot and went into a large brick building overlooking the river. Chabal parked on the street, and they gave the woman a few minutes before following her into what turned out to be a pub. Mrs. Peach was sitting alone at a table in the corner, and they asked for the empty table adjacent to hers.

Her horn-rimmed glasses were gone, suggesting they were reading glasses, and she'd no need to glance at a menu. Her skin, other than her cheeks, were pasty white, indicating that she didn't get outdoors much, at least in the winter. She was staring out the window to where the river trickled over the dam.

"Oh, hello," Chabal said as they were about to be seated. "Funny running into you here."

"Excuse me?" Mrs. Peach frowned. "Oh, yes, right, the Jordans. How did your visit with Mr. Peccance go? And did I hear you were also talking to Rick?"

"It went well, but I forgot to ask a few things and have been kicking myself for it," Chabal replied. "Are you eating alone?"

"Please join us," Richam said.

"Oh, I couldn't do that."

It took less than a minute to persuade her to switch tables.

"Do you come here often?" Chabal asked.

"Whenever I can," Mrs. Peach replied.

They exchanged pleasantries for several minutes before Chabal began steering the conversation back to MECI. "I found it interesting that Mr. Peccance is the longest serving employee with you being a close second."

"We're the two old birds, that's for sure, even if 14 years isn't all that long." Mrs. Peach took a bite from her vegetarian wrap. "The elders of the faculty and administration, that is. The janitor has been there for ages."

"What's his name?" Richam asked.

"Why do you want to know that?" Mrs. Peach snapped.

"My husband has a thing for names. It's a hobby of his, trying to identify a region by the names of the people there." Chabal smiled reassuringly at Mrs. Peach.

"Oh, really? That sounds fascinating. Have you done a study on Skowhegan?"

"I, uh, have only dabbled a bit, but French-Canadian seems to be a prevalent ethnic contributor to the area," Richam said.

"His name is Levesque," Mrs. Peach said. "Paul Levesque, and he still has a heavy accent, even though he's lived here since he was a young man."

"Aha, right on the button," Richam said. He was more than a little proud of himself for having pulled the ruse off. "We can look in the handbook for the current faculty, but how about some of the teachers who left after you were hired?"

"You mean their names?"

"Yes, were they largely French-Canadian?"

"No, I don't think so, there were a few, like Tim Leroy and Sarah Boucher." Mrs. Peach's face creased in thought.

"What were the names of the last to leave?" Chabal asked.

"Oh, the very last would have been John Flanagan."

"Irish," Richam said.

"I suppose so, but he was born right here in Skowhegan, I believe. His family has lived her for generations," Mrs. Peach said.

"Does he still live around here? If I wanted to talk to him?" Richam asked.

"No." Mrs. Peach shook her head. "He moved away."

"How about any of the others who left MECI? Are any of them around?" Richam asked.

"Not that I know of."

"None of them live in the area?" Chabal asked.

"Well, maybe, but not that I know of. I was friends with a few of them, including John, but they all moved away as far as I know."

"Where did this John Flanagan move to?" Chabal asked.

"The day after his house burned down, he packed up his wife and kids and moved to California," Mrs. Peach said.

"His house burned down?" Chabal asked.

"Yes. That was truly the straw that broke the camel's back. He had a run of bad luck, and, when his house burnt to the ground, that was it.

He was out of here. It was right before summer break. He didn't even finish the semester off."

"Do you have his phone number?" Richam asked.

"Whatever for?" Mrs. Peach asked. "That is an odd thing to ask for."

"I just, uh, wanted to ask him when his family came over from Ireland," Richam said.

"Oh, look at the time! I have to be getting back to work." She placed 12 dollars over her bill. "Thank you both for your company." She stood up and walked straight out the door.

"You got our bill?" Chabal asked Richam. "Give me a few minutes." She followed Mrs. Peach out the door.

Chapter 12

Jamal tried to remain impassive on the ride back to Brunswick, but this proved difficult between Coffee Dog licking his face and the running banter between 4 by Four and Langdon. They had already covered exercise and health—or rather, 4 by Four's lack of either—and were now onto Langdon's marital status.

"Yo, when's my court date?" Jamal asked. He wanted to be left alone but not ignored.

"They didn't set a date yet," 4 by Four said.

"Why not?"

"To be perfectly honest, because I am doing my best to delay it."

"Why's that?"

"In a case like this, the more time passes between the crime and seeing your face in court, the better. Let people forget about it. Everything is a little too raw right now, between the storm and the damage to the homes."

"How long we talking?"

"At least six months."

"I can't be driving around with you two for another six minutes, let alone six months." Jamal had been slouched in the backseat as if his body was absent of bones, but he now sat up.

"You want me to drop you at your car?" Langdon asked 4 by Four.

"Nah, I'll just come over to your house and get it later. I got nowhere to be," 4 by Four replied.

"I think I'd rather stay in jail than with you white dudes," Jamal said.

"We should be able to get you permission to return to Roxbury while you await your court date," 4 by Four said.

"How long for that?"

"No more than a week." 4 by Four could have made this quicker, but Langdon had asked for him to put it off, knowing that it was going to be that much harder to get to the heart of this case with Jamal down in Massachusetts.

"You can probably even finish up your year at MECI if you want," Langdon said. He was looking in the rear-view mirror to judge Jamal's reaction, but he needn't have bothered.

"No, I can't do that," Jamal said, his head leaning forward between the two men in front.

Langdon pulled into his driveway hitting the remote for the garage and easing the boat of a car into the tight space. He turned to face Jamal. "Why not?"

"I just can't go back, that's all."

"Why throw away what your mom says is a promising basketball career? Or at least a shot at a college education?" Langdon asked.

Jamal stared impassively at him, not giving the slightest hint of his thoughts.

"I went to see your Uncle Eddie last night," Langdon said.

"Yeah, so?"

"When's the last time you saw your uncle?"

"Couple times over break," Jamal said.

"This past holiday vacation?" Langdon was not really surprised.

"Yeah, sure."

"I thought your mom forbade you from seeing him?"

"We going inside, man, or we just staying in the car?" Jamal asked.

"Sure." Langdon opened the car door and got out and pulled the seat forward. Coffee Dog shot past Jamal and almost bowled Langdon over.

"You got to train your dog, man," Jamal said as he squeezed his large frame out of the car.

"He doesn't follow orders very well," Langdon said. "Sort of like teenage boys."

"Look, my mom threw some hissy fit years ago and told me never to see Uncle Eddie again, but you know, the man is family."

"How often you see him?"

"Often enough." Jamal said as he followed Langdon into the house. "Look man, you ain't gonna say nothing to my mom about this, are you? Don't we have some sort of deal, you know, where you can't tell my secrets?"

"I don't see why I'd have to," Langdon said. "But I should call and let her know you're out of jail." He went and dialed the number. It went to voice mail and he left a short message.

"She's probably working," Jamal said.

"Did you ever do any work for your Uncle Eddie?"

"Like, you mean, did I ever rip off houses for the man?"

"Yeah, I guess that's what I was getting at."

"When I was fifteen, Uncle Eddie sat me down and told me that if I ever did anything illegal, he'd personally beat me to a pulp. He said I had a gift, and if I messed that up by doing stupid shit, he'd ghetto university my ass."

"Sounds like you shouldn't be going back to Roxbury," 4 by Four said. "You got anything to eat, Langdon?"

"Nope, probably not."

"I'm starving," Jamal said.

"Okay, then, everybody back in the car. We'll go out for lunch." Langdon figured he'd pushed Jamal enough for the moment.

They resumed their positions in the car in silence. Langdon had sensed the truth that Uncle Eddie hadn't wanted Jamal to get caught up in criminal activity, which seemed to rule him out as the main suspect behind the robbery spree. Who, then? Maybe nobody? Sometimes kids do stupid things all on their own.

"I'm sorry about Stanley," Langdon said.

There was neither reaction nor answer.

"Was he from Boston, too?"

"Yeah, from Southie."

"You two know each other before you came up to school?"

"We played ball against each other a few times. He was real tough."

"You have any idea why he'd go and hang himself?"

"His parents were real middle-class, Irish Catholic, and hard-working folks. They lived up in Dorchester Heights, not down in the ghetto. There's no room in their thinking for what Stanley done." Jamal had obviously given this a lot of thought.

"Can't say that I get it, either," Langdon said. "But I'm willing to listen."

They pulled into the parking lot behind Goldilocks without anybody making a move to get out. "We gonna eat, man?" Jamal asked.

"Did you know that MECI has a history of suicides?" Langdon asked.

"No, I didn't know that," Jamal said.

"This is all tied in, I can feel it in my bones. What the hell is going on?"

"It's got nothing to do with Meese, okay?"

"I don't believe that."

"It was just some guy from the streets. I was home for break and then longer because of the ice storm. Maurice was staying with me because he'd flown back from his home in California, and we was loafing around killing time, and this dude I know kicks the idea at us."

"Kicks what idea at you?" Langdon asked.

Jamal shifted his eyes to look at the back of 4 by Four's head. "He was talking about how the ice storm had knocked all the power out up in Maine and somebody with a bit of initiative could make a killing robbing houses."

"Did he provide you with the van?"

"No. We didn't talk no more about it, but later that night me and Maurice got to tossing the thing around, and in the morning, we called Stanley up. He'd told us about how he'd stolen a couple of cars before just to take 'em for a joyride."

"So you stole the van?"

"Yeah, didn't even have to hot-wire it, some dude left it running on the side of the street."

"But you didn't just take it for a joyride? Did you?"

"No."

"What day was this?"

"The day we got caught, man."

"The day you got caught was the fourth day of houses being broken into."

"That wasn't us, man. We did it the one time. It was our third house when we got caught."

"What's the name of the man on the street who gave you the idea?"

They ordered two large pizzas for lunch but should have gotten more. Jamal ate like he'd been in jail for a few weeks rather than a few days. Goldilocks approached the table as the three men were wiping up any traces of food, not a word having been uttered while the pies were demolished.

"I make a damn fine pizza," Goldilocks said by way of introduction.

"This is the Goldilocks on the sign," Langdon said, and then nodded at Jamal. "Jamal Jones. He's staying with me for a few days."

"Hey, Jamal," Goldilocks said and was met with an impassive stare.

"Jamal, here, is supposed to be pretty good at hoops," Langdon said. "I thought we might test that out a bit later. You up for some ball around four?"

"Sure," Goldilocks replied. "I got coverage coming in at three. She should be fine for a few hours without me, until the dinner rush anyways."

"I'm not sure three drunks eating peanuts counts as a dinner rush," Langdon said.

"Whatever. Who you got so far?"

Langdon held up three fingers and then looked over at 4 by Four.

"Not full court? Please?" 4 by Four looked terrified.

"Nah, it might just be the four of us. I'll check in with Bart and Chabal, so six at the most," Langdon said.

"Bart was coming by at three. I'll corral him into coming," Goldilocks said.

"You could have told me before I had nine slices of pizza," 4 by Four said. This was an exaggeration by approximately six.

"Yeah, well I was trying to get an edge on Jamal. I figured if I tried to tell you in private, you'd run your big yap and spill the beans."

"Before I forget, Richam's stopping by in a few minutes to pick up some cherries for his bar," Goldilocks said. "Guess his order got shorted this week or something. I think he's got Chabal along with him."

"Good to know," Langdon replied.

"Where we playing?" Goldilocks asked. "I got to run home and grab some duds."

"Bowdoin."

"Upstairs?"

"Yeah, I'm pretty sure the big gym is open for practice now that they restored power."

"Okay. I'll see you there. I best get back over to Jeff before his liver begins to breathe again or he'll be pissed." Goldilocks hustled off behind the bar.

"Hey, you mind if Coffee Dog clears the leftovers from that table?" Langdon called, pointing to a table a young couple had just departed.

"Tell him not to break anything," Goldilocks said.

Once given the okay, a remarkable show of patience by the Lab, Coffee Dog jumped upon a chair, balancing precariously while plucking the remnants from the plates.

"Who says I want to ball?" Jamal asked.

"I do," Langdon said. "You live for the game."

"Says who?"

"Ask me that again in a year, after you drag your tail back down to Roxbury, take the beating your uncle is going to hand out, and go to work for him at the most menial job he has, probably cleaning out shitters. The one enjoyment in your life will be playing some pick-up with the boys."

"I am not going to work for my uncle," Jamal said.

"Seems to me you got two choices. Take your ass back to MECI and get your scores up so you can go to BC for free and get a college education. If you are able to turn pro, that's just gravy on the turkey, because you will have already filled your belly. Or, go to work for your uncle."

"What if I don't get my scores up?"

Langdon shrugged. "Only one way to find out."

"What if I wash out of BC and lose my scholarship?" Jamal spoke angrily. "Do you know how many rookies make NBA teams every year?"

"Not many," 4 by Four said.

"Less than that," Jamal said.

"I don't imagine you got any good playing ball by being a quitter," Langdon said. "So, what's the deal?"

"Maybe I should make my own way."

"What's that mean? Walk on at UMass?"

"I got the marks to get in there, at least."

"There isn't any such thing as a walk-on in D1," Langdon said. "Especially not from somebody who quit his prep school and has a criminal record. Basketball is about more than talent. It's about discipline, teamwork, and moxie. Do you have the moxie to play ball or not?"

"Oh, I can ball. But I need some shorts and my kicks."

"I got some you can wear."

"Size 16?"

"I'm just messing with you. Your mom gave me a bag of stuff for you. It's in the trunk of my car. She said she put an old pair of basketball sneakers in there for you."

"Don't let him bother you, kid," Chabal said as she walked over to their table. "Langdon used to think he was some hotshot basketball player himself, but he didn't make the team in college and he's been waddling around with a shoe in his ass ever since."

Langdon grinned. She was not too far off the mark. "Jamal. Chabal."

Jamal smiled as well; the usual reaction Chabal produced in people. Her inner positive attitude, friendly nature, and non-threatening demeanor caused people to like her.

Richam came out from the kitchen with a bucket, presumably of cherries. "I got to get to work."

"You need a ride?" Chabal asked.

"No. I can just walk across the street."

"Phew. He would have been an odd number," Langdon said once Richam had gone up the stairs.

"Odd number?" Chabal asked.

"Yeah, for basketball. You're in, right?"

"Sure. It just so happens I got my gym clothes in the car, as my husband thought I was working out this morning, instead of driving up to Skowhegan on a Langdon investigation," Chabal said.

"Skowhegan?" Jamal jerked his head around.

"We can talk about that later," Langdon said. "We need to swing by the bookshop and check in on Starling."

"Can one of you two swing me by my house so I can get some shorts?" 4 by Four asked. "Or better yet, drop me at my car over at the diner?"

"Sure, I'm right out back," Chabal said. "I'll meet you at the store?" she asked Langdon who nodded his agreement. Chabal and 4 by Four went up and out the back while Langdon and Jamal went out the front.

The sky was beginning to darken as Langdon and Jamal crossed over Maine Street. Billy, the maintenance man, was in the hallway as they entered the building. He trundled over to them as if he had important information to share, but it was only that he'd been asking around the other businesses in the building if they'd seen anybody suspicious the day before. They had not.

Starling was waiting on a customer when they entered. Once he was done, Langdon pulled up the daily report on the computer and realized that the man had had a busy day. "You've made us some money," he said.

"I sure as hell did and haven't had a chance to pee since I opened," Starling said. "I'll be right back to finish my grumbling." He walked out the door, the bathroom being down the hallway.

Langdon waited on a few customers while Jamal browsed through the aisles.

"This place ain't bad," Jamal said, coming to the counter. "I like the vibe."

"Thanks," Langdon said, astonished that the young man had thrown out a compliment.

"You got any Walter Mosley books?"

"Sure," Langdon said. "Right down that aisle over there."

Starling came back and went to the office to retrieve his lunch, tuna on rye bread with a pickle he'd brought from home. "Chabal coming in?" he asked as he bit into the sandwich.

"Not for long, if that's okay with you?" Langdon was leafing through the mail and disposing the bulk of it in the trash without opening it.

"Hey, I get paid either way. I'd rather be busy than bored to death," Star said.

"That's the spirit," Langdon said.

"Are the two of you up to something?" Starling asked as Chabal came into the store. "Working undercover?"

"Slow your jets, old man," Chabal replied. "We're going to play some ball."

"Sure you are," Starling replied.

"What'd you find out up in Skow-town?" Langdon asked her.

"How about we go back in the office?"

"Sure," Langdon said coming around the counter. The two of them walked towards the back.

"I'll knock if I need anything," Starling called after them.

"The first thing is that I'll probably be sending Jack up to MECI when he gets to high school," Chabal said as they closed the door. "The headmaster is one smooth dude."

"He didn't strike me as particularly smooth," Langdon said. "But I think I rubbed him the wrong way."

"You were an investigator, and I was the mother of a star athlete," Chabal said. "The place is like a college campus and the classes they offer? Wow."

"So, you liked Peccance. Did you get a chance to talk to the coach? Rick Pious?"

"Yeah, he wasn't quite so likeable. More like an arrogant asshole. When we asked if we could talk to some of the players, I think he may have shit himself."

"Sounds like a red flag."

"What do red flags sound like?"

"You know what I mean."

"I don't know," Chabal said. "They do have to abide by privacy laws and whatnot. It just seemed odd."

"You get anything from either of them?"

"Not so much, but we followed the receptionist or secretary or whatever when we were leaving. She was having lunch, so we 'bumped' into her and joined her. She was quite a chatterbox, until the end when Richam scared her off a bit."

"What'd he say that scared her?"

"He was trying to get the phone number of the last teacher let go."

"Why?"

"Get this, Peccance was hired as headmaster fourteen years ago and in nine years replaced the entire staff, all except the janitor, I guess. This guy was the last one to go, after his house burned down."

"I guess that's a bit odd, but not really criminal activity."

"This guy, Flanagan, was the last one. He'd been there twenty-nine years. One more year and he'd have his thirty in, just saying, because I know you're not that good at math. It was the end of the school year, just a few weeks to go, and his house burns down, and a day later he and his family move to San Diego."

"Kinda wish I was in San Diego now," Langdon said.

"Well, Mrs. Peach agreed to call me with the man's number, which she did on our way back."

"Yeah, that's good. Give him a call when you get a chance. Is that all?"

"Is that all?" Chabal walked out of the office into the bookstore.

Langdon followed her out, wondering what he'd said.

"Hey Langdon, you think I can get a book on credit?" Jamal asked. He was holding up a Walter Mosley book, *Black Betty*.

"Yeah, no problem. I have connections. Just let me run it through the computer." He took the book and walked to the counter. "You read *The Devil in a Blue Dress*?" he asked.

"Yeah, that Easy Rawlins is pretty badass."

"You want me in all day tomorrow as well?" Starling asked.

"If you can," Langdon replied. "Hey, Chabal, can you work tomorrow? We should have two people on, it being Saturday and all, and I don't know what my schedule holds."

"Shouldn't be a problem," Chabal replied. "The marriage counselor has been coaching me with tips on how to broach awkward conversations with my husband."

"Sorry. I need to hire somebody else. Who would have thought getting shot in the head would be such good advertising?"

"Yo, man, you got shot in the head?" Jamal asked.

Langdon pushed his red hair back from his forehead, exposing the jagged scar. "Couple years back on a case I was working."

"*We* were working," Chabal said.

"That's dope, man, tell me about it."

"Come on, I'll tell you on the way," Langdon said. "You all set?" he asked Starling.

"Sure thing, boss."

The teams were Langdon, Chabal, and Bart against Jamal, 4 by Four, and Goldilocks. They played half-court, one point per basket, games to eleven. After forty-five minutes, Jamal's team had won every game with him scoring the bulk of the points.

"I thought you said you were good," Jamal trash-talked after crossing over and sailing by Langdon as if he were a post planted in the court.

"Just getting warmed up," Langdon said.

"Maybe you weren't bad before you got old?"

"Old?" Langdon asked. "How about we play for something?"

"What do you want to play for?"

"We win, and you give me the name of the man who put the idea of robbing houses into your head," Langdon said.

"And when my team wins?" Jamal asked.

"What do you want?"

"You buy the beer."

"Okay, then, let's play," Langdon said. "Two out of three."

"You take the ball first," Jamal said, flipping it to Langdon a little harder than necessary.

Langdon bounce-passed the ball to Bart in the post and then went and knocked 4 by Four to the floor, leaving Chabal wide open. Bart tossed her the ball, and she made the short bank shot.

4 by Four climbed to his feet in time to check the ball. He passed it to Goldilocks, who immediately gave up the ball to Jamal. Jamal faked and went baseline, and Langdon hip-checked him, knocking him out of bounds with the ball.

The gloves were off, and the game was on. So far, it had been a game of rules, but the rulebook was now moot, and it became a battle.

Langdon's team won the first game 11-9.

Jamal's team won the second game 11-7.

By the time the third game rolled around, Bart's catching the ball in the post was reason enough for Goldilocks to elbow him in the back of the head and vice-versa. Chabal had a ragged scratch on her cheek, and 4 by Four had stuffed Kleenex into his nose to staunch the flow of blood. Langdon and Jamal had been talking a steady stream of trash, and on several occasions had almost come to blows. A small crowd of Bowdoin students had gathered to watch the unusual game, none of them so much as speaking.

Langdon's team was up 9-4 when Jamal took over the game. He sank three shots in a row from outside and defensively blocked two shots and had a steal. When Langdon was forced out into space to cover him, Jamal went by him like a cool breeze, and Langdon wasn't able to get close enough to hit him. With the score tied 9-9 and nobody bothering to cover Goldilocks or 4 by Four, Jamal split between Langdon and Chabal and pulled up short of Bart for a short jumper and the lead. When Langdon tried to muscle his way to the basket, Jamal shivered him with a forearm and took the ball like candy from a baby.

"Check it up," Langdon said, breathing raggedly. A tendril of blood was sliding down his forehead from the cuts he'd received from the falling ice. He probably should have gone for stitches. Too late now, he figured.

Jamal took the ball at the top of the key, stutter-stepped past Langdon, pulled up like he was going to take the mid-range jumper, bringing Bart flying out at him, and then juked and went past the heavy man with ease. He took two huge steps and went airborne over the top of Chabal with a monster dunk that shook the rafters, coming down on top of her, his knee driving into her face and crumpling her to the floor.

"Chabal! What the hell are you doing?" Langdon said. "Why'd you let him score? You just cost us the game."

"What's that?" Chabal rolled over, a puffy red spot on her cheekbone promising to turn into a bruise. "Game?"

"Go up with him, girl," Bart said. "Reject his sorry ass. Don't let him run all over you."

Jamal looked at Chabal on the ground, suddenly realizing he'd just slam-dunked on a five-foot tall woman and kneed her in the face in the process.

And then everybody started laughing. Jamal looked around in astonishment. Who laughed at some lady getting slammed to the ground? Some white woman by a Black kid from the ghetto, nonetheless. These people are crazy, Jamal thought, but kind of fun all at the same time.

"Anybody want to go for a beer?" 4 by Four asked.

"Got to get home," Chabal said. "Dinner with the fam."

"Me, too," Langdon said. He looked at the clock on the wall. He was supposed to be to Amanda's house in fifteen minutes. "Maybe later, though. I suppose I lost the bet."

Bart and Goldilocks thought a few beers was a grand idea.

Chapter 13

A quick shower and a five-minute drive later, Langdon and Jamal pulled into Amanda's house. It had been Langdon's house at one point, but he'd moved out when she ran off with the golfer, and he couldn't see himself moving back in. He should have called to tell her he was bringing a guest. Every time he had thought to do so that busy day, something had come up, and now here they were.

Unfortunately, Amanda was not one for surprises. "You should have told me you were bringing somebody," she said when she opened the door.

"I'm sorry about that," Langdon said. "This is Jamal."

Jamal stuck out his hand. "Hey."

"Amanda," she said, her own hand disappearing into his. "No worries, we have plenty of food." She looked nervously at the clutter behind her.

"Hello," Missouri said, hiding behind her mother's legs.

"Hello, little girl. You got a name?" Jamal asked.

"Missouri."

"Like the state?"

"I don't know."

"Missouri, will you take Jamal to the kitchen to get another plate and silverware?"

She gamely slid out into view and raised her hand up for him to take. "Come with me, Jamal."

Langdon smiled as he watched his two-foot tall daughter walk down the hallway to the kitchen with the six-foot seven-inch young man.

"Who is he?" Amanda asked.

"It's a case I'm working on," Langdon said.

"That doesn't tell me who he is."

"He, uh, got himself in some trouble and I'm trying to untangle why an otherwise good kid would do stupid things."

"What kind of trouble?"

"He broke into some houses and stole some stuff."

Amanda's eyes widened. "He's one of those boys?"

"Yep."

"Then, that was his friend that just…"

"Yep. Hung himself from the rafters of his jail cell."

"Maybe I better go check and make sure they find the right plate," Amanda said, hurrying down the hall.

Dinner was chicken smothered in cream sauce, green beans, and white rice. There was an open bottle of white wine in a chiller. It seemed that the rumor of Langdon being off the wagon had reached his wife.

"Will you pour us some wine, Goff?" Amanda asked as she brought Jamal and Missouri into the dining room with her. "How about you, Jamal?"

"I'll have some wine," Jamal said. He had, after all, won the bet, and had yet to see any beer, but this would do.

"You're not twenty-one," Langdon said.

"You lost the bet," Jamal said.

"Does your mother let you drink?"

"Does *your* mother let *you* drink?"

Langdon winced. He had lost the bet, after all. "What about training? There must be a rule about not drinking?"

"I think I'm on suspension. Give me some wine, man."

Langdon shrugged. Jamal was in his custody, after all, so the rules were up to him. Hell, he'd been drinking since he was fourteen. He poured the wine.

The conversation at dinner was dominated by Amanda telling Langdon about her art show down south, her mother maybe coming for a visit in the spring, and discussion of who was still without power. Missouri was the first to disappear from the tedious adult-dominated table, but Jamal was not far behind. He'd brought the new Mosley book and sprawled out on the couch to find out what Easy Rawlins was up to.

"So, is Jamal staying with you?" Amanda asked.

"Yeah, the court released him to my custody."

"What about his mom and dad?"

"His dad died years ago, and his mom got called into work. She should be back up tomorrow afternoon."

"I was hoping you might spend the night," Amanda said.

"If I stay, so does Jamal," Langdon replied.

"Maybe tomorrow night would be better?"

Langdon did the dishes and then went to find Missouri for a goodbye. He read her two short books, wondering when he'd be able to turn her on to Nancy Drew.

"I've got to go now," Langdon said.

"Why can't you stay?"

"Maybe another day."

"I miss you, Daddy."

"I miss you too, E."

"Where to now?" Jamal asked when they were back in the car.

"I don't know," Langdon said. He was trying to hold on to the warmth of his daughter's presence for as long as possible. "What time do you go to bed?"

Jamal laughed and shook his head. "You're too much, man. Do you ever stop and take a look at yourself in the mirror?"

"What?"

"*What time do you go to bed?*" Jamal asked. "That's just lame."

Langdon didn't answer.

"What would you be doing if I wasn't here?" Jamal asked.

"I guess I'd be going down to see if the boys were still drinking beer."

"Sounds good to me. I seem to remember you losing a bet, which means you buy the beer."

"You're not old enough to drink in Maine bars."

"Tall Black people never get carded in Maine," Jamal said. "I don't know if it's because they think we look old enough, or they're afraid we'll knife them, but I haven't been asked for ID since I been up here."

"I take it you get carded down in Mass.?"

"Pretty much everywhere, but I've been going to the Glitter Club the last couple years. I'm dialed up there."

"Goldilocks is a bit tamer than the Glitter Club, but I'm dialed up there," Langdon said.

"Don't even try." Jamal said, shaking his head. "Don't ever say that again."

Langdon grinned. "In this college town, I can guarantee you are going to get carded anywhere you go."

"Unless you happen to know the owner," Jamal said.

"So, I *am* dialed up?"

4 by Four and Bart were coming up the steps when they got there.

"Langdon!" 4 by Four yelled. "We were just talking about you and that Black kid, Jamal. Why wasn't I covering him? I would have shut him down." He turned away from Langdon and eyeballed Jamal. "Oh, hi there, kid."

"You were on his team," Langdon said.

"Ah, yes, the winning team," 4 by Four said, a stupid smile plastered on his face.

"You giving him a ride home?" Langdon asked Bart.

"Yeah, I got him," he replied, putting an arm around the lawyer and steering him away.

Goldilocks was throwing darts when they came down the stairs. Even though they'd eaten lunch there earlier, it had a different vibe at night, Jamal thought. It was a bit rougher around the edges. Two weather-beaten men were playing pool and drinking Budweiser. Music blared from the jukebox, and lights flashed over the small dance floor in the corner. In an hour or so, the young crowd would show up, and the place would be pulsing with sexual energy. This underlying current often led to fights, especially as the weekend crowd included such disparate elements. Friday night was a mix of locals, fishermen and clammers, military personnel from the Naval Air station in town, and Bowdoin College students. Now, at just before nine o'clock, there were only about fifteen people in the place, but anticipation rippled through the air promising more excitement to come.

Langdon got a pitcher of beer and two glasses from the bar and walked over to a table by Goldilocks with Jamal in tow. Goldilocks was a fantastic dart player and Langdon enjoyed watching him throw much like he appreciated listening to a master violinist—that is to say, for about a minute and then he was bored. There was something about the gentle rhythm as he worked through the numbers and finished with a bull's eye.

Langdon had known Goldilocks for years. When Langdon's father had run off when the boy was eight, Goldilocks had hired him to work on his lobster boat, filling bait bags and banding the bugs when they came out of the traps. Mainers didn't really believe in charity but offered a helping hand without being asked. Later, when Goldilocks bought the restaurant/bar, Langdon had worked as a busboy, waiter, bouncer, and on occasion, bartender until he had graduated college. It was Goldilocks who taught Langdon to play darts, a skill he used to make money and win drinking games while in college.

Now in his fifties, Goldilocks still retained the golden blond curls that had earned him his nickname from an early age. He was single, with a daughter who had moved out of state, and he lived upstairs from the bar. He didn't even own a car, as everything he could want was within easy walking distance. Shop 'N' Save, the health food store, a movie theater, video store, and of course, his own place to eat and drink. He still had his lobster boat, and in warmer weather, rode a bicycle out to Nate's Marina to work the few traps he still kept. He made more money than he needed and funneled the excess into a college scholarship program he'd started at the high school, Langdon having been the first recipient some twelve years earlier.

"He can't be here at this time of night," Goldilocks said, coming over to their table.

"It's okay, man, we're dialed up," Langdon said.

Goldilocks shook his head, as did Jamal. "Whatever, but he can't drink."

"I bought us Sam Adams, so consider it a history lesson on Boston."

Jamal tipped his glass at Goldilocks. "The spoils of victory," he said.

"How about a game of darts?" Goldilocks asked. He should have known better than to try and argue with Langdon. Besides, the kid looked like he was thirty.

"Only if there's a wager," Langdon said.

"Sure," Goldilocks replied.

"Go get him, Jamal," Langdon said.

"What?"

"The man played your game earlier. Now it's time for you to play his game." Langdon looked at Goldilocks. "We passed the boys leaving," Langdon said. "I think 4 by Four may have been slightly over-served."

"Take a few practice throws, kid," Goldilocks said, turning to look at Langdon. "I think something's going on with him. He's been in an awful lot lately—hitting the sauce pretty hard."

It wasn't until about eleven o'clock that the place began to really hop. A group of Bowdoin girls showed up and were making eyes at Jamal, who had enough beer in him to go over and sit at their table. He was somewhat humbled, having lost nine games of darts in a row to Goldilocks. To his credit, he'd refused to give up until the pressing crowd made throwing sharp objects while drunk a hazard.

At one, Langdon pried Jamal away from the coeds, and Goldilocks shoved them both into a cab and sent them home. When Goldilocks went back down into the bar, he realized Coffee Dog was still there. He called and left Langdon a message that he had the dog for the night.

It was supposed to be his night off, but he stayed around to help clean up before going up the stairs to his apartment. It was times like this that sometimes the loneliness snuck up on him, so it was nice to have the companionship of the dog for the night. Maybe one of these days he'd get a dog of his own.

Goldilocks slid *True Romance* into the VHS player, having rented it earlier. He usually needed a couple of hours to come down from a busy bar night, and movies had become his addiction. For a change, he had company to share the flick with, and the dog certainly was happy to partake of some popcorn as well. When they got to the scene where Christopher Walken is torturing Dennis Hopper, a sudden shiver went through Goldilocks' body. It was as if the punishment was being inflicted on his own body, and he hastily hit 'stop' and turned the television off, but it would be quite some time before sleep would embrace him.

Chapter 14

The phone was ringing. Or maybe it was his head?

"Hello," Langdon said into the receiver as alertly as possible. He saw sleep as a sign of weakness and hated to be caught visiting the sandman.

"Do you know where your dog is?" The voice was pitched low and sinister.

"What?"

"The brown mutt called Coffee Dog. Do you know where he is?"

"Who is this?"

"If you ever want to see your dog alive again, you will pay your bar tab at Goldilocks along with a hefty tip for the bartender who had to put up with you last night."

Langdon swore at the man, and then paused in thought. "Do you really have my dog?"

"For sure," Goldilocks said. "You forgot him here last night, or should I say this morning. I left a message on your machine."

"Things got a little hazy," Langdon said. "But, yeah, now I remember getting the message."

"There's probably a reason you didn't drink for the past year."

"You got that right. I can be right over to grab him."

"Don't worry about it. I was just calling to see if it was okay if I give him bacon, eggs, and potatoes for breakfast?"

"I would say you would have a new best friend, then," Langdon said.

"He does make good company. We both got freaked out by a Tarantino flick and cashed in early, though. I was going to go up to the Town Commons for some snowshoeing after I eat. How about I take the dog, and you can come by around noon to get him?"

"That works for me. Hey, Goldilocks? Thanks."

Langdon hung up the phone and looked at the clock. It was eight. He stumbled to the coffee machine and put a full pot on. This morning called for drastic measures. His mouth was fuzzy, and he tried orange juice to dispel the thick dryness, but this made his stomach churn over in a threatening manner. He peeked in on Jamal, who hung off the single bed on all sides, dead to the world. In sleep, he was more like the young boy he was than the man he was becoming.

A cold shower was in order, one of the penalties Langdon imposed on himself for overconsumption, and he managed to shave without cutting himself. He rewarded himself with a cup of hot coffee and then was ready to face his wife, or at least, to talk to her on the phone.

"Amanda, hi. Can we get together sometime today?" He was missing his daughter.

"I'm meeting some friends for lunch down in Portland. Maybe later?"

"How about I pick up Missouri and hang out with her today? Then you can do your thing with your friends."

"You still got Jamal with you?"

"Yeah."

There was a long silence on the phone.

"He's a good kid, Amanda, really."

"I don't want my daughter hanging around with criminals."

"Okay, okay. His mother should be up this afternoon. How about I grab Missouri around four for some dad time, and then we can all get together later?"

Langdon's next call was to Chabal. He held his breath, hoping that her husband didn't answer the phone. He didn't. "Hey," he said when she answered. "You working out this morning?"

"Working out? I'm not sure I can even walk this morning," she said.

"What's the matter with you?"

"Oh, I don't know. It might have something to do with being run over by a huge man-child yesterday, who, as far as I'm concerned, should have assault charges added to the burglary stuff."

"That little bump?" Langdon laughed. "I still don't understand why you handed the game away like that."

They bantered back and forth before agreeing that it should have been a charge, and therefore, the game a tie.

"I could use a workout," Chabal said. "I told Star I'd come in at noon today, and had planned to do some chores, but I'm sure the laundry and cleaning can wait."

Jamal merely grunted when Langdon shook him and told him he was going out. Langdon doubted the boy was going anywhere anytime soon. Unfortunately for Langdon, he and Chabal arrived at the gym just as a Power Pacing class began. The instructor cajoled them into the room with Langdon dragging his feet, and the next forty-five minutes were spent being screamed at by some tyrannical instructor with masochistic tendencies over blaring rock music.

"That was great!" Chabal said as she helped pry Langdon's hands from the cycle.

Langdon sank to the floor while she went to refill her water bottle. He was vaguely aware of a distant voice, the instructor's, expressing concern over the color of his skin and the fact that he was curled into a fetal position. When the fit young woman got the owner from the front desk, he merely gave Langdon a kick and told him to stop being a baby. And, they hadn't even gotten to the weights yet.

"Ya know, I'm not so sure this drinking thing is all that good for you," Chabal said as they were super setting pull-downs with bicep curls.

"Not so good for my body, that's for sure," he replied.

"What's that supposed to mean? It's good for your mind?"

"It helps reduce my angst, takes the edge away."

"You're the most laid-back man I have ever met."

"Ah, on the outside," Langdon said. "On the inside, I'm a seething cauldron of complications."

"Sounds like a cop-out to me," she said, but inside wondered if perhaps it wasn't true.

"Yeah, probably, but I did feel the routine of life starting to smother me."

"We done?" Chabal asked. "Time for a shower?"

"Together?" Langdon looked sideways at her.

"Sure. Which locker room should we use?"

"Definitely the women's room."

"You'd fit right in. Nobody would notice anything out of the ordinary."

"Okay, no shower together. How about some brunch?"

"Sure."

Langdon spent the brunch thinking about Chabal in the shower, or more specifically, the two of them in the shower together. He knew it was inappropriate. He was married. She was married. He was her employer. She was his employee. None of these realities banished thoughts of the two of them in the shower together.

They chatted amicably while he had a Reuben and she had a Caesar salad. They laughed and joked, and to tell the truth, Langdon couldn't remember a word of what was said. In his version, they were in the shower together and tongues and lips had better things to be doing than talking.

They made it back to the bookshop ten minutes before noon.

"Morning, Star," Langdon said as they walked in. "You look terrible." And he did, his skin was ghastly pale, his eyes were twitching from lack of sleep, black blotches puffed out below his eyes.

"I spent the night here researching MECI," Star said. "Totally lost track of time."

Langdon looked down guiltily. He'd gone to play basketball, had a nice dinner with his wife and daughter, and then gone drinking. Instead of coming in to give the man a break, this morning he'd gone to work out, and then out to eat again.

"Find anything?" Chabal asked.

"Yep," Star said. "I sure did."

"What'd you find?" Langdon asked.

"Rick Pious was all over the internet. He had some pretty good teams at Las Vegas. They never won the big dance, but they had a few Sweet Sixteen appearances, and once even made it to the Final Four."

"We know all that," Langdon said. "The man is a future hall of famer, if not in the country, at least in Maine and Nevada."

"Then I got to wondering what would make a man move from the mecca of civilization and the limelight of big-time coaching to backwoods Maine?"

"Yes?" Langdon and Chabal said together.

"He was accused of rape."

"Rape?" Chabal had just met the man, and while he seemed extremely arrogant, he didn't seem to fit her idea of a rapist.

"Who?" Langdon asked. "A student?"

"More than just a student," Starling said. A bit of color was returning to his face with the satisfaction of his knowledge.

"A cheerleader?" Chabal asked.

"Nope."

"Out with it," Langdon said.

"His starting point guard."

"What?"

"It took some digging, but I found several articles. The boy said that Coach Pious had bullied and intimidated him into performing oral sex on several different occasions."

"Was he arrested?"

"I was unable to find anything else other than just a tiny blurb about six weeks later that the charges against Coach Pious had been dropped. No reason why. That's what I was trying to dig up, but the whole story seemed to have just blown away. So to speak…"

"The school fired him?" Langdon asked.

"He was up for a new contract, and they chose to not renew it," Starling said.

"And with controversy swirling around him, there wasn't another college in the country that would touch him," Langdon said.

"So, that still doesn't explain why MECI would hire him. Do you suppose they don't know?" Chabal asked.

"That's a good question," Langdon said.

They were interrupted by a small flurry of customers, and the three of them went to work taking care of them.

"You need to go check on Jamal," Chabal said as the last woman walked off with several Marcia Muller books.

"He's fine," Langdon replied. "Plus, it looks to be a busy day, and Star might collapse at any moment."

"Is he fine?" Chabal asked.

"What do you mean by that?"

"The school has a history of suicides. His friend just offed himself. And now we find out his coach might be forcing his players to perform sexual acts?" Chabal's eyes were blazing. Any thought of hurting kids, no matter their age or size, got her dander up.

"He was pretty adamant he never wanted to go back there," Langdon said.

"I can stay around and help," Starling said.

"Go get some sleep and come back at four when the afternoon rush kicks in," Chabal said to him, and then turned to Langdon. "Get home now."

"Okay, that makes sense," Starling said. "I'll be back in a few hours." He went to the office and got his jacket and left.

"I guess I should go. Maybe I can bring Jamal back here with me."

"I'll be fine, Langdon. Get out of here."

Langdon walked across the street and up to Goldilocks' apartment.

The door was unlocked, and he found man and beast sleeping on the couch. Coffee Dog jumped down excitedly, somehow not waking the man up, and they slipped back out the door.

When they got home, they found Jamal wrapped up in a quilt, watching college basketball in the living room. Langdon would've guessed that he hadn't been awake for more than a few minutes. Coffee Dog cleared away any vestiges of sleep by licking his face, and Jamal, cocooned in the quilt, was unable to defend himself.

"Did you get any food yet?" Langdon asked.

"Not yet."

"Hungry?"

"I could eat."

"I got cereal, bread, and maybe even some muffins kicking around somewhere."

"What do you got for cereal?" Jamal, having freed his arms, pushed the dog away. "Man, its freezing in here. Don't you have any heat?"

One battle at a time, Langdon thought. He walked over and notched the thermostat up a tad. It was true that he liked cold better than the average person. "Why don't you drag your butt into the kitchen and take a gander. Cereal is in the pantry next to the fridge. You know where to find the milk?"

"Ugh," Jamal said. He gamely rose to his feet, extending his long frame into a standing position.

"I got a TV out there, so you won't have to miss any of the game," Langdon said.

The kitchen had a counter in the middle with stools along one side facing a television. This is where Langdon ate most of his home meals, watching sports, and perhaps the occasional Clint Eastwood movie. Jamal was draped over a stool eating a bowl of cereal when Langdon followed him in.

"I need to know the real reason Stanley hung himself," he said to Jamal as way of preamble.

"I told you, man. His parents were real uptight and shit."

"Yeah, you said they had some cash. Stanley wasn't exactly hurting, was he?"

"He was usually pretty flush."

"So, I don't get why he was ripping off houses in the first place. I mean, you grew up with nothing, but he was raised with a silver spoon in his mouth."

"You don't understand nothing, man."

"Why don't you tell me, then?" Langdon said. "What's the real reason you all were riding around ripping off things and smashing up homes?"

Jamal put on his tough inner-city face and gave Langdon the thousand-yard stare.

"Come on, Jamal. Don't close me out. What was really going on?"

"We just got a little carried away, man. That's the whole deal."

"Are you okay?"

"What do you mean?"

"You're not going to do anything stupid, are you? Slit your wrists? Take some pills? Hang yourself?" Langdon leaned across the island with his face inches from Jamal's.

"What are you talking about, man? What do you know?"

"Talk to me. What's really going on?"

Jamal held his stare silently.

"Who really put you up to robbing houses?"

Nothing.

"Has Coach Pious ever made sexual advances to you?"

Chapter 15

Jamal had stormed off to his bedroom, slamming the door, and didn't come out until his mother arrived. Langdon left them alone in his place to catch up, and went to hang with his daughter. Missouri was waiting for him at the front door when he arrived.

"Daddy!" she yelled. "I've been standing here waiting for you for days."

"Hey girl, I missed you, too," Langdon said, picking her up and swinging her around in circles.

"Faster!"

Langdon spun her until he thought he might fall down. His stomach lurched, but he kept going, for hangovers were not allowed with daughters around.

Amanda came down the hall with a smile. "I miss you, too, Goff," she said.

Langdon gave her a kiss on the lips, just a brush. "And I miss you. Maybe the three of us can do something together?"

"What are we doing?" Missouri asked.

"I told you I had plans today," Amanda said. "I'm supposed to go down to Portland. Maybe later we can catch up? After Missouri goes to bed?" Amanda looked at him with her eyes wide and inviting.

Langdon looked back at her, wondering if she really wanted him to sleep over and have sex, or if she was merely not ready to give up on what was clearly a losing game. He figured that if he was becoming disinterested in their weekly rite of fornication, then she most certainly must be, for he wasn't sure how interested she'd ever been in the first place.

"I need to get back at a decent time to have a conversation with my client," he said after a bit. "His mother just got into town, and I need to sit down with the both of them."

"Can't it wait until the morning?" Her face showed relief, but her words suggested exasperation.

"I feel like I'm on the verge of cracking something wide open with Jamal. There's something he needs to get off his chest, and I want to give him the chance," Langdon said doggedly.

"Fine." Amanda took her coat off a hook.

"Maybe I can come over after speaking with him?"

"Whatever." She flinched and stepped to the door.

"Can I bring my Barbie doll with me, Daddy?" Missouri didn't wait for an answer but ran back into the house to retrieve it.

"It's gotten bigger than just theft and vandalism," Langdon said. "I think there might be sexual abuse involved."

"Jamal was sexually molested?" Amanda was openly skeptical. "You mean some older woman tempted him into her bed? And that's why he's running around breaking the law?"

"There are some indications…" Langdon stopped himself. He couldn't go around slandering Coach Pious without more concrete proof, not even to his own wife. "There's more to it, is all. He's not a bad kid."

"That might be the case, but until I'm certain, I don't want my daughter around him," Amanda said. "I'm probably a bit jealous that he's taking all your time, is all."

Langdon bit his tongue on commenting that it was her who had been gone for the past ten days. "I'll bring Missouri back here at seven, give her a bath, and read her some books."

"I should be back by eight," Amanda said.

Missouri and Coffee Dog came racing down the hallway. She had a slight lead and bobbed left just as he went to pass her, and an ugly collision occurred. "Daddy, Coffee runned me over," Missouri said with big gasping sobs.

"Well, I think we'll leave him here, then. If you're okay, we have plans to pick up Tangerine, go to McDonald's, and then to see *Alice in Wonderland*?"

"*Alice in Wonderland*?" The tears immediately dried up. "Yay." She started dancing around the room, and then suddenly stopped and got very serious. "Coffee Dog didn't mean it. He can come, too."

"I don't think he likes plays," Langdon said. "He'd rather take a nap."

The three of them went out the door together, leaving the dog behind, but then went their separate ways.

"What are we doing here?" Missouri asked as they pulled into the parking lot behind the Coffee Dog Bookstore.

"I thought we'd say a quick hello to Chabal. That okay?"

"We won't miss the movie?"

"Actually, it's not a movie, but a play with real people, over at the School Street Theater."

"Whatever." Missouri rolled her eyes, a look of exasperation most likely learned from her mother. "We won't be late for the *play*?"

"No, we have plenty of time."

"Okay, then."

The counter was three deep when they got there. Langdon pitched in to help while Missouri went over to the small play area in the corner and played with the wooden train. He knew that he shouldn't have left Chabal alone at the store on a Saturday afternoon, but it seemed his life currently had too many moving pieces.

The last customer had just walked out the door when Starling arrived. Chabal ran off to pee, and once she was back, Langdon told them he was out the door.

"You're leaving?" Chabal asked.

"You okay to stay until close?" Langdon asked.

"Yeah, sure, but I think you need to be around more. It's not really a local store if the owner isn't ever in it," she said.

"Maybe I should make you part owner?" Langdon asked, more than half-seriously.

Chabal waved her hand dismissively. "There were points this afternoon when people had a ten-minute wait in line."

"You know the hot dog stand theory, right?" Langdon asked.

"Hot dog stand?"

"Yeah. There are two hot dog stands, side by side. One has a really long line, maybe fifteen minutes wait, and the other has nobody at all in line. Which one would you go to?"

"Is one of them Barnes and Noble?" Chabal asked. "Because you can get the same books there for a cheaper price."

"Okay, okay." Langdon raised his hands in mock surrender. "Monday morning I'll call up the Bath paper and get an ad in that we're hiring. Maybe we'll be able to get a pretty college girl in to help out."

Chabal hit him, not gently, in the arm. "Where are you rushing off to?"

"We're going to go pick up Tangerine and go to McDonald's and then over to School Street to see *Alice in Wonderland*." Tangerine was Richam and Jewell's daughter.

Chabal grinned. Her eyes went from flat to all sparkles in an instant, and her cheeks, round to begin with, puffed out in an adorable way with the force of her smile. She wished that her own husband, John, was as doting of a father as Langdon. John was a good man in so many ways, but he was of the belief that raising children was the mother's duty.

"Okay then," she said. "You go and have a great time."

Leaving the store, busy as it was, was no big deal, but leaving Chabal behind was a bit more difficult. "For sure. And I'm serious about making you a partner," Langdon said.

"We can talk about that another time." What, exactly did he mean by *partner*, Chabal wondered? Was she just imagining the chemistry between the two of them? They had such a good time together. She'd been deeply attracted to him the first time she ever saw him, which was months before they officially met. Chabal knew that she would leave her husband for Langdon in a heartbeat if the opportunity presented itself, but did he feel the same way? He said, albeit without much conviction, that he was trying to reconcile with Amanda. If the two of them got together, that would make two broken families. It was all such a mess. Enough so that it made her knees weak.

"Thanks, Chabal. I'll see you tomorrow."

"Bye," she said. "And Langdon? This time stay out of the ball pit."

"Don't worry, I'm not allowed back to that McDonald's. We're going over to the one in Bath."

Richam and Jewell owned a ranch house with a spectacular view overlooking Maquoit Bay. As soon as they pulled up, Missouri was out of her car seat and running inside, no knock needed. Langdon followed more slowly. There'd been a time when he would have entered just as unthinkingly as his daughter, but things between him and Jewell were still a bit stiff after he'd put her family in danger a couple years earlier with a villain named Shakespeare.

As it was, he knocked loudly on the door Missouri had left open. Tangerine had whisked Missouri up to her room to show her some new toy, or so Richam said as he met Langdon at the door. Jewell was upstairs. Langdon updated him on the latest information on the case before gathering the girls and herding them into the car.

It was a fifteen-minute drive to the McDonald's in Bath, but it was worth the trip as it had, by far, the best playground in the area. Langdon ordered the food while the girls went screaming through the tunnels and slides. He spread it out for them, making sure to hide the toys for the car afterwards, before calling them to the table to eat. After about five minutes they appeared long enough to scarf down a few Chicken McNuggets and fries before heading to the ball pit. Langdon shrugged, and finished their food. He hadn't ordered anything, knowing this would happen. He was of the belief that if a kid were hungry, then they'd eat. And if they weren't, well then, they didn't.

He was about to bus the trays when a familiar face caught his attention. Standing at the counter placing an order was a burly man with black hair that was most likely a wig. Who was that? Then it came to him. It was the assistant coach at MECI. What was his name? Helot. Ed Helot. It was the same man who'd come to confront him when he'd gone up to Skowhegan to pay Coach Pious a visit. What was he doing in Bath? Langdon glanced over at the girls. They were fine. He went out to his car and retrieved his cell phone.

He called 4 by Four first, and when there was no answer, Bart, but the policeman also didn't pick up. Jeff answered the phone at the pub and passed the phone over to Goldilocks. The two of them must have been standing next to each other at the bar.

"Hey," Langdon said. "Can you get away from the bar for a little bit?"

"Should be able to. It's pretty slow. Why?" Goldilocks asked.

"I'm sitting here at McDonald's in Bath, and guess who walks in?"

"No idea."

"Ed Helot."

"Who's that?"

"He's the assistant coach up to MECI."

"So?"

"Don't you think that's sort of peculiar? Like maybe he came down to look up Jamal?"

"Yeah, but I can think of a thousand other reasons that are more likely. Like, maybe he came down to see a Bowdoin game? I think they played this afternoon. Or maybe he's visiting a friend? Maybe his mom lives in Bath?"

"I don't know," Langdon said. "It seems like a bit of a coincidence to me. I got a hunch he's hiding something."

"And what do you want me to do?"

"Can you come tail him?"

"You've been watching too many episodes of *Rockford Files.*"

"Just do me a favor, would you?"

"Why can't you do it?"

"I got Missouri and Tangerine with me."

Goldilocks sighed. "Okay. I think Jeff will let me use his car. I'll be right over."

"Thanks. I owe you."

"Yeah, I'll put it on your tab," Goldilocks said and hung up.

Ed Helot sat down by himself at a table but was joined by a second man after a few minutes. The other man was thin, had wire-rimmed glasses, a fancy watch on his wrist, and wore an expensive suit. They leaned in so that they were almost touching and conversed back and forth in whispers. Langdon would have loved to have heard what they were talking about but was afraid to move closer. If he were spotted, the hope of anything coming of Goldilocks' surveillance would evaporate.

Goldilocks arrived just as the two men rose to leave. Langdon pointed at them and mouthed a thank you to his friend, who followed them back out the door. Langdon put his private detective hat away and went back to being a father. Missouri and Tangerine were separated from the playground with minimal fuss, especially after offering to buy them a cookie and hot chocolate at the theater. As they struggled into their coats, Langdon looked out the window and saw Goldilocks drive by, apparently tailing Ed Helot.

He was probably wasting the man's time on a fool's errand.

Chapter 16

Goldilocks pulled onto Route 1 South behind Ed Helot, who was, in turn, behind the man he'd left McDonald's with. They pulled into the passing lane and buzzed up to 10 miles an hour over the speed limit. They seemed to be in a hurry. Maybe Langdon had been onto something after all. Goldilocks thought this was pretty thin, but he'd seen Langdon's hunches play out before. It was irritating, but the man was more often right than wrong. Besides, what else did he have to do?

Goldilocks had seen him grow up from a scared lad of just eight into the scared man he was today. Goldilocks realized that most people fell for his outward demeanor—that he was a tough guy and that nothing bothered him. In reality, he took on every problem his family and friends had as if they were his own. It most likely stemmed from becoming the man of the family when he had been all of fourteen years old.

As the three cars got off at the New Meadows exit, took a left, and then a right on the road heading towards Cooks Corner, Goldilocks pondered the turns his younger friend's life had taken. When he had seen an infatuated Langdon bring Amanda home from college, he'd hoped it would wear off. But it hadn't, and they'd gotten married. He had wanted to stand up at the wedding and stop it, the way they do in the movies. Instead, Goldilocks had kept his mouth shut.

When Amanda then took off with some guy a couple years back, Goldilocks had silently rejoiced, particularly because his fervent wish of seeing Langdon getting together with Chabal Daniels had started to blossom. Then Amanda had returned, and Langdon seemed to have again fallen under her spell. Goldilocks was not going to stay quiet any longer. He was working his nerve up to whack Langdon upside that thick head, point at Chabal, and say "*there* is your destiny, dumbass!"

The two cars pulled into the Greenlander Motel, which consisted of about thirty units in a horseshoe shape around a central office and an above ground pool. Goldilocks drove on past and turned around in the Walmart parking lot. He pulled into the motel from the opposite direction, just as Helot came out of the office, got back in the other man's car, leaving his own parked where it was. They pulled into the back and parked, as did Goldilocks, four trucks down. The trucks were all heavy-duty and with out-of-state plates, The Greenlander apparently the lodging of choice for utility workers who'd come to Maine to help restore electricity.

He watched as the two men got out, each carrying a small bag, barely larger than man-purses. As Helot was unlocking the door, the other man came up behind him and wrapped his arms around his torso and laid his cheek on his back. Helot pushed the door open, and then turned and kissed the man, before easing into the room locked in an embrace and kicking the door shut.

Goldilocks waited for about ten minutes and then called Langdon. The call went straight to voice mail, reminding him that Langdon was at a play. He left a message saying that it appeared to be nothing more than a lovers' get together, and that he'd give it another half-hour, but it looked like the two men were in for the night.

After twenty minutes, he started the car up, but as he did, a BMW pulled in and a Black man in an expensive overcoat got out and went into a room two doors down. In a motel filled with utility workers, this wealthy man and Ed Helot were the oddities, and Goldilocks wondered if there was some connection. He had just decided this was a foolish notion when a Toyota Corolla pulled in and a woman got out and went to the door that the man had just entered. She looked over her shoulder as she knocked, and Goldilocks immediately recognized her.

It was the woman who had hired Langdon on his latest case. Goldilocks' mind buzzed. What was her name? This was indeed getting interesting. Goldilocks sat in the idling car running multiple scenarios through his head. The adrenalin of being on to something coursed through his body, banishing the sluggishness from a poor night's sleep after that disquieting Tarantino film of the night before.

Slightly less than an hour later the door reopened. Latricia Jones— whose name Goldilocks had finally remembered— and the man both came out and went to their respective cars. There was no lingering kiss or hug to indicate they'd been together. Latricia's face was drawn tightly, while the man overflowed with a confident satisfaction.

This seemed to be a better lead than watching a motel room all night, but which one to follow? Goldilocks chose the man because he thought that Langdon would be very interested in finding out his identity. He thought about calling him, but then remembered that Langdon was probably still at the play. It could wait. Maybe he would have more information to relay soon.

The BMW went down the Bath Road and swung around Bowdoin College, heading out of town towards Freeport. It was dark, and Goldilocks doubted that his headlights behind the man were a tip-off, but he made an effort to stay back. When he turned right off the road, Goldilocks had to race to catch up, and barely saw the car turning into a driveway and disappearing through the trees, presumably to a house tucked back in the dark woods.

Goldilocks pulled into the driveway and turned his headlights off. He wondered what the next step was. Should he go up to the door and knock? He could claim to be lost, but that wasn't any guarantee he'd learn the man's identity. There was a mailbox with the number 579 on it, and he found a pen in his pocket and jotted that on his hand. The first thing to do was to call Langdon. He grabbed his phone and went to dial just as his side window was smashed in, glass fragments showering him like the icy pellets of the recent storm that had driven Maine into darkness.

The man he'd been following stood there with a pistol held casually only about a foot from his forehead. Goldilocks did not know much about guns, but it was black, and the opening at the end of the barrel looked like it was the size of a trashcan.

Chapter 17

It was almost nine before Langdon dropped Tangerine off. The girls had loved the show and got into the car yelling and laughing, but both were asleep before they'd completed the five-minute drive. He handed the sleeping Tangerine to Richam at the door, and then drove Missouri to Amanda's house. He carried his daughter in and tucked her into bed, slightly disappointed he hadn't gotten a chance to read to her, as this was one of his favorite moments in life.

Amanda was annoyed, as he'd told her they'd be back by seven. He really was quite bad with time. She also looked tired and put up no argument when Langdon said he really had to go. Then she told him not to bother trying to stop by later. In the driveway, he checked his phone and saw he had a message from Goldilocks. It was short and to the point. It had been a fool's errand, unless discovering Ed Helot was gay was somehow pertinent to the case.

When he got to his house, Latricia and Jamal were watching basketball in the living room.

"Welcome home, honey," Latricia said. Jamal made a face, not appreciating the joke.

"Good to see you've made yourself comfortable. Can we talk for a few minutes before you leave?" Langdon asked.

"About that," Latricia said. "You know how you offered we could stay here?"

"Not a problem."

"I really can't afford a hotel room, and I don't know how long it'll be, but maybe we can stay a night or two until we figure something out?"

Latricia Jones was a beautiful woman. The haggard lines had disappeared from her face, if not the tightness. Her black hair was out of its bun, descending upon her shoulders in voluminous waves, and her skin was a rich black and without blemish.

"Do you have a bag in the car?"

"Jamal already brought them in," Latricia said. "I brought him some things, too."

"Great. Maybe we can talk?" He looked at Jamal who clicked off the television.

"Jamal has something he wants to tell you," Latricia said with the air of someone turning a truant student into the principal.

Langdon sat down in his leather recliner facing the couch upon which the Joneses sat. "Okay."

"Well, my mom, she, uh, says you're just trying to help, and that you're, uh, on my side," Jamal said. "And you, uh, seem like a straight-up kind of guy." Jamal was struggling to find the right words, almost like he was reciting an oral report in class without notes.

"What do you want to tell me?"

"The guy who suggested the whole thing, that's what you want to know, right?"

Langdon nodded.

"It was Larry the Fish."

"Does Larry the Fish have a last name?"

"Yeah, I imagine, but I don't know it."

"Where'd you meet him?"

"He hangs out at the Glitter Club."

Latricia's nostrils flared but she didn't say a word.

Langdon was in a quandary. Just when he'd gotten around to thinking that MECI was the Pandora's box, here was Jamal pointing him in another direction.

"What was the deal?"

"What do you mean?"

"What was your cut? What was his cut?"

"Fifty-fifty."

"The three of you split half and he kept the other half?"

"Yeah."

"Does your Uncle Eddie know him?"

Jamal cast a nervous look at his mother. "Yeah, sure. Larry lays down the numbers for Eddie."

"So, Larry is a bookie." Langdon leaned back and put his feet up on the footstool. "What else does Larry do?"

"Like I said, he's connected."

"You mean the Italian mob?"

"Yeah, what's left of it. They got busted up pretty good the last few years."

"Yeah, it was that Irish boss, Bulger, or something like that that who was snitching for the FBI and got them all arrested," Langdon said, remembering the recent news stories.

"Yeah, Whitey was his name, go figure. He ratted them all out, and so Larry's been laying low. Eddie throws him a bone once in a while, figuring it can't hurt to have one of the few Italians not in jail on his payroll."

"Do you know this Larry dude?" Langdon asked Latricia.

She shrugged. "I heard of him."

"I guess your worst fears have been realized," Langdon said.

"What's that mean?"

"You didn't want Jamal hanging around your brother-in-law because he was a thug, and you were afraid that he would get caught up in it somehow. Well, here it is."

Latricia said nothing. Her eyes were blank, devoid of emotion.

Langdon waited for a reaction, anything, but when none was forthcoming, he turned back to Jamal. "Okay, let's hear the whole thing from the beginning."

Jamal had known Larry for several years, but when Bobby Russo had been indicted last year, the last in a lengthy line of Italian mob arrests in Boston, Larry had become more of a regular fixture at the Glitter Club. Jamal had gone home when the ice storm knocked out power at school. He'd been complaining to Larry the Fish about having no cash, not like the white kids at school who were probably all home driving their sports cars around and taking their girls out on dates and shit like that.

Larry the Fish had offered up a solution, which was to make some quick cash—and not pocket change either, but some real money. When Larry the Fish pointed out that all the flush white families in Maine had moved into hotels or gone to stay with relatives, leaving their big homes unguarded with no working alarms, Jamal had seen the dollar signs flash in front of his eyes.

The deal had been a 50/50 split. Larry the Fish supplied the van, which he boosted somewhere, and he handled the sale of the stolen goods. Jamal and his buddies took the risk, but how risky was it, really? Or so he'd thought.

Once the story was complete, Jamal sighed as if finishing an extremely unlikeable task. Langdon caught Latricia studying his face, and thought that odd, instead of showering her son with maternal concern. The phone rang, interrupting his musing. It was Chabal.

"Hey Chabal, what's up?"

"How was the kid time?"

They made the mandatory small talk for a few minutes before Chabal got down to business. "I called that former teacher at MECI, you know, the one who left after his house burned down?"

"What'd he have to say?"

"Not much. He was quite rude, actually."

"Okay. Is there something else?"

"Yes. I think John Flanagan is the key to the whole puzzle," Chabal said.

"John Flanagan?" Langdon was preoccupied with the story of Larry the Fish and how to proceed with Latricia and Jamal.

"That's his name, the teacher I called." Patiently.

"Why's that?"

"Don't you think it's remarkably odd that over the course of nine years Jerry Peccance replaced every single member of the faculty? And that the last holdout had his house burn down, helping him to decide to leave?"

"What are you saying?" Langdon was in the kitchen on the phone but lowered his voice anyway. "You think something happened at MECI, and Peccance covered it up by getting rid of everybody?"

"Don't go all skeptical on me, or I'll be forced to come over and knock you upside the head," Chabal said. "Put all the pieces together, would you? You're supposed to be the detective."

"That's what I'm trying to do," Langdon said.

"What do we have so far?" Chabal asked. "Fourteen years ago, Jerry Peccance becomes headmaster and over the next decade replaces absolutely everybody. One of the new recruits is Rick Pious, a basketball coach and health teacher who left Las Vegas under a cloud of suspicion that he was sexually molesting one of his players. Over the course of Peccance's tenure as headmaster, there have been a rash of suicides amongst the students there."

"Keep going," Langdon said, now drawn into this new theory.

"Just this week, three star athletes and otherwise good kids with no criminal background get arrested for robbing and vandalizing homes. Not just vandalizing, but spewing hatred and anger. Why? Where did it come from? The one thing they all have in common is MECI." Chabal's voice was tinged with both excitement and alarm. She truly believed she was onto something, but what would happen if she was right?

"What you seem to be saying is that the entire faculty is involved in sexually molesting their students?" Langdon made sure to deliver the line deadpan.

"Or at least turning a blind eye. Maybe it's just him and Pious who are the pervs, but he carefully hired a staff that doesn't like to make waves, engage in conflict, and who are only too happy to avoid confrontation."

"What do you suggest we do?"

"I think we need to talk to John Flanagan face to face," Chabal said.

"Didn't you say he moved to San Diego?"

"Yes."

"Do you know where?"

"Yes. Mrs. Peach? The one who we went to lunch with? She got me his address and phone number. He didn't leave it with the school, but her sister is an insurance agent in town, and she handled the payout when his house burned up with all of his possessions. She had to send him a check and talked with him several times on the phone."

"Yet, you said the man was rude and unwilling to talk to you. What good would it do for me to go see him face to face?" Langdon had to admit there was merit to this whole line of reasoning, but then there was Jamal in the other room just having revealed that it was all Larry the Fish's idea.

"We."

"We?"

"I booked us two tickets. Last minute so they were marked way down."

"You booked tickets to San Diego? When?"

"Tomorrow night."

"What?"

"Like I said, they were a great deal. If you don't want to go, fine, I'll go alone."

Langdon sat down at the island. Go to San Diego? With Chabal? Just the two of them? "Your husband will never let you go. You had to lie to the man to be able to go up to Skowhegan for a few hours. And if you tell him that I'm going with you, and we're spending the night together? No way."

"Two nights."

"You're serious?"

"I need to get away," Chabal said. "To think. Things aren't so good at home."

"Maybe you should go alone…"

"I was hoping you'd go with me," Chabal said. "You know, over the past year, we've kind of lost our connection. The shootout at Fort Andross. Your wife coming back. The bookstore doing crazy business with all the publicity, and on top of that, you taking all these cases as well. My husband's barely speaking to me."

"The two of us going away for a couple of nights to San Diego is not going to rekindle that fire," Langdon said.

"You're probably right."

"I don't think I can get away right now, Chabal. I have a young man staying with me who may have just ruined his life. His mother is here, and she just made him tell me who put him up to this whole thing. Long and short of it is, it wasn't anybody from MECI, but rather, a mobster dude named Larry the Fish from Boston. My wife is angry with me. My daughter misses me. 4 by Four has been acting real strange. And I don't think they let dogs on planes."

Chabal laughed. It was almost a relief. Almost. "Okay. I'll go myself. It'll give me a chance to do some soul searching. If you change your mind, the flight is out of Portland at 6:30 tomorrow evening. I'll hang on to your ticket for you." She hung up the phone.

Langdon thought that was perhaps an abrupt goodbye. After all, he knew—and assumed she knew—that he would be at the airport tomorrow for the flight. He returned to the living room where Latricia and Jamal were arguing over whether to watch the Celtics/Lakers game or a Marlon Brando movie.

"Anybody want something to drink?" Langdon asked.

"Do you have any wine? White?" Latricia asked.

"I'll have a beer," Jamal said avoiding his mother's eyes.

"What?" She glared at him while he studied his reflection in the window.

"Tell you what," Jamal said, turning to meet her gaze. "If I can have a beer, then we can watch the old black and white movie. It's not one of those silent things, is it?"

"Okay," Latricia replied, surprising all three of them.

Langdon found a bottle of Pinot Grigio and returned to the living room with it in his hand. "Okay if I drop a couple of ice cubes in the glass to get you started?" he asked. "It's not chilled. If you'd been here a few days ago, it would've been cold even though it was in a rack on the counter."

Latricia agreed to ice, and he returned to pour their drinks. He'd always liked to drink his beer out of a glass. He poured Jamal's carefully into a tall glass as well. He brought the drinks out and went back for chips and salsa, as well as Triscuits and cheese.

"I'm thinking about asking your Uncle Eddie to check in with this Larry the Fish," Langdon said once he returned and settled into his recliner.

"Whatever, man," Jamal said. "My ass is already grass. I'm packing my bags and going to Mexico."

"Put a sombrero on you, and you'll fit right in," Langdon said.

"The man's gonna kill me no matter if you give him the Fish's name or not. Especially if he finds out I'm a rat."

Langdon looked at Latricia. "Is that true?"

"If Eddie Jones has any loyalty at all in his body, it's for family," Latricia said. "He'll be pissed off at Jamal, but he won't hurt him."

"What about Larry the Fish?" Langdon asked.

"Oh, that man is dead."

"I don't think so," Langdon replied. "Fast Eddie strikes me as far too intelligent to kill Larry as long as I can impress upon him how important the Fish's testimony in court will be for Jamal. You do realize, Jamal, that you're going to have to give a statement placing the blame squarely on Larry the Fish, and maybe even testify to that."

"Yeah, I get that. I don't think it'll come to that, though," Jamal said.

"Why not?"

"I think, uh, like my mom said, the man is as good as dead."

Somehow, their glasses were all empty and Langdon went to the kitchen to replenish, determining that the wine for Latricia still needed a single cube of ice. *On the Waterfront* had started, and the three of them were silent, lost in their own thoughts.

"This is a very apt movie for the situation," Langdon said.

"What do you mean?" Jamal asked.

"Pay attention to it," Langdon said. "Sometimes you have to stand up for what is right, even if it means going against your supposed friends."

"Whatever, man."

"You know the number to the Glitter Club off the top of your head?" Langdon asked him. He had the card Eddie had given him but wanted to test Jamal.

"I don't know about the Glitter Club, but I got Eddie's cell phone," Jamal said, giving him the number with a sidelong look at his mother.

Langdon went to the kitchen to use the landline, repeating the numbers in his head to not forget. Still, he was surprised to have gotten it right.

"This is Eddie."

"I got your name," Langdon said.

"The dude behind this whole mess with my nephew?" Eddie must have recognized Langdon's voice. The man was sharp as a tack and didn't seem to miss a thing.

"Yeah, that's the one."

"So, give it up."

"Not so fast," Langdon said. "I need you to promise me something, first."

"I won't kill him. Now spill it."

"Or have him killed."

"Maybe a bit roughed up, but the man will live."

"It's somebody you know. Larry the Fish."

"Larry the goddamn Fish?" Eddie went off on a string of obscenities. "Are you sure?"

"Pretty sure. Remember, we need him alive. We'll have Jamal give up the name to the police tomorrow. You make sure he can be found, say, late morning?"

"He'll be here at the Glitter Club. I'm always happy to do a favor for the police department," Eddie said. "Eleven o'clock."

"What's his last name, by the way?"

"Ciampi, not the boss, just a second cousin or something."

"Can you spell that for me?" Langdon asked.

Eddie did, and then hung up the phone.

Langdon poured himself another beer and returned to the living room. "Tomorrow we tell the police that Larry Ciampi was the man running the operation, and that he can be found at the Glitter Club in Roxbury around eleven," he told the mother and son.

"Whatever, man," Jamal said. "Let's finish watching this movie."

Marlon Brando was on the screen arguing with his brother, who was the right-hand man of the mob boss. "I coulda been somebody. I coulda been a contender," Brando said to his brother. "Instead of a bum, which is what I am—let's face it."

Langdon snuck a glance at Jamal, who was eating up the movie, quite contrary to his earlier resistance. There might have even been a tear at the end when badly-injured Marlon Brando is supported by the other dockworkers and goes into the garage, the door closing behind him, and the movie ending.

Langdon left the mother and son to talk, making sure they were all set with their beds and had what they needed, and then excused himself to go to sleep. This proved more difficult than he thought, as he worried about whether or not he could trust Eddie, Jamal, Latricia, and what a trip to San Diego with Chabal might entail. He had some ideas on that last item, and it was this that kept him tossing and turning.

He must have finally drifted off, because his cell phone ringing woke him at just past two in the morning.

"Langdon?"

"Yep."

"This is Fast Eddie. You awake?"

"Getting there."

"I got bad news for you."

"You didn't?"

"It wasn't me or any of my men, I swear to God."

"What happened?" Langdon swung his legs to the floor to stop Coffee Dog from licking his face.

"The police found the body of Larry the Fish this afternoon in the Charles River. It appears that he couldn't breathe underwater. I know what you're thinking, but the man was found dead this afternoon. My sources with BPD tell me he took his final swim sometime last night. You didn't give me his name until a few hours ago."

"Okay, okay. Unless, of course, me telling you wasn't exactly when you found out," Langdon said.

"I told you it was a complete surprise to me," Eddie said. His voice had gone dangerously quiet.

"Sure, to coin a phrase from your nephew, whatever," Langdon said.

"How about we get on the same page as to how we're going to move forward."

"Forward?" Langdon asked. "We're back on square one. We gotta start the game all over again."

"Not exactly," Eddie said. "Jamal can still finger the man as the one who put him up to that whole crime spree. The only difference is Larry the Fish can't lie through his blowhole and claim he didn't."

The man had a point.

Chapter 18

It was one of those small commercial airplanes, the kind you have to walk out onto the runway to board, go up the stairs, and in Langdon's case, duck your head when you entered. It was only going as far as Boston, where they would switch to a larger jet for the direct flight to San Diego.

"Glad you could make it," Chabal said.

"I wouldn't have missed it," Langdon said. Of course, he had misgivings about leaving a young man who'd confessed to vandalizing homes in his house, as well as leaving Star alone at the bookstore, but he wouldn't have missed this opportunity was the absolute truth.

The plane taxied down the runway and lifted into the air, a slight wind bouncing them around just a bit.

"Are you afraid of flying?" Chabal asked.

"No."

"You sure look like it. We are going to sunny California for two days, so lighten up man."

Langdon sighed. "4 by Four gave me a ride down. He's had some bad news."

"What's up? Another girl break his heart?"

"He thinks he might have HIV," Langdon said.

"What?"

"Yeah, he's going down to Boston this week for some blood tests, I guess."

"But, how?"

"Last week, Darla Brunette, a woman he dated for a bit, told him she'd just tested positive for HIV and that he should know." Langdon shook his head.

Chabal was stunned. "Just because he had sex with somebody infected doesn't mean he is, right?"

"All week he's been fighting a fever, headache, aching muscles, and sore throat. He was hoping it was just the flu, but coupled with what Darla told him? He said those are the symptoms of Stage One HIV."

"It's times like these that it would be nice to believe in God," Chabal said, taking his hand and squeezing.

"Damn right," Langdon said, and they both half-smiled.

They had a four-hour layover in Boston and bantered about getting a motel room, but in the end, Langdon called Fast Eddie to see if he could meet them for dinner. Twenty minutes after landing they were in a cab heading to Faneuil Hall and a bar called the Golden Goose.

"It's not a strip bar, is it?" Chabal asked.

"I don't think so," Langdon said. "Why?"

"Oh, come on, the Golden Goose? That sounds a little racy to me."

They beat Eddie to the restaurant and waited at the bar. Chabal ordered a Tequila Sunrise while Langdon had a Sam Adams. In the natural course of life, Chabal was not much of a drinker, but the dislocating combination of being on a semi-vacation mixed with the latest upsetting news, they were both on their second when Eddie arrived, and they moved to a table.

"And who is this lovely woman who is not your wife?" Fast Eddie asked.

Langdon stared at him, wondering how Eddie knew he was married, and if so, how he knew that Chabal was not his wife. "Eddie Jones, meet Chabal Daniels, my assistant."

Chabal smirked at her description. "Hello, Fast Eddie. Why do people call you that? I'm thinking it best if I keep one hand on my purse and the other holding up my pants." Two drinks were a lot for Chabal.

"Dice," Fast Eddie said charmingly, cupping his right hand around imaginary dice and making a throwing motion. "I got the nickname because when I was eighteen, I made a fast 50K at the craps table one night in Foxwoods." He called the waitress over and ordered a Woodward Reserve. "So, you can loosen your grip." He winked at Chabal.

"Phew," Chabal said. "I was feeling bad for you, thinking some girl had saddled you with that name due to you know what."

"Perhaps we can move the conversation back to Larry the Fish," Langdon said.

Chabal smirked.

"What do you want to know?" Fast Eddie asked.

The waitress returned with the Woodford Reserve and took their order. Chabal ordered the crab cakes, while Langdon got a burger, and Fast Eddie a Mediterranean salad.

"Who killed him, for starters?"

"Wait, that's the guy who was the ringmaster behind Jamal's break-ins? He's dead? How?" Chabal took a gulp of the sunrise.

"He drowned," Langdon said.

Chabal smirked again.

"Not much of a fish," Fast Eddie said.

Langdon and Chabal had always worked well together. Chabal softened Fast Eddie up with her appearance of naïve innocence, and Langdon pushed for the hard questions in a quasi-good cop/bad cop routine. Larry the Fish had started off as a numbers runner back in the '70s in Roxbury, and then moved on to Somerville when the state lottery system started to supplant illegal betting.

In Somerville, he went to work for Whitey Bulger and the Winter Hill Gang. When the Winter Hill Gang went into debt to the Patriarca family of the Italian mob, Larry the Fish acted as a go-between, when he wasn't rigging horse races. With an Italian father and an Irish mother, he was the perfect intermediary between the organizations. Whitey Bulger's stock rose drastically when the Patriarca family came tumbling down in the early 1990s under a wave of indictments some claimed may have been the result of him informing on their workings to the Feds, possibly with the help of Larry the Fish.

When Whitey Bulger was forced to go into hiding in late 1994, Larry the Fish officially cut his ties with the Winter Hill Gang. Again, rumors circulated that he might have been a stooge for the FBI, and he sought protection with Fast Eddie, whose star had risen as those of the Irish and Italians had waned. There were plenty of people who wanted to kill Larry. Even if Bulger was in hiding, it was likely he'd extended his hand to finish the man off for ratting him out, which Langdon thought to be an ironic twist of fate.

Between an overload of information and booze, Langdon and Chabal lost track of time and had to rush from the restaurant and into a cab to the airport. They made a spectacle skipping through the terminal arm-in-arm singing the Laverne and Shirley theme song and barely made it to their gate before the door closed.

"Rum and Coke and Tequila Sunrise please," Langdon said to the stewardess who greeted them at the door.

"Peanuts, no pretzels, please," Chabal said.

"Seats 19 A and B," Langdon said.

They were not brought drinks before takeoff, even though people in first class seemed to be imbibing.

"What do you think of Fast Eddie?" Langdon asked.

"He's a real smoothie, no doubt about that," Chabal said. "I bet you he has his way with the ladies."

"He had his eye on you," Langdon said.

"I noticed that," Chabal said. "I was hoping you'd walk off, and I could sneak him into the broom closet for quickie. Always been a big fantasy of mine."

"You could've given me a signal. I'm not one to get in the way of somebody's fantasies."

"Speaking of, are you a member of the mile-high club?" Chabal draped her hand seductively on his inner knee.

"Not yet, but I'm hoping to check that one off the list soon." Langdon's body was a pinball game with a short circuit, the ball zinging back and forth, and threatening to burst into flames. "As in, immediately."

"How did Fast Eddie know I wasn't your wife?" Chabal asked. "Why couldn't I be your wife?"

"You caught that, too, huh? I'm thinking he did some checking up on me. He did not seem to catch on that you work at the bookstore, though, so maybe just family?"

"He might be a good-looking man, but he has dead-fish eyes." Chabal shivered.

They chatted about the case, their kids, their friends, and nothing at all. After a bit, Chabal lay her head down on his shoulder, and they fell asleep together. At some point her hand draped across his chest, and he rubbed her back lightly. She liked the smell of him. He liked how her hair tickled his face. It was the thirty-something married to another with children version of the mile-high club. A mildly naughty moment in time that neither of them would ever trade nor let fade.

Chapter 19

They were the last plane to land at Lindbergh Field Airport for the night—early morning actually—but somehow the rental car agency had remained open long enough to hand them a key to their Mazda 626. With the windows open and no traffic at this late hour, it was no time before they arrived at the Horton Grand Hotel in San Diego's downtown district facing Coronado Island.

The room only had one bed, but it was a king, and they kept to their respective sides, fighting the magnetic attraction that pulled at them. Langdon woke up to find Chabal curled up inside of his embrace, her back to him, as big spoon and little spoon. He lay there for several long minutes, comfortable, but then embarrassed to walk past her to the bathroom. Finally, he slid his arms from around her and walked quickly to the shower, his body turned away. The beauty of a cold shower is that you don't have to wait for it to warm up.

He emerged twenty minutes later with a towel wrapped around him to find Chabal at the window looking out at the Pacific Ocean. She had on a pair of boxers and a white T-shirt and he almost had to flee back to the cold shower.

While Chabal took her turn in the bathroom, Langdon got dressed, and went to the lobby for coffee and the morning paper. He called his wife and daughter, but neither conversation lasted very long, so he sat in a fat armchair and browsed through the news, giving Chabal some privacy in the room.

He had just finished reading the paper when Chabal got off the elevator. She had on a white tank top and yellow shorts that made Langdon's insides melt. They decided to go out for breakfast, stepping out into a humid-free seventy-degree day. Maine, responsibilities, and spouses seemed a long way away. It felt like a real vacation.

They ate at a Mexican café. Langdon had a spicy omelet with salsa and guacamole while Chabal stuck with pancakes and powdered sugar. The tables were made of stone and were old and cracked. The breeze from the ocean rippled the air. They flirted gently—harmlessly—laughing in the sunshine.

When they left, they held hands. They were just good friends wanting to touch. Or, at least that was what Langdon told himself, not believing the lie, but too content to question it deeply.

"I guess it's time to go find this John Flanagan," Langdon said.

"He owns a gift shop in the Old Town," Chabal replied.

Even now, on a Monday in the middle of the day, there was very little traffic. Langdon idly wondered why it was that he didn't live here. Perfect weather year-round, spicy breakfasts, and no traffic? It sure beat ice storms and freezing weather. Then he thought of the fires and mudslides that southern California had to put up with and was somewhat mollified. Not to mention the gangs and drugs.

They rode with the windows down, the wind tousling Chabal's short hair. Her white tank top left little to the imagination. Her laughter caressed Langdon with a sensuous exhilaration. Her faint scent was a bouquet of pleasure. He found it very hard to keep the car on the road.

"I think we were supposed to exit back there," Chabal said. "Sorry."

"No worries. Let's do the whole loop anyway and get a feel for San Diego."

Eventually, they found the Old Town, which was exactly what its name indicated. It was comprised of stone buildings, cracked streets, and wide sidewalks. It was far from tourist season, and thus, there were few people strolling along and even fewer cars. The occasional families browsed the shops, dad with a camera, and mom yelling at

MAINELY FEAR   167

the kids to stay out of the street. The businesses seemed to consist of restaurants and gift shops. It was not hard to find John Flanagan's gift shop.

Chabal burst into squeals of pleasure when Langdon spotted the sign over the shop. *Mainely Mexican*, it read. There was not much of Mexico in Maine, nor Maine in Mexico, as far as either one could tell, but it certainly made an impression. Ever since tracking down Flanagan on the internet and finding the website for this shop, Chabal had been bursting with excitement, more to share it with Langdon than for herself.

"I've been dying to see what they have here," Chabal said. "It would have been worth the trip even if Flanagan didn't own the place."

Inside, there were lobsters in sombreros, paperweights with cactuses that you shook to cause a snowstorm, skiers on sand dunes, and bumper stickers that read WHERE THE HELL ARE THE MOOSE and CINCO DE MAYO IS MAINE'S GROUNDHOG DAY.

The short, wiry man behind the counter wore colorful shorts and a red T-shirt that proclaimed ALLEN'S MARGARITAS. He had a bushy mustache, hard cheekbones, and eyed them carefully as they browsed the shelves.

"Can I help you?" he asked when he'd tired of waiting.

"Yes, yes you can," Langdon said. "If you are John Flanagan."

"Who wants to know?" His fluttering eyelids gave away his nervousness.

"Are you the John Flanagan who used to teach at the Molly Esther Chester Institute in Skowhegan, Maine?"

"I don't know what you're talking about. I must ask you to please leave." He turned his back as the cowbell over the door rang, and a couple came into the store.

"Students are being hurt, John," Chabal said.

His body seemed to deflate when she said that. Flanagan turned to face them, his face showing the anxiety giving way to reluctant acceptance, and perhaps a tinge of self-loathing.

"I can't talk here, not now," Flanagan finally said. "I have a store to run."

Langdon understood that. "What time do you close?"

"Eight."

"We'll meet you here."

"Fine."

Langdon and Chabal went to leave. Almost as an afterthought, Chabal turned back and found Flanagan's eyes watching them. "John, children are being hurt," she reminded him.

They drove up the coast, discussing what they knew of HIV, which was very little, and wondering what they could do, if anything, to help out 4 by Four. Langdon parked on the side of the road by two other cars and they followed a path down to an isolated beach. There were several surfers in wet suits out on the waves, but the beach itself was empty, and theirs alone. For the average Californian, this was probably freezing. They walked down the beach, shoes off, getting their feet wet, holding hands, and sat on some rocks and watched the waves crash. Up behind the rocks was a small stretch of sand, warm from the sun, protected from the wind, and they lay down and dozed, their bodies touching.

The tide coming in woke them as it tickled first, their toes with its chilly fingers, and then trickled up their legs, sending them crawling hurriedly to safety, laughing the entire way. It was rush hour when they returned to the Horton Grand Hotel, and this was busier, more like Brunswick in August, but still not atrocious. They changed into dry clothes not dotted with wet sand, back-to-back and promising not to look, but both peeking over the shoulder at the other.

The concierge recommended Croce's for dinner and jazz music. It was just around the corner, both hotel and club in the Gaslamp Quarter of San Diego. The music rose and fell and jumped and jived like neither of them had ever heard. Langdon had a steak with blue cheese and Chabal gorged on rich duck with a sour cherry sauce. Langdon drank a beer from Stone Brewing recommended by the waiter, and then had a second. Chabal had a glass of the Joseph Phelps Vineyard Insignia.

"Did you call home this morning?" Chabal asked.

"Yep."

"How'd it go?"

"Amanda was a bit snippy," Langdon said.

"Yeah, John told me that I shouldn't come back."

"Did he mean it?" Langdon wasn't sure if he was horrified or tantalized by the concept of staying here together forever.

"I don't know. I suppose he'll get over it. At this point, I don't really care, to tell you the truth. I just can't do it anymore."

"Yeah, I know what you mean. I've been trying hard to make my marriage work for the past couple of years, but lately I'm starting to wonder if it should be so hard?"

"People say marriage *is* work," Chabal said.

"Stupid people, maybe," Langdon replied.

"So, are you getting divorced?"

"It's looking that way."

They ate in silence for a bit, then moved the conversation to safer topics. When the waiter asked if they wanted anything else, Langdon looked at his watch, and realized they were almost late for their appointment with John Flanagan. He looked at the check, tucked cash into the bill holder, including a healthy tip, and out the door they went. Langdon's phone had a voicemail from Bart. It was the normal curt Bart, letting him know that Goldilocks had never shown up for work, and nobody seemed to know where he was. Langdon called him back, but there was no answer.

Flanagan was pacing in front of his shop, walking down the sidewalk like he wanted to keep going, and then jerking around and reversing direction. They pulled up next to him and Chabal leaned out. "John," she called and waved. He came over and climbed into the back seat.

"Can we go somewhere where nobody knows me?" he asked.

"Sure," Langdon said. "You tell me where."

He directed them to a dive bar back in the Gaslamp Quarter where their hotel was.

"Do you mind if I smoke?" Flanagan pulled out a cigar the size of a blackjack.

"Is it legal in here?"

They were sitting at a round wooden table in a dimly lit corner of a barroom that was forty feet long by maybe twenty feet wide. The adobe building was stuck between two new large and modern business towers. A jukebox next to them was playing a Smash Mouth tune that Langdon liked called "Walkin' on the Sun."

"Ah, officially as of the first of this January, smoking was supposed to be banned from bars." Flanagan lit his cigar. "It'll be awhile for that to kick in, especially here," he said, looking around.

"You got any more?" Chabal asked.

Langdon gave her a look. He occasionally liked a cigar, but nothing about Chabal had ever indicated that she smoked them. He mentally put another plus in her column.

Flanagan produced two more cigars, and the three of them lit up. A waitress in a slinky leather skirt and a fishnet top covering her black bra brought them a round of drinks.

"Who are you?" Flanagan looked at Langdon.

"I'm a private detective."

"Did some parent hire you to investigate Meese?"

"Sort of," Langdon said. "Why did you leave the school?"

"My house burned down."

"Some people would have rebuilt, or perhaps bought a new house somewhere closer than 3,000 miles away," Langdon said. He liked that the cigars had somehow made the three of them friendlier.

"It was good timing, actually. The school year was just about over.

My wife had family out here." Flanagan shrugged. "I don't know what you're hoping to hear."

"The truth."

The three of them stared at each other, and Langdon thought it eerily similar to the final standoff in *Reservoir Dogs*, but with cigars instead of guns. In the background, the music droned on.

"What do you care? What's your angle?" Flanagan was the first to break.

"We're investigating a scandal at MECI," Langdon said.

Flanagan actually squirmed in his seat. He raised a hand, and he and Langdon ordered another round while Chabal demurred for the time being. "What type of scandal?"

"What do you know about the suicide rate at MECI?" Chabal asked.

"I know nothing about that."

"There were three suicides in your last five years," Langdon said. "That seems high, now, don't you think?"

"A bit, yeah, I guess."

"Would it surprise you that there have been seven more since you left?" Langdon blew out a puff of smoke. "Seven in the last five years."

"Seven? Seven attempted suicides?" Flanagan choked on his cigar.

"Seven successful suicides," Chabal said. "If you call killing yourself successful."

"Why?" Flanagan's mask of indifference was slipping away to reveal a deeply troubled face.

"That's what we want to know from you."

"Ask away."

"Does Jerry Peccance have a thing for teenage boys? Young men? Is he a pedophile?" Langdon asked.

"I don't know."

"What *do* you know?"

"I was against hiring Coach Pious," Flanagan said. "As a senior faculty member, I was on the search and hire committee, but I was strongly overridden by Jerry Peccance. You know, I trust, why Pious left Las Vegas?"

Langdon and Chabal nodded.

"It was never proven, but still, why take a chance? Besides, there was something I didn't like about the man. Not just a personality difference, mind you, but something that set off my warning systems."

"What do you know, John?" Chabal asked.

"That's it, I don't *know* anything."

"What is it that you suspect?" Langdon asked.

"I never wanted to be anything but a teacher, even when I was in school and all my friends hated teachers," Flanagan said. "When I got a job at Meese in my hometown, well, I was tickled pink. And I loved it. I mean, there were trying incidents, and many times I came home exhausted and depressed, but the next day I would bounce back and it would all be worthwhile again." He took a long sip of his Tequila on the rocks.

"And then Peccance was hired." Langdon spoke calmly, his words a gentle prodding.

"He started getting rid of teachers, and at first I was okay with it because they were the weak ones, dead wood, but then he moved on to teachers I knew were good teachers, real teachers, men and women who cared about and were excellent at their jobs."

"How about the students?"

"The school climate had become toxic. The white boys closed ranks against the Black outsiders, and the girls were caught somewhere in the middle. There was anger that erupted again and again, and I could never quite understand where it was coming from."

"Race seems to be a pretty raw topic for a lot of people," Chabal said.

"It was more than that. Sure, I know that lily white Skowhegan might not be the most tolerant place for Black kids to go to school. I know all that. But I sensed something deeper."

"What did you do about it?"

"I brought it up at the weekly faculty meetings. I tried to form a committee to look into the school culture. I held open office hours for students. I tried…" Flanagan buried his face in his hands. "For my troubles, I was mocked by Peccance and gradually became an odd outcast in the school hierarchy."

"Did they try to get you to quit?"

"Peccance suggested early on that I might move, and then became less gentle, and began looking for reasons to fire me. But I was the union rep, you know, and he was scared to dispose of me without proper provocation."

"And then your house burned down," Langdon said.

"I ran," Flanagan said. "I packed up my family and ran away as fast as I could. It was like when you're a kid, and you hear a noise in the dark, and you start running, and that only makes it worse? I drove us across the country in seventy-two hours. I was manic." He slammed the last of his Tequila down and waved for another.

"You never reported anything?" Langdon asked.

"Reported what?"

"So, you had no proof that anything was going on?"

"One day, I, uh, found some pictures on his desk. They were male nudes, young men, but probably over eighteen I would guess, but much younger than him," Flanagan said.

"Peccance's desk?" Langdon asked.

"Yes."

"What'd you do?"

"There's nothing illegal about a man having nude pictures, now is there?" Flanagan asked. "I asked myself, what if these pictures had been of women? Would that make it different? I mean, it was creepy that they were young, and he shouldn't have them on his desk at work, but his sexual interest was none of my business, right?"

"So, you did nothing?"

"I confronted him about the pictures. After three days of tossing and turning at night, I walked into his office and asked him if he was sexually abusing the students. I told him that I'd found the pictures on his desk, of boys, some with erections, almost all naked."

"And what did he say?"

"He asked if he was on fucking *Candid Camera*, I believe, were his exact words. He said that Ed Helot had taken the pictures from one of the female students, she was sharing them around sitting out on the green on one of our rare warm spring days, and he'd brought them to Peccance."

"And you believed him?" Chabal asked.

"No, I didn't believe him one whit. I demanded that we get Ed to come down to the office, which he did, and without giving Peccance a chance to give any warning, I demanded his version of where the pictures came from."

"And he backed it up?"

"One hundred percent. They hadn't told me the name of the student because of the delicacy of the situation, but yeah, he totally supported what Peccance had told me."

"So, it was nothing?"

"I thought I'd gone crazy. I apologized and stumbled toward the door. As I was about to exit, Peccance called to me. He was smiling—no, he was leering at one of the photographs in his hand. He never looked up at me but suggested that I might consider a leave of absence. Then he licked his lips and sighed."

"And that was it?"

"Two days later my daughter talked to a man in the street. She brought an envelope inside that he had given her addressed to me. Inside was a note that said: '*Too bad I don't like girls. Maybe next time your son will be outside.*' She was twelve. My son was ten."

"Shit," Chabal said.

"The next day my house burned down. As I said, I threw everyone in the car, and we drove straight through. My kids were bickering and fighting and crying. My wife was screaming at me. My entire world was caving in, and I was sure the boogeyman was after us. Then we got here, rented a place, opened the business, then bought a house, and gradually, day-by-day, I forgot about all of it. That is, until you called me the other day." Flanagan looked at Chabal.

The three of them sat in silence finishing their drinks.

"Will you testify?" Langdon asked.

"To what?" Flanagan asked.

It was a fair question.

Chapter 20

The trip back for Langdon and Chabal was subdued. The conversation with John Flanagan had dulled the honeymoon aspect of the trip. They had gone back to the hotel lost in their separate thoughts and dropped into dream-filled sleep. In the morning, they did not share the strange images their unconscious minds had summoned forth in the night. On the flight, their thoughts were consumed by possible abuse of innocent young men at MECI, the missing Goldilocks, and fears for the health of Jimmy 4 by Four. The air was almost too thick to breathe, much less talk.

"What now?" Chabal finally asked as they were walking through the Portland Jetport.

"I need to have a talk with Jamal," Langdon said.

"We need to stop it."

"Stop what?"

"I don't know. Whatever's going on."

"We have our suspicions, but what do we really know? Flanagan supported our theory that there *might* be something dark happening at MECI, but he had nothing more substantial than we do."

"So, the key is to get Jamal to talk," Chabal said.

"He is hiding something. I know he is."

"What would you do? Put the boy on a witness stand?"

"I don't know. Maybe he can give us a direction that we can build a case on without his testimony."

"So, you think he was sexually abused?"

"Everything seems to be pointing that way," Langdon said.

"And we can't do anything about it?"

"I am very close to taking a baseball bat and going to pay a visit to Peccance to get some answers. Perhaps ask for his resignation. The sane part of me suggests that this won't accomplish anything except to get me arrested. But it would make me feel better."

"Let's not forget Coach Pious. He is the only one ever accused of any sort of abuse, as far as we know."

They had no checked baggage and breezed out of the airport, crossing the street to the parking garage across the way. The temperature was a rude awakening after San Diego.

"How about Amanda's friend the state trooper? Jackson Brooks?" Chabal asked.

Langdon rolled this around in his mind. Brooks had helped them out with vital information in a recent case, but what Chabal didn't know was that Amanda had slept with the handsome trooper. Plus, he didn't really see his wife willing to help him out as he was summoning the courage to tell her he wanted a divorce.

"He can get things done that we can't," Chabal said.

"We need more proof. If he starts asking questions in an official capacity, they will circle the wagons. No, we need to do some more digging on the sly."

"At least no more kids would get hurt."

"For a few months until the whole thing blew over, and then the abuse would start up again."

In the parking garage they hugged, more a gesture of emotional support than blinding want, their selfish desires dampened, for the time being at least.

~ ~ ~ ~ ~

"I need to talk to you," Langdon said to Jamal when he walked back in the door of his house. "Alone."

Latricia told him she had managed to get the entire week of work off, and she and her son had taken up residence. The place was cleaner than it had been in a while, and the fact that Langdon noticed this was statement enough.

"What do you have to say to my boy that I can't hear?" Latricia asked.

Langdon didn't know how to reply to this.

"Who we need to be talking to is our lawyer," Latricia continued. "I've been trying to get hold of him the whole time you were gone. He won't return my calls."

"He's, uh, sick," Langdon said. "I believe he might have to withdraw from representing you."

"Sick? You mean the damn man has the flu?"

Langdon was knocked back a step. Latricia's tone was hard and flat and not at all like the gentle and concerned woman he thought he knew. This was the backbone of a woman who'd raised a boy in the ghetto without any support.

"Answer me." Latricia's eyes were hard. "This is what I get for hiring a private dick in a hick town along with his hippie lawyer friend?"

"Mom," Jamal said. "Relax. Everything is okay."

"I am not at liberty to discuss Mr. 4 by Four's illness with you," Langdon said.

"Was it because I turned him down when he tried to get into my pants?"

"Mom, cut it out," Jamal said. He gave her a beseeching look before turning back to Langdon. "Should I be getting a new lawyer? I mean, I'm sorry the dude is sick, I really am, but I'm scared shitless. I can't walk into court all alone, now, can I?"

"It's for the best, Jamal," Latricia said. "I don't know what I was thinking hiring a lawyer who is named after a truck."

Jamal glared at her. "You're not helping."

"It would probably be wise to seek new legal counsel," Langdon said.

"Eddie has offered his legal team to represent me," Jamal said. "I told him no, but if Mr. 4 by Four is sick? I think it might be the right play."

Langdon nodded. Eddie probably had a top-notch lawyer. Or legal team, as Jamal had said. They would probably join up with a Portland firm with local connections. It *was* for the best. But where did that leave him? It was quite possible that he was about to be dropped from the case. No, it was more than likely that he was about to be fired.

"You have to do what you have do," Langdon said.

"And we're going to move out of here and into a hotel," Latricia said. "We got to start looking out for Jamal."

"Fine," Langdon said. At least he'd gotten a clean house out of the deal. "But, can I speak privately with Jamal for a minute? Just the two of us?"

"Fine," Jamal said.

"No way," Latricia said. "I won't allow it. You're just trying to drive a wedge between me and my boy."

Langdon's phone rang. "Hey, Bart, let me call you back, I'm right in the middle of something."

"He was found dead just a few hours ago," Bart said.

"Who?" Langdon asked, but he had a suspicion rushing at him like a runaway steer.

"Goldilocks. Out on the town commons. Not far from your house."

"He snowshoes there on Sundays," Langdon said dumbly. "What happened?"

Bart took a deep breath, and Langdon could hear him grinding his teeth. "Somebody killed him. Carved him up something awful."

"Killed him?"

"Slow-like, tortured, or so it appears. There is no official autopsy report back yet."

Why? What for? Thoughts rampaged through Langdon's mind, and he tried to slow them down, control them, organize them. "Are there any leads?"

"No. Nothing. He was beaten with a blunt object. A club of some sort. Maybe a baseball bat? Then they carved him up with a knife." Bart snorted and choked over the phone. "Somebody has to pay."

"Where are you?" Langdon asked.

"The parking area at the Town Commons. The forensics people just cleaned the area out. The Chief told me to go home." Langdon's house was on one side of the commons, the entrance and trails for the wooded acres' walkers, skiers, and snowshoers accessed from the opposite side on Harpswell Road.

"Come over here. I'll call the gang and we'll figure out how to deal with this."

"On my way," Bart said. "And Langdon?"

"Yeah?"

"Somebody *is* going to pay for this. There will be a reckoning." He hung up.

Latricia and Jamal were staring wide-eyed at Langdon.

"Somebody was killed?" Jamal asked.

"Goldilocks." Langdon sat down heavily in his leather recliner.

"The dude from the restaurant? Shit, man."

"Why?"

Langdon shook his head. "The police have no leads so far. It sounds personal. He was beaten and tortured."

The three of them, strangers until just a few days ago, sat quietly contemplating the vileness.

"We'll get out of your hair," Latricia said.

"I just saw him Saturday night," Langdon said. "He was following a man for me while I went to a play with my daughter." He was staring out the window lost in pain.

"What man?" Latricia asked.

"It doesn't matter. It turned out to be nothing. He tailed him to the Greenlander Motel and that was it. He left me a message while I was at *Alice in Wonderland*." If Langdon hadn't been so far down the rabbit hole, he might have seen Latricia twitch and hurriedly look away.

Latricia started to say something to Langdon, and then closed her mouth and shook her head. "Come on, Jamal, let's leave the man to his sorrow."

Once they'd got their things together and walked out the door, Langdon dialed Chabal's cell. She didn't answer. He tried home.

"Hello." It was her husband.

"Hi, John, can I speak with Chabal?"

"Is this Langdon?"

"Yes."

"I've had enough of you two sniffing around each other like dogs in heat. You can have each other. I told her to pack her bags and get the hell out. And you can go to hell, too." John Daniels hung up.

Langdon called the Denevieuxs. Jewell answered.

"Hey, Jewell, this is Langdon."

"Hello, Goff." Her voice was chilly.

"I've got bad news."

"Bad news is that you're dragging my husband into another one of your cases," she said. "I won't have it."

"Jewell? Goldilocks is dead."

"What?"

"He was murdered."

The silence enveloped both of them in its forlorn embrace. "Does this have anything to do with the case you're working on?" Jewell asked.

"I don't know."

"Stay away from us, Goff. Just stay away from us." The phone went dead.

He stared at the phone in anguish. 4 by Four's phone went straight to voicemail.

A strange voice answered Amanda's home phone. "Who is this?" he demanded.

"Jax. Is this Langdon?"

"Yes. Hi Jax." Jax worked at The Cellar of Fitness and was Missouri's regular babysitter. "Amanda's not there?"

"She left about fifteen minutes ago, some art lecture at Bowdoin or something like that, but she left a message if you called." Jax spoke in a tentative and careful tone.

"What is it?"

"She called you a bunch of obscene names I won't repeat and told you to leave her the hell alone." Jax giggled.

"Thanks, Jax. Is Missouri still up?"

"I'm not supposed to let you talk to her."

"Jax…"

"Here she is."

"Hi, Daddy," Missouri said over the phone line.

"Hi, honey. How are you?" It was a much-needed balm to hear his daughter's voice.

"Jax is here, and we're watching the *Swan Princess*, and we…" Her voice bubbled on like a brook rushing down the side of a mountain, talking about things that meant nothing, but meant everything in her world.

When Langdon finally hung up with a promise to come over first thing in the morning, he'd gained a bit of sanity back, and was no longer contemplating driving straight through to South America and beginning a new life. There was at least one island of sanity keeping him from losing his marbles and throwing in the flag, and it came in a two-foot high package.

Langdon walked to the kitchen and poured himself a glass mostly full of rum with just a splash of Coke. He set it down on the counter. When the doorbell rang, he'd been staring at the glass for several minutes.

It was his wife. Amanda stepped forward and hugged him firmly. She brought Coffee Dog with her, as she'd had custody while Langdon was on his trip. For once, the dog was subdued, sensing the despair filling the air.

"I was coming to drop Coffee off when Jewell called me with

the news," she said. Of Langdon's friends, only Jewell had a tight connection with Amanda.

"He was like a father to me," Langdon said. "Only much better than my real father."

"I know."

Langdon had not cried. Now was not the time for tears. They would come later, but for now, he rolled his anguish into a tight ball that fueled his growing anger.

Bart came into the house without knocking. He enveloped both of them in his mammoth arms, his eyes red and puffy. "What they did to him was not right." He sniffled loudly.

The doorbell rang again. It was Chabal. "What's going on?" she asked.

Langdon told her the little they knew. Her eyes immediately welled up and overflowed, the tears running down her full cheeks like white water on a river.

Bart went into the kitchen to find a beer, and Amanda went to the bathroom to check what damage tears might have done to her make-up. This gave Chabal a chance to hug Langdon, if for just a moment.

"John kicked me out," Chabal said.

"He told me." Langdon clasped the back of her head against his chest. "He seemed rather angry with the both of us."

"Do Jewell and Richam know?"

"I spoke with Jewell. She was none too happy with me. She thinks I'm dragging Richam into a mess."

"He's not a child." Chabal stepped away, knowing the door was closing on their few seconds of intimacy. "How about Jimmy?"

"4 by Four went down to Boston today for some medical tests," Bart said, returning with a beer in either hand. He walked on past and into the living room.

Langdon went to follow, but the doorbell rang again. Jewell stepped in and embraced him as soon as he opened the door. It was a maternal embrace of forgiveness, apology, and sorrow all wrapped into one.

Richam and Starling followed her through the door, Richam clasping Chabal tightly, and then they all went into the living room, where Amanda had joined Bart.

They talked of inconsequential things, one by one wandering to the kitchen to find their booze of choice, except for Starling, the recovering alcoholic, who had a ginger ale. Memories and anecdotes of Goldilocks began to filter their way into the conversations, and the group laughed and cried together.

"What happened to him?" Amanda finally had the gumption to ask.

"He was murdered," Langdon said, avoiding what he knew to be the real question.

Amanda shot him a look that she was not to be put off.

"We need to know," Jewell said.

Langdon nodded to Bart.

Bart stared around, his eyes resting on each person for a few seconds. "A little bit after noon today we got a call at the station. A guy out on the Town Commons walking his dog found a dead man. I wasn't the first to the scene, but I was the one who positively identified the body as Robert Southie, or Goldilocks, as everybody knew him."

"I don't think I've ever heard his real name," Starling said.

"It took me a bit to be sure, as his face was mashed in pretty good. Teeth broken, broken jaw, I don't know what else." Bart clenched his own jaw tight and glowered. "He was also sliced up pretty good. Somebody carved him up like a Thanksgiving turkey."

"Was he on the path or off in the woods?" Langdon asked.

"On the path," Bart replied.

"So, they wanted him found." Chabal asked. "I mean, they didn't make any effort to hide his body. Don't murderers usually try to hide the people they kill? Bury them or drop them in the ocean tied to a rock?"

"Yeah, usually they do," Bart said.

"So, why was he left on a public path in broad daylight?" Jewell asked.

"Serial killer?" Richam asked. "I mean, they often kill people for the perverse pleasure of the media exposure, right? They bask in the public eye and that makes them feel special."

"Or, they're sending a message," Bart said. "Gangsters will leave the body to be found if they are warning somebody off their turf, to stay away from their girls, don't be selling drugs in my house, or whatever."

"I haven't heard of any turf wars happening in Brunswick," Langdon said, looking at Bart, who shook his head. "I suppose it could be some sicko wanting publicity, but I don't think so."

"What, then?"

"Saturday night I called Goldilocks and had him meet me at the McDonald's in Bath," Langdon said. "I was there with Missouri and Tangerine when Ed Helot, the assistant basketball coach at MECI, walked in. I thought that was kind of strange, so I asked Goldilocks to tail him."

Jewell grimaced at the fact that her daughter had been there but kept her mouth shut.

"He left a message on my phone that Helot went to a motel, The Greenlander on the Bath Road, with another man, and that it looked to be romantic in nature. They went in the room and that was it. He said he was going to give it half an hour and then go back to the pub," Langdon said. "Has anybody," he paused and took a deep breath all the way from the depth of his stomach. "Has anybody seen him since Sunday night?"

Nobody had.

"Ed Helot has to be the prime suspect, then. I'll go down to the station first thing in the morning and tell them what I just shared here," Langdon said, looking at Bart for approval, which was given by the smallest of nods. "I don't know what happened afterwards, but it would seem that there was some sort of altercation between Goldilocks and Helot."

"You think that a gay assistant basketball coach beat the shit out of Goldilocks, carved him up, and dumped him in the Town Commons?" Bart was openly incredulous.

"The morning that 4 by Four and I confronted Pious, Helot showed up and was overly aggressive in demanding we leave. He certainly seemed threatening, and he isn't some shrinking violet. He's built like a brick shithouse, even if he's pretty short," Langdon said.

"I did some research on Coach Pious and learned that he left a plum college coaching career under a cloud of suspicion that he sexually assaulted one of his own players," Chabal said.

"And we talked to a former teacher at MECI who suggested that there is something dark going on up there, and that the headmaster, Jerry Peccance, is most likely involved," Langdon added.

"Something dark?" Richam asked.

"Perhaps tied to sexual abuse of students," Langdon said.

"But he doesn't have concrete proof?" Bart asked.

"Nothing," Langdon said. "Just suspicions."

Bart stood up. "I'll go shake some proof out of those bastards."

"Sit down, Bart," Langdon said. "Let's think about this, come up with a plan."

"What do we have so far?" Jewell asked. "First, we think that your client was put up to robbing houses by somebody at MECI? And the likely candidates are his basketball coaches or the headmaster?"

Langdon shook his head. "No, Jamal told me Saturday night that it was a man named Larry the Fish from down in Roxbury who put the idea in his head."

"And that in no way can be connected to Goldilocks death, right?" Richam asked.

"The only connection between the two is Jamal," Chabal said.

"Have you reported this Larry the Fish guy to the police?" Bart asked.

"He's dead," Langdon said. "He was found Saturday afternoon floating in the Charles River."

"Fortuitous," Richam said.

"What's that?" Langdon asked.

"Jamal finally decides to rat the guy out, and he turns up dead—and with such great timing?" Richam said. "So, the blame can be placed on the guy without him being around to defend himself?"

"You've got a point," Langdon said.

"Have you or 4 by Four reported this to the police, yet?" Richam asked.

"No. As a matter of fact, Jimmy has withdrawn from the case due to his, uh, illness, and I might have just been fired, as well," Langdon said.

"You need to speak with Jamal," Jewell said. "If for no other reason than to clear MECI of any suspicion."

"I was about to have that heart to heart when Bart called to tell me about Goldilocks. He and his mom took off to get a hotel room and give me some space, or to get away from me," Langdon said. "I think I may have missed that boat. Latricia seemed pretty upset with me for some reason."

"What else we got, then?" Bart asked.

Langdon turned to Chabal. "How about Mrs. Peach? You think you could get anything else out of her?"

Richam laughed, a dry and humorless chuckle. "She didn't care for me much, but she sure took a shine to Chabal."

"She seems to know everything about the school and everybody who works there," Chabal said. "So, sure, why not? I'm not going up there by myself, though."

Richam was out, Langdon thought, having already upset Mrs. Peach. Starling was going to have to work the bookstore. Amanda? No, that was a terrible idea. Bart should keep his ear close to the pipeline at the police station. Maybe Jewell? No.

"I'll go up with you around noon," Langdon said. He was oblivious to Amanda's glare. "First thing in the morning, I'll tell the police what I know about Ed Helot, and then I'll try to have a conversation with

Jamal."

"I take it you want me working the bookstore by myself, again?" Starling asked.

"We can close down if you want."

"For what reason?"

"Ah, we could give no reason, and it would be a mystery."

Starling shook his head in disgust. "I'm fine. Now that people have their power back, they're all catching up on their shows anyway."

"Richam and Jewell?" Langdon looked at the couple. "You don't have to be part of this if you don't want."

"We're in," Jewell said.

"Where are your kids now?"

"My cousin's house in Falmouth," Richam said.

"Do you have to work tomorrow?"

"Already traded the next couple of days out."

"Good. Why don't you two stick together and at home? We'll use you as command center. Anybody finds out anything, report in to Richam and Jewell. Maybe you can see what you can dig up via the Internet in the meantime?"

"I should see if my friend, Elaine, will take Missouri for the next few days as well," Amanda said. "If this thing doesn't tie up soon, I might take her back to my parents in Atlanta."

"Let me know if Elaine can't watch her," Langdon said. "It wouldn't be a bad idea for you both to get clear of this mess either way. In any case, do you think you can have a chat with Jackson Brooks? The Incident Team might eventually get called in on this, and it would be good to open that connection." Langdon avoided Amanda's eyes as he asked her to contact her former lover.

"I can do that," Amanda said, perhaps too readily.

"I'm not on the case, but I'll keep my ears open. Cause of death and any evidence found at the scene should be forthcoming soon," Bart said.

With the business taken care of, Amanda left to relieve the

babysitter, and Jewell and Richam decided to leave as well. Bart, Chabal, Starling, and Langdon stayed up talking until late into the night. After the first few drinks, Langdon tapered off, but Bart kept slamming beers with no apparent side effects. One by one, they fell asleep where they were seated. It had been a traumatic day, and there were no promises the following days would be any better.

Chapter 21

Langdon woke restless and uneasy. He had a thin line of saliva from the corner of his mouth, and his eyes felt crusty. It was 4 a.m., meaning he'd only been asleep for about two hours. He eased his way out of the recliner, careful not to wake the others, Bart snoring heavily, and Starling talking feverishly in his sleep. Langdon realized that Chabal was missing. He wondered if she'd gone home, or merely had found a bed. When he went to pee in the bathroom attached to his bedroom, he heard the water running.

He knocked lightly. "Chabal?" He heard a muffled reply that might have been an invitation to enter. He turned the knob and pushed the door open. "Hey, are you decent?"

"What do you mean decent?" she asked from the shower, the steam filling the room with its hazy warmth.

"I guess you're pretty decent, at that," Langdon said. "Do you mind if I pee?"

"Just put the lid down when you're done."

"Are you all soapy in there?"

"All lathered up. Shaved my legs, too. I'm talking smooth as a baby's butt."

"Is that supposed to be a good thing?"

"I'll let you decide that in just a minute."

"Where are you going to find a baby's butt?"

The water went off. "Hand me a towel."

Langdon grabbed a purple towel from the closet. He reached

his hand around the shower curtain and his hand brushed against what must have been her boob and she gave a small squeal, and then giggled. "I'll take it from here," she said, removing the towel from his quivering hand. "You can take your hand back now."

Langdon turned to the sink with a sudden urge to brush his teeth. He caught sight of his large frame housed in wrinkled and rumpled clothing in the mirror. He grasped his toothbrush and went to work scraping the accumulated crud of bad news from his teeth. His red eyes stared back at him under thick eyebrows and an unshaven face. He splashed water across his ragged features and smoothed his hair down, somewhat.

When Chabal emerged from the curtain behind him, his eyes enveloped her in the mirror. Her body glowed from the shower, the skin soft, smooth, and totally inviting. Her wet hair made him wonder if he'd ever get to see her emerge from the ocean on some future Caribbean vacation together. Her eyes were amazingly alert after such little sleep and promised mischief in the making.

"I couldn't sleep," she said.

"Me, neither. The shower is a great idea. Do you mind if I jump in?" Langdon rinsed his mouth, turning to face her.

"I have to dry my hair, but I promise I won't look." Chabal stepped past him, brushing against him slightly, tremors cascading through both their bodies. "Look, you do have a hairdryer. I wouldn't have guessed."

"Missouri likes to dry her hair, now," Langdon said thickly.

He stepped over to the shower and took his shirt off, turned the water back on, and slid his pants and boxers off, then his socks. He looked up to see Chabal's eyes staring at him as he slipped behind the curtain.

His shower lasted exactly as long as her hair drying. "Hey, you there? Hand me a towel, would you."

"I can't believe John kicked me out of my own house." Chabal handed a towel around the curtain to Langdon.

He didn't know what to say to that. "I never should have had Goldilocks follow Helot. That was my gig." He realized the towel was damp and purple.

"You couldn't know what was going to happen. You don't know what happened. It's not your fault," Chabal said.

"Is this your towel?" Langdon opened the shower curtain.

Chabal was standing facing away from the sink with not a stitch on. He took in her rock-hard nipples and carefully trimmed pubic area, but his attention was focused on the hunger so plain on her face. Her eyes looked deeply into his, and her lips twisted with an animal ferocity, as if she meant to devour him.

Langdon stepped from the shower, leaning to kiss her roughly on the mouth. She was too short to kiss and embrace properly at the same time, and so he lifted her onto the counter and pulled her tight, his hands on her backside, and his mouth on her neck. When his eyes looked up to see the image of Chabal's naked backside in the mirror, his mind clouded over with a desire so strong he would have trouble remembering the next few minutes. When they climaxed together, it was not a signal of the end, but rather an opportunity to move into the bedroom to continue on after the briefest of intermissions.

When the sun was just beginning to glow in the sky two hours later, they were both finally able to sleep the slumber of the sated. Langdon dreamed of being on an isolated island alone with Chabal. They swam naked in the ocean, read books in the shade of the palm trees, and made love wherever they wanted. This was interrupted by the arrival of a boat, and a man with no face stepped off. He had a huge knife, more like a shovel with a blade, and started chasing them. The island was too small to hide from him for long, so eventually Langdon ventured forth with a pocketknife to confront this villain. A dark storm cloud swept across the sky and sleet began to fall, pelting his naked body with the tiny projectiles. The man was on the beach just in front of him, and as Langdon approached, he turned with a huge grin upon the face that had magically appeared. It was Goldilocks.

"Nice ass, but you might want to cover it up before it gets you in trouble." Bart was standing in the bedroom doorway. "I just wanted to let you know I was headed into the station. I'll keep you or Richam updated with anything I find." He took a moment to appreciate the scene. It was none of his business who got naked with whom. Bart knew both of their spouses, of course. But he also knew that Langdon and Chabal getting together was inevitable, as they all had, all except for the two idiots doing the getting together, that is.

When he left, closing the door behind him, Langdon and Chabal were left with adrenalin coursing through their bodies. Waking suddenly had been followed by fighting to pull up the blankets, not sure whose ass Bart was talking about. Now guilt snaked through their thoughts, but this was followed by excitement and desire.

"Wow," Chabal said.

"That just happened," Langdon agreed.

"I'm an adulteress."

"A very pretty and sexy one." Langdon wondered if Amanda planned on coming over this morning. It was 8:30.

"Bart won't say anything, will he?"

"Bart? No way. He'd shoot himself before he'd gossip."

"One thing's for sure, we can't do that again," Chabal said.

"Absolutely not."

"Not that it was bad."

"Might even say it was pretty good."

"Delicious?"

Langdon moved his arm under the covers so it was just barely touching the outside of her thigh. "We should probably get dressed."

"We could pretend it never happened."

"That would be best."

"Although…" Chabal said.

"We've sinned, this is true, but we haven't left the bed yet." Langdon's fingers brushed over the top of her thigh.

"Technically speaking, this is just a continuation of the sin we've already committed." Chabal's breathing grew ragged at his touch just grazing down there.

"If you're going to sneak into the cookie jar?" Langdon asked.

"Might as well take more than just one cookie." Chabal reached her own hand out and grasped him firmly.

Chapter 22

Langdon and Chabal showered together to wash the sin away and then got dressed. It was ten in the morning when they finally emerged.

"I need to have a talk with John," Chabal said.

"What are you going to say?"

"I'm not going to lose my kids." Chabal was adamant. "If he wants the house, fine. He can have everything. I don't care. But I get the kids."

"Technically, you were kicked out before you even did anything wrong."

"I guess you could say, then, that we were separated, which makes adultery a lot more palatable for most people."

"It was certainly palatable for me," Langdon said.

Chabal hit him in the arm. "I guess I might need a place to live."

"You could move in with me?"

"I don't think that would be smart. Let's keep us on the down-low for a bit while we sort out our baggage."

"That would be wise," Langdon agreed, nodding sagely.

In his heart, though, he felt deflated. He'd waited long enough, hiding his true emotions, and now that Chabal and he had taken that step, he wanted to spend every moment with her. But he knew the kids must and would always come first. In his own case, Amanda had been the first to cheat, so his position in any divorce was not as tenuous. For Chabal, however, it was a potential disaster. Either way, he knew that this was the final step of his own crumbling marriage, and whatever came of his relationship with Chabal, he would soon be speaking with Amanda about making it official.

"I best go home and have a conversation with John," Chabal said again, as if reminding herself to make a dentist appointment. "And you need to go talk with Jamal about everything."

"I need to stop by the police station and pass on what I know about Goldilocks following Ed Helot to the Greenlander first," Langdon said.

"How about we meet back here at noon to go up to Skowhegan to visit with Mrs. Peach?" Chabal went to the door and opened it but paused before leaving. "Langdon?"

"Yeah?"

"Thanks."

Langdon contemplated the meaning of that single word, said with such heart. He had an inkling that it had nothing to do with the sex, but more with just being a good friend.

He nodded. "Good luck."

Once Chabal was out the door, Langdon put on a pot of strong coffee. Even though he'd drunk too much alcohol and gotten hardly any sleep, was mourning the death of one friend and worried about the health of another, he felt remarkably clear-headed. He got out the phone book and began working his way through the motels and hotels in the area. Near the bottom of his list he hit pay-dirt at the Admiral Perry House, which was a bit of a surprise, as it was fancy and expensive. The room was under the name Eddie Jones. He asked to be put through.

"Latricia?"

"Yes?"

"This is Langdon. I'm sorry about last night, but I do need to speak with Jamal. Can I come over?"

"I'm sorry. Jamal can't talk with you."

"What? Why not?"

"We spoke with Eddie last night. He had his lawyers come and visit us in our hotel. They have told us to not speak with anybody about the case."

"But you've hired me to investigate the case, and I think I'm getting somewhere."

There was silence on the phone. "We are going to have to let you go, Mr. Langdon. Please send me a bill if we owe you anything."

"Shouldn't this be up to Jamal?"

"I hired you, Mr. Langdon, and now I am firing you." The phone went dead.

"She dumped you, huh?" Starling entered the kitchen rubbing his eyes.

"Yeah, it sounds that way," Langdon said. "Why aren't you at the bookshop?"

"Yeah, sorry about that. There was some banging in the middle of the night that kept me up. I think I nodded off when I should have been getting up."

Langdon tried to discern the meaning of his innuendo, but Starling's craggy face was completely unreadable. "Again, we can close down if you want. As a tribute to Goldilocks, if nothing else."

"Nah, what else've I got to do? Hang out with you fools tempting me to fall off the hay wagon and get drunk? Gives me something to do other than thinking about the bottle."

Langdon's phone rang.

"Langdon. Bart. Don't talk. Just listen. Someone reported seeing you leaving the Town Commons yesterday carrying a large knife. They didn't think much about it until they heard the news about Goldilocks being killed and deposited out there in the woods."

"What? Who?"

"It was an anonymous tip. They called the station, said their piece, and hung up."

"When did they say they saw me?"

"We'll talk later. Right now, there's a squad car on its way to your house right now. If you don't want to be tied down answering questions for the next twenty-four hours, you best vamoose."

Langdon hung up with a thousand different thoughts churning in his head. Where had he been when Goldilocks had been found dead? Had they established time of death yet? Chances were, he was still on the plane and had a firm alibi to prove his innocence. Who supposedly saw him leaving the Town Commons with a knife?

"What's up?" Starling asked.

"I gotta roll," Langdon said. "You probably want to clear out as well."

"I need a cup of joe."

"It seems I've become a suspect in Goldilocks' death."

"The boys in blue on their way here?"

Langdon was pulling on his jacket. "Yep."

"I can't see getting myself out the door in a hurry. I'll stay and face the music. Have I seen you?"

"Last night," Langdon said. "But I was gone when you woke up this morning."

His car was in the garage. As he opened the driver's side door and gestured for Coffee Dog to jump in, the canine whined low in his throat and hunched over, refusing to get in the car. Langdon's eyes adjusted to the dim light and he saw a brown stain on the seat and reached his hand down. It was sticky, and when he looked at it, he realized it was blood. He hurriedly wiped his hands on his pants. He carefully inspected the inside of the car without climbing in, noticing nothing else out of the ordinary, but Coffee Dog was now at the rear of the car, whining. Langdon went slowly to the trunk and turned the key, swinging the heavy lid up. There was much more blood splattered in the trunk, as well as a large carving knife glistening red in the dim light cast by the single bulb of the garage.

A car pulled up in the driveway, and Langdon risked a look out the window. It was a police cruiser. He had blood on his hand, on his pants, coating the inside of his car, and somehow, he knew that the knife in his trunk was the weapon used to murder his friend and mentor Goldilocks. Shocked, he realized that somebody must have planted this evidence in his car last night while he had been commiserating the death of Goldilocks with his friends. The true murderer had been right outside his house.

Coffee Dog barked, and Langdon hushed him with a low word and a look. Two officers, who Langdon knew slightly, got out of the police car. Max Carpenter and Harold Smith. The two men were traversing the walkway to the front door, or Max was, while Harold stayed back about ten feet.

There was a back door to the garage. Langdon motioned for Coffee Dog to follow him and out they went. The ice was crusted over and he was able to walk across the top of the snow. There would be no footprints to follow and hopefully no reason to get out the dogs to track him. It was forty feet to the thin woods that led to the backside of the Town Commons, and the garage would block him from the officers' view. Langdon slipped into the trees without a backward glance.

The Town Commons was over 100 acres of woods and trails that was rarely used by anybody in the winter except the occasional skier or snowshoer. Langdon and Coffee Dog were exceptions to that rule, as in the normal course of events, they were out there for a walk almost every day. And Goldilocks. He snowshoed the trails at least once a week. Or he had.

Langdon wiped the blood from his hand on the crusted snow and began to walk, his thoughts raging in his head. There was no question he was being set up for the killing of Goldilocks. Who would go to such elaborate lengths to incriminate him? It must have something to do with the Jamal case. Larry the Fish was dead. Ed Helot? Jerry Peccance? He needed to dig deeper. He needed to speak with Jamal. He needed to poke around more up at MECI. How was he going to do that as the main suspect in a murder investigation?

If he could find out the time of death, that would certainly clear him. He was almost certain he'd likely been on the plane, or maybe still in San Diego, things that he could prove. But if he turned himself in now, it would take some time to produce witnesses and receipts and boarding passes, and maybe that was what the people setting him up were counting on. They just wanted him temporarily out of the picture while they tied up whatever loose ends they needed to in order to protect themselves.

~ ~ ~ ~ ~

As Chabal was driving home, her thoughts turned to her husband. Would he be there or at work? Maybe he'd gone to his parents? What had she done? She shrugged and mouthed the words, oh well. She giggled, reflecting that, now the deed was done, it felt like it had been inevitable. She and Langdon were as natural as the rain. For the first time in quite a while she felt whole and happy. Her body tingled, letting her know she was alive. The air was crisp, and the sun brilliant.

Looking at herself in the rearview mirror, Chabal realized she had a goofy grin plastered to her face. She hadn't properly dried her hair, and it was crazy on her head, the wildness somehow exciting her. For the first time in a blue moon, she'd done something for Chabal Daniels. Not for her husband. Not for her kids. Not for her family. No, not even for Langdon, but for her and her alone. It had been a totally selfish act, even if Langdon had reaped some pleasure from her abandon, Chabal thought, a smile creasing her face.

It was with some relief that she found the house empty. The kids were off to school and daycare. John had probably dropped them off on his way to work. Whatever his faults, the man was a responsible dad. She had half-expected him to be sitting here, though, and she feared he might use her kids as a weapon against her. At least he hadn't changed the locks on the doors. This was a good sign. Chabal let herself in, grabbing an apple from the kitchen, her teeth crunching through the skin and into the crisp fruit of the Granny Smith. She briefly wondered how it was that apples could be fresh in January when their season had ended months earlier.

She called John at work and left a message that she was coming to see him and hoped they could talk. Even though she'd showered, clean clothes were a necessity, and she added a hint of perfume and a smidgen of make-up. She teased her hair with some spray and raised it up close to where she wanted it. All the while, her thoughts reran lascivious scenes with Langdon, and she shivered in anticipation at seeing him in just a bit more than an hour.

When she came out the front door, the police were waiting for her.

Chapter 23

Langdon needed a ride. He called Chabal's home number but hung up when a strange voice answered. He thought it best not to call Bart at the police station. Neither one of them were answering their cell phones, which was no surprise. Bart thought that phones that you carried with you spoke to the world coming to an end, and Chabal rarely knew where her cell was. Well, it had been decided that the Denevieuxs would be command center.

"Richam? This is Langdon."

"What's up?" His voice was wary.

"I need help."

"Where are you?"

"Can you pick me up out behind the Bowdoin Field House?"

"Do I have a choice?"

"I'm wanted by the police."

"Ten minutes good?"

"That works."

So much for the plan of stopping in and sharing his theory with the police that Ed Helot was the killer. Langdon wondered where in these woods Goldilocks' body had been found. He was sure there'd still be a crime scene investigation, investigators searching meticulously for clues, but he didn't stumble upon them as he worked his way to the back of the Bowdoin College Campus. He arrived at the same time as Richam's 1990 Honda Accord was pulling into a parking spot close to the woods.

Langdon looked carefully up and down before emerging with Coffee Dog and moving towards the vehicle. Halfway there, a squirrel darted across their path, and Coffee Dog went in hot pursuit. Langdon waited patiently, not bothering to call him, as he knew that the dog had selective deafness and would return in his own good time. Finally, he came trotting back with a large smile plastered on his face at having driven the ferocious rodent off.

The warmth of the car felt good.

"You going to tell me what the police want with you?" Richam asked.

"They think I killed Goldilocks." Langdon told him about the tip, the police visit, and the blood and knife in his car. "I'm sure they are searching the garage by now. I'm screwed."

"How about you turn yourself in and tell them what you know about that Helot guy?"

"Yeah, they're going to believe me now? I need to find out the time of death. If I can prove I was in San Diego or on a plane, I might have a chance. Otherwise? With the bloody murder weapon in my trunk? No, I've got to solve this one, or I'm going away to the clink for most of my formative years, or I hope they're still to come anyway."

"That's right. I forgot you were in San Diego when Goldilocks was murdered."

"Maybe. I got to get hold of Bart and see if there is a time of death yet. He said it looked like it may have been a couple of days, anyway."

"And what's the deal with you and Chabal?"

"How about we figure out how to keep me out of jail and solve this thing before sharing secrets."

"I suppose you got a plan?" The exasperation in Richam's voice was evident.

"I need to talk with Jamal. Something about this whole Larry the Fish thing doesn't smell right. Everything with him was just such a mess—and now it's all been cleaned up. And the way his mom seems to have caved to Eddie all of a sudden, I don't know. And then there's MECI, also a puzzle."

"Just because of that guy in California? Flanders, was it? Had some suspicions that something was going on at MECI? If you ask me, it's more likely that organized crime or gangsters from Boston were involved in a rash of burglaries in town than a couple of coaches and a headmaster from Skowhegan."

"I just have a hunch something is amiss at MECI."

"So, you want me to bring you where?" Richam asked.

"The Admiral Perry House."

Richam whistled. "Nice digs."

"You got your phone?"

"Yeah, I got it." Richam pulled into the parking lot of the fancy inn down by the Androscoggin River on Water Street.

"Do you think I can borrow Jewell's car? My car's out of the question and Chabal's sticks out like a sore thumb."

"You still going up to Skowhegan?"

"All fingers seem to point there," Langdon said. "I guess we should clue 4 by Four in at some point as to what's going on."

"Should I keep the engine running?" Richam asked wryly.

"If you don't want to freeze to death, yes." Langdon told Coffee Dog to stay, climbed out of the car, and ambled into the inn like he was any other wealthy out-of-towner and not a wanted fugitive with bloodstained pants.

It was up a flight of stairs to reach the classy lobby and the reception desk. "I'm here to meet my friend Latricia Jones," Langdon told the young woman seated there.

"I'll call her room."

"It's a bit of a surprise," Langdon said. "If you can just tell me her room number?" This was against the rules, but after all, this was Brunswick, and small-town courtesy still applied.

They were down the hall on the next floor up, and a minute later,

Langdon was rapping on the door. Latricia pulled the door open with a smile that crashed to the floor as soon as she saw him standing there. She had obviously been expecting somebody else.

"Mind if I come in?" Langdon strolled past her without waiting for a reply.

Jamal was lounging on the bed watching ESPN. The room was spacious, with two queen beds split by an oak center table. There was a small sitting area with two cushioned armchairs and an ornate lamp.

"Hello, Jamal." Langdon walked over to sit in one of the armchairs. Latricia stood by the open door looking like she was hoping he might leave as suddenly as he had arrived.

"Hey," the teen said without looking up.

"What do you want?" Latricia asked.

"I need to talk with Jamal," Langdon said. "Alone."

"Absolutely not." She shut the door hard.

"Jamal, my man, I need your help." Langdon focused his gaze on the young man on the bed. "Somebody killed Goldilocks. You played ball with the man. I think he's dead because of all this, and I don't know what *all this* is."

Jamal flipped the television off and sat up. "What do you want from me?"

"I need to ask you some questions about Meese." Langdon slid into the slang for MECI to ease the conversation along.

Latricia walked over until she stood between them. "You know what the lawyers told us."

"Mom, I am going to talk with the man. Why don't you run down and get us something to eat from the restaurant? I'm starving over here." Jamal stared hard at his mother.

"Okay, it's your funeral." Latricia stormed out of the room.

"Why's she so angry with me?" Langdon asked.

"She's just scared, man," Jamal said. "What do you need to know?"

"Why'd you give me the old shove off?"

"Damn, man, what would you do? I'm the one with my ass on the line, and on the one side I got you and some hippie lawyer and on the other I got these guys in suits wearing watches worth more than your bookshop. Uncle Eddie is down on me. My mom is freaking out. They told me not to talk to you, so I said okay."

"So, am I fired?"

"I don't got no money." Jamal turned his palms up. "My mom don't want nothing to do with you, and Eddie thinks you're playing me for a fast one."

"That's rich," Langdon said. "Fast Eddie saying I'm pulling a fast one."

"Whatever, man, I'm telling you it's time to go our separate ways."

"Okay. But tell me something. Just so I know. What's going on up at Meese?"

"Nothing, man. I do my work and play ball."

Langdon let the silence hang until Jamal shifted uncomfortably. "Let me tell you what I know. Coach Pious left college ball because of a scandal involving sexual assault on one of his players. Headmaster Peccance has forced out all of the teachers serving prior to his tenure. I talked to one who had his house burned down and had suspicions of some sort of cover-up but couldn't prove anything. Saturday night I ran into Coach Helot in Bath and asked Goldilocks to follow him. That was the last time Goldilocks was seen alive." Langdon was talking fast knowing his window of opportunity was small and closing rapidly. "And my guess is that you got caught up in whatever the hell is going on, and it made you angry. So, you took it out on a bunch of homes, a general 'fuck you' to whatever pain had been inflicted upon you."

"I didn't do nothing." It wasn't clear what Jamal meant by this.

"Tell me, Jamal."

"I was one of the top basketball players in the country," Jamal said in a monotone. "A bunch of places were throwing free rides at me, that and more. Money. Girls. I wanted to stay close to home and go to Boston College. But that's a bit harder to get into than some of the other schools, so I thought if I could bring my SATs up, I could stay close to my mom, at least, until I could make some money balling and give her what she deserved. You know what I mean?"

"What happened up at Meese?"

"I looked at a bunch of programs, but the chance to play for Coach Pious? Man, the dude is a legend, and Meese was less than five hours from my home. The place spits out NBA players like a baseball player spits out sunflower seeds, know what I mean?"

"Tell me, Jamal."

"I was treated like a king at first, but soon that started to change. Coach Pious started tearing me down. 'You're not quick enough. You're too short. Your defense sucks.' If I turned the ball over, he sat me down on the bench, and that destroyed my confidence. I was afraid to drive to the hoop. I was afraid to pass anywhere but on the perimeter. If I missed a shot, he sat me down. I couldn't make a basket after that. All that was in my head was if I miss, I sat. You know what I'm saying? You can't play ball like that."

"I agree," Langdon said. "Keep going."

"After two months of this, I was a mental wreck. I second-guessed everything I did. One night, just as I was about to turn out my light, there was a knock on the door. The hall monitor gave me a note from Coach Pious asking me to come down to his office. I threw on my jacket and shoes and headed over to the gym. I figured the note would clear me if anybody asked why I was out of the dorm after curfew, but I didn't see a single person. The lights were all out in the whole building, all that is, except a sliver of light from under Coach's door. I walked over and knocked, and the door swung open under my knuckles."

"Close the door behind you," Coach Pious said.
Jamal shut the door.
"Come in, come in." Pious was looking at some papers.
Jamal walked over and stood uncomfortably in front of him for what

felt like hours. There was no chair for him to sit. He was about to clear his throat when Pious looked up at him.

"I'm afraid I have some bad news," Coach Pious said.

"What?"

"We're going to have to cut you from the team."

"What about my scholarship?" Jamal managed to ask as a thousand other dark thoughts tumbled through his head.

He could kiss BC goodbye. Everything his mom had done to get him here was gone. She would be devastated. He'd have to return to the 'hood and maybe, if he was lucky, work for Eddie.

"We're going to give it to another young man who wants to transfer in," Coach Pious said.

"You have to give me another chance." Jamal was pleading with tears streaming down his cheeks.

"I don't have to do anything." Coach Pious picked the papers back up. "Shut the door behind you."

"Please, I'm begging you."

"I'm sorry, Jamal, but you're not enough of a team player."

"I'll do anything you want, just don't cut me."

"Anything?"

"Anything."

Coach Pious put down the papers. "I suppose I haven't signed off on the transfer yet. We might be able to keep your spot if you can prove that you know what it means to be a team player."

"Please, Coach. You tell me what to do and I'll do it."

"Lock the door."

"What?"

"Lock the damn door."

Jamal turned and did as he was commanded. When he turned back around, Coach Pious had rolled his chair back and unbuttoned his pants…

"What the hell is going on here?" Fast Eddie stood in the doorway of the room at the Admiral Perry House.

Jamal turned his back and pushed Latricia away when she hurried over to him.

Langdon attempted to mask his surprise at Eddie's sudden appearance. "Why are you so intent on driving me away when I'm one of the few people who can help your nephew?" Langdon asked, throwing up his hands in feigned exasperation.

"All you've done so far is screw things up," Fast Eddie said. "One boy dying by suicide isn't enough for you?"

"I can't get past the feeling you're hiding something from me," Langdon said.

"Aren't you wanted by the police?" Fast Eddie spread his hands out palms up. "And I'm the gangsta bad guy?"

"How do you know I'm wanted by the police?"

"That don't matter. I know."

"Who killed Larry the Fish?"

"Who killed Robert Southie?"

Langdon was surprised that the man knew Goldilocks' real name. People who had known the bar owner for years didn't know his real name. At that moment, Langdon's phone rang. He took the opportunity to buy some time and answered it.

"Langdon?" It was Richam. "A police car just pulled up out front. I don't know if it's for you or not, but you should probably scram."

"I asked you a question," Fast Eddie said, but some of the initial bluster was diminished. "Did you really kill your friend? And now you wonder why I don't want you on the case?"

"No," Langdon said. "I didn't kill my friend. But, now, I'm wondering. Did you?"

"Get the fuck out of here." Fast Eddie snarled, pulling a pistol from the pocket of his suit jacket. "Or you'll wish you had."

"I was just leaving," Langdon replied. "Jamal? Don't worry. I'm going to bring them down."

Langdon went down the back stairs and out to the parking lot in the back. Richam had wisely moved the car to a position in which he could see the front of the inn. He had to shoo Coffee Dog out of the front seat. The canine started to protest, and then something in Langdon's voice made him realize now was not the time, and he gamely jumped in back.

"Bart called and said they brought Chabal in for questioning." Richam put the car in gear and eased out past the black and white parked in front.

"Chabal?" Langdon's mind was ninety minutes north in Skowhegan.

"You know, Chabal, who works for you? The one you asked me to call? The cute one with the sexy cheeks that you may or may not be sleeping with?"

"What do they want with Chabal?"

"Because she works for you and you're wanted for murder. Remember?"

Often at the end of the night, behind the bar, Richam had many similar conversations. Gentle and non-confrontational was as important as patience in getting a point across to a drunk to avoid violence.

"Jamal just told me what they did to him up at MECI," Langdon said. "Pious tore him down, stripped him of his confidence, and then forced him to perform oral sex."

"That old white dude forced Jamal to give him head?" Richam was openly incredulous.

"Power isn't always about physical strength or size."

"Will he testify?"

"I don't know."

"Should he testify?"

"What do you mean?"

"If Jamal stands up in court and details blowing his coach, his life as he knows it is over," Richam said. "The media hype will drive any colleges away from recruiting him. Hell, he won't even be able to go back to Roxbury. They'll be merciless, worse than Pious."

"That's not right."

"No, it isn't. But that's the truth, though."

"The man has to be stopped."

"Yeah, I suppose Jamal has to take one for the team, so to speak," Richam said.

"Not necessarily." Langdon's hushed words were beginning to turn harder.

"What do you mean?"

"What if I can stop Pious without involving Jamal?"

"How?"

"You don't believe that Jamal was the first or the only one, do you? Pious has been coaching for at least twenty years now. How many kids has he done this to? How many lives has he destroyed?"

"Don't do anything rash. A couple days of reflection isn't going to hurt anything."

"Yeah? What if the police catch up with me and throw me in jail? Who's going to stop Pious then? The clock is ticking."

Richam's silence conceded the point.

"What did Bart say about Chabal?" Langdon asked.

"He's going to take her back to my place when they're done questioning her, and we're supposed to meet them there."

Langdon dreaded making small talk with Jewell, but it was another hour before the policeman showed up with Chabal, so he had little choice. As it turned out, it was a good thing, for Jewell wasn't holding a grudge and seemed fine with him. Perhaps it was his telling her about the hideous act of the MECI basketball coach that had turned her ire away from Langdon, but whatever, she was all in on his side now.

"That new Chief of Police guy really doesn't like you much," Chabal said to Langdon without preamble once she walked in the door. "What'd you do? Sleep with his wife?"

"What'd he say?" Langdon asked. He considered asking if her husband, John Daniels, was the new police chief, but managed to refrain.

"He was very interested in what time we flew to San Diego," Chabal said.

"Time of death is estimated to be between eight a.m. and two p.m. on Sunday," Bart said.

"Giving me plenty of time to kill the man and dump the body in the Commons," Langdon said.

"He said as much, that he thinks you were using me to try to create an alibi for you," Chabal said.

"What did you tell him we went to San Diego for?"

"I told him nothing," Chabal replied. "But I… led him to think that we were lovers."

"That rumor is spreading through the station right now," Richam said with a wry grin.

"Rumor?" Bart asked.

Langdon shot him a warning look. "Do they know when the body was dumped in the Commons?"

"The preliminary forensics suggests late Monday night or early Tuesday morning," Bart replied.

"And I have witnesses placing me in California, or at least on a plane for those times," Langdon said.

"Which doesn't give you the freedom pass," Bart said. "The idea is that you must have had an accomplice."

"Great," Richam said. "I suppose I'm the next one to be brought in for questioning?"

"Or me?" Bart asked. "Or 4 by Four or Starling?"

"Don't forget I'm Black," Richam said. "No, I'm sure I'm next on the list."

"It appears in this case that us women are higher up on the ladder of suspicion than Black people," Chabal said. "Just for the record."

"So, what's the game plan?" Bart asked.

"Well, if Richam is right and he's the next one to be picked up, I don't want to be hanging out here much longer," Langdon said.

"Did you get a chance to talk to Jamal?"

"Jamal just spilled all to Langdon," Richam said. "How the boy was forced to give Coach Pious a blow job, or lose everything."

"You're fucking kidding me," Bart said. "I'm going to put a bullet in that man's head right now."

"Sit down, Bart." Langdon leaned over to peek out the window.

"That sick fuck can't get away with that." Bart walked to the door.

"Give me a break," Chabal said. Her voice was low but cut through the air cleanly and clearly. Her tone brooked no argument and stopped Bart in his tracks.

"What?"

"You make it sound like it's the end of the world. So, Jamal had to perform oral. Don't think most women aren't pressured into the same thing in their lives at some point, usually starting way too young and usually to get a job or a promotion, maybe a loan or an apartment. That's the damn line in the sand you want to draw?" Chabal looked in turn at the three men in the room, holding their gaze until they turned their eyes away. "Goldilocks is dead. Our friend was chopped up. Jamal will be okay."

"Chabal is right," Langdon said. "Jamal may have suffered, *is* suffering, but Goldilocks paid with his life and suffered terribly." He paused and fought back the tears for a moment. "But there is nothing we can do for Goldilocks. We can't bring him back."

"Going up to Skowhegan and killing some basketball coach isn't going to make anything better," Chabal said, Jewell nodding strongly.

"That is where you are right again," Langdon replied. "This has to be handled delicately." Here, he looked at Bart with a warning glance. "Coach Pious has to be held accountable, but with as little further damage to Jamal as possible."

"Isn't this the kid who just dropped you from the case?" Bart asked.

"I think he and his mother are both being controlled by Fast Eddie. She seems to have truly gone to the dark side, but I sense Jamal is reaching out for help, that's why he finally told me about Pious."

"Don't you think that his mother and uncle would know what's best for Jamal?" Richam asked. "Certainly more so than some bookstore owner who has known him for a couple of days?"

Langdon appeared to consider the question. "Jewell and Chabal, correct me if I'm wrong, but *this* mother and *this* uncle? I was hired to do a job," he continued, "and I aim to finish that job."

"And what is that job?"

"To find out who put him up to burglary and vandalism."

"Didn't you say that Jamal fingered that guy, Larry the Fish?"

"Yeah, that's what he said. If it's true, maybe that covers the burglary part, but it doesn't explain the vandalism." Langdon said.

"What are you thinking?" Richam asked.

"If we can prove that Jamal was being sexually abused by his white basketball coach, that might justify him acting out in anger, and then I'm pretty sure the D.A. would drop the hate crime charges."

Chabal nodded. "That makes sense."

"So, what now?" Bart asked.

"We follow the original plan," Langdon said. "Chabal and I will go poke around MECI and see what we can uncover."

"Best to not get pulled over," Bart said. "Not only are you wanted by the police, but your face is on every news channel in the state. Stay low."

"I think we should keep an eye on this Fast Eddie character," Richam said. "And probably Latricia and Jamal Jones as well."

"Good idea," Langdon said. "Can you get back over to the Admiral Perry House and keep watch?"

"Sure."

"Don't get too close. The man just pulled a gun on me. If he catches on that you're watching him, it might go bad. *Real* bad."

"Roger that," Richam said.

"I think if 4 by Four's up to it, we should get him back up here," Bart said. "As much as the little puke irritates me, it would probably be good to have some legal advice when this all comes crashing down."

"I wasn't sure if we should bother him in the middle of what he's going through," Langdon said.

"He's going to be some pissed when he finds out we didn't," Richam said.

"Yeah, okay, I'll give him a call," Langdon said.

"I'm going to go pick him up in Boston," Bart said.

"Wouldn't it be easier for him to just jump a bus to Portland?" Chabal asked.

"I was thinking I might like to poke around down there a bit. I know this Fast Eddie is a gangster and all, but how does that tie in with Latricia and Jamal? I'm not sure I'm buying this blood is thicker than water thing."

"What do you mean by that?" Langdon asked.

"I'm not sure," Bart said. "If Fast Eddie is really the boss man down there, he would've known that Larry the Fish was sending his nephew out to burglarize homes. I ran a background check on him, and he's been suspected of everything from dealing drugs to pimping prostitutes to committing murder, but none of it has stuck."

"Yeah, it's all a little too tidy, laying the blame on a dead man."

"You think Fast Eddie and Latricia are a little tighter than they're letting on?"

"Could be," Bart said. "Or maybe it was actually that prick who sent Jamal out to pay back some of his debt."

"OK, it can't hurt," Langdon agreed. "Why don't you take Star with you? I got Latricia's address right here." He pulled a notebook from his pocket and ripped out a piece of paper and handed it to Bart. "As a matter of fact, I think I have another address for Latricia Jones. Why don't you swing by this place as well? I thought it was her work address, but it didn't match up. I have no idea what it is." He dug around in his wallet and came up with the card that had fallen on the bar in Portland just the week before. It read: QUEEN LATRICIA, 15 WARREN STREET, ROXBURY, MA. He handed it to Bart.

"Queen Latricia?" Bart asked looking at the card. "What's up with that?"

"I don't know." Langdon shrugged. "Sounds like it's worth a look, though."

Chapter 24

Amanda Langdon was busy cleaning. This was what she did when she needed to think. Things were not working out with Goff. She knew it. He knew it. Hell, everybody knew it. One didn't have to look far to point a finger at whose fault it was; most likely, the woman who'd slept with a friend and then run off with some dipshit golf pro thinking life would be more glamorous.

The dipshit's professional status involved working at a small course in Florida and trying to stay sober long enough to pick up other golfers' wives in the lounge. He was actually less successful at sobriety than golf, if that was possible, so as far as she knew, his fornication was limited to once a week sidling up behind her in bed if she slept in too late and was too tired to fend off his advances.

Her affair had thrown a solid marriage to a good man into turmoil. But, if she were to be honest, their marriage hadn't exactly been built on the strongest of foundations. Sure, she and Goff had had some fun together when they were younger, and their creation of Missouri was a wonder to be marveled at, surely their greatest achievement. The reality was that they were two very different people. Maybe they'd grown apart. Maybe they'd always been that way.

Perhaps it was time to stop trying to fit a square peg into a round hole. Amanda sensed the sexual tension between Langdon and Chabal. Maybe it was time to step aside and move on with her life. A sudden rapping on the door interrupted these thoughts. She hurriedly crossed the living room to open it before whoever it was woke Missouri from her nap.

"Amanda Langdon?" A police officer stood at her door with another one a few feet behind. "I am Officer Carpenter, and I was wondering if I could ask you a few questions?"

"Hi, Max," Amanda replied. "Why are you asking who I am?"

"Mrs. Langdon, Officer Smith and myself are investigating a murder. Is your husband here?"

"No, we don't live together." *Why were they looking for Goff?* She wondered. "What's this all about?"

"Do you mind if we come in?"

"My daughter is napping."

"Ma'am, your husband, Goff Langdon, is wanted for questioning in a murder case." Officer Harold Smith stepped up onto the porch beside his partner.

"What murder? You mean Goldilocks?" Amanda looked from one man to the other in shocked disbelief. "You know better than that, Max. You've played basketball with both of them. Goldilocks was like a father to Goff, the good kind, not the shitty kind that runs out on you or beats you or worse."

"Your husband was seen in the vicinity of a crime scene," Officer Smith said. His face was red. He had never liked Goff Langdon and this southern belle wife who thought she was better than everybody else. "The trunk of his car was splattered with blood, which I'm betting will match up to the murder victim. The bartender at Goldilocks Pub said that Langdon called him at the bar Saturday evening. Nobody saw him after that until he turned up as a corpse in the woods."

"Easy, easy, Harold," Officer Carpenter said.

"We could probably clear this up quickly, but your husband seems to have disappeared." Officer Smith took another step forward into her space.

"As I said, I don't know where he is," Amanda said.

"Can we come in and ask you a few questions?" Carpenter asked.

"I think I should speak with my lawyer."

"If necessary, we can drag you down to the station," Smith said.

"You bringing my five-year-old into jail as well? Or just leaving her here alone?"

"Nobody is bringing anybody anywhere," Carpenter said. "When did you last see your husband, Mrs. Langdon?"

They beat around the bush for about fifteen minutes. Amanda was able to verify that she had seen Goff the previous Saturday night when he dropped off Missouri after taking her to a play. She refrained from mentioning that she'd seen him just the night before as soon as she'd heard about Goldilocks' brutal murder. As the police cruiser pulled out of the driveway, Amanda immediately got out her cell phone and called Jackson Brooks.

~ ~ ~ ~ ~

Bart stood nervously across the desk. For all of his bluster, he didn't much like confrontation. He had never gotten on very well with Chief Mark Batchelder. It didn't help that Bart had secretly coveted the man's job, even though he knew he was too much of a maverick and not enough of a politician for the position. It still rankled him that they'd brought in an outsider to fill the spot vacated just two years earlier.

He'd figured it best to take the bull by the horns and put the fact that he was acquainted with Langdon out on the table, and maybe also gain some insight into the case being built against his friend. True to his nature, Bart had entered the office without knocking and now stood rocking back and forth from foot to foot.

"I want to be put on the Goldilocks murder case," Bart said.

"I'll be right with you," Chief Batchelder said. Inwardly he was seething. After twenty years in the military it was hard to put up with the kind of insubordination that seemed a hallmark of Lieutenant Jeremiah Bartholomew's every interaction with his superior officer.

"Have a seat."

"I'm fine standing."

The Chief made the pretense of finishing up some paperwork, but it was just for show to make the officer in front of him uneasy. It did not appear to be successful.

"What can I do for you?"

"I want in on the Goldilocks case."

"Lieutenant Carpenter and Sergeant Smith and their squad appear to be well in control of the situation," the Chief said.

"Those two couldn't find their way out of a paper bag. Hell, you could've appointed them to be dog catchers except for the fact we'd then be overrun by strays."

"That's enough, Lieutenant. You will treat other officers with respect."

"I'm sorry, sir, but I knew Goldilocks."

"That's exactly why I don't want you on the case. You're too closely connected emotionally." A small smile leaked from the corner of Chief Batchelder's mouth, his pencil-thin mustache doing nothing to hide the pleasure he was taking in rejecting Bart's involvement.

"But my knowledge of the victim can bring insight to the case."

"I am sure that Lieutenant Carpenter and Sergeant Smith will want to talk to you, in regard to, not only the victim, but your relationship with the main suspect as well." Chief Batchelder no longer tried to hide the grin filling his face. It was about time this relic was put in his place, he thought, or forced out of the department entirely.

"You might as well've assigned Laurel and Hardy to solve the murder," Bart said.

"And why is that, fat man?" Lieutenant Carpenter walked into the office with Sergeant Smith on his heels.

"Does nobody knock?" Chief Batchelder asked. "And don't—"

"Any time you want to try me, dough boy." Bart had turned to face Carpenter. "I'll knock your damn block off. Otherwise, keep your yap shut."

"Lieutenant Bartholomew, that is quite enough," Chief Batchelder said.

"Are you in here sniffing around trying to protect your pal, Goff Langdon?" Smith took a step towards Bart in a threatening manner.

"I know the man didn't murder his friend for no apparent reason," Bart said.

"Yeah, well maybe his 'friend' discovered that Langdon was behind all the ice storm robberies and confronted him about it and—"

"Smith! Stand down." Chief Batchelder stood, his thin face pinched and red.

"Bullshit," Bart said.

"Yeah, sure," Smith said. "Why was his basement full of stolen items, then? Brad Parker has already identified a bunch of stuff, and we have others coming in as we speak. Oh yeah, he's the mastermind alright."

"It's a setup," Bart looked at the chief.

"Why don't you take some time off, Lieutenant Bartholomew," Chief Batchelder said. "And get the hell out of my office. Smith, you stay here, and Carpenter, too."

"Sure thing, Chief." Bart strolled to the door where he paused and looked back. "Thanks for the info, Harry."

~ ~ ~ ~ ~

Langdon and Chabal borrowed Jewell's less obtrusive Lincoln Continental for the drive north. Jewell had expressed her frustration at sitting on her hands at home, and Langdon suggested she go over to Amanda's and check in with her. Richam had already called and told her he was on stakeout duty for the foreseeable future.

Once on 295 North, Langdon settled the sedan into a steady 60 miles an hour. He wore purple sunglasses that matched the stripes of his Oxford shirt. Chabal's glasses were an emerald green, and she had a velvet black beret on her head. There was something exciting about being outlaws. The day was bright and hard, and the road whipped by in black and white.

"What's the plan, flatfoot?" Chabal asked.

Langdon smiled. "We take this tin can up to MECI and see if we can't find a stool pigeon to spill the beans on Pious."

"We got to avoid the coppers."

"For sure. I'm just an average Joe out for a drive with his doll."

"I think I'd rather be a moll."

"I'm certainly dizzy with you, dame," Langdon said.

Chabal flushed in a fabulous way. "We going to start with Mrs. Peach?"

"Do you think she can be trusted?" Langdon turned serious. "I mean, she is the assistant to the headmaster, has been there the longest amount of time since the man arrived, and I'm pretty sure that Peccance is either involved or at least knows what's going on there."

"You think he might be molesting the boys as well?"

"Yeah, or maybe the girls?"

"That would be downright diabolical," Chabal said.

"Or maybe he just covers for Pious because of the prestige the basketball program brings to the school?"

"I think Mrs. Peach trusts me. You just stay quiet and play nice and maybe we'll find out something."

"If she plays it straight, I won't have to rough her up." Langdon was watching Chabal out of the corner of his eye.

"Well, I get the feeling that Mrs. Peach is pretty loyal to the school, so let's not go in with gats blazing. Besides, I bet that old lady can kick your ass."

Langdon's phone buzzed, and he wrestled it out of his pocket. It was Bart, telling him that the police had found a bunch of stolen items in the basement of his house.

"I always wondered what was down there," Langdon said. "But, as

I'm scared of spiders, I never went down. Not even sure I knew I had a basement."

"Well, Carpenter and Smith have you arrested, convicted, and sentenced to Thomaston already," Bart said.

"Somebody's going to a lot of trouble to make me out to be the villain."

"That they are."

"Do you think they planted the stuff in my basement while I was in San Diego?"

"Most likely," Bart said. "You didn't notice anything when you got back? Like, maybe the lock on the door was busted or a window smashed?"

"Nope. To be honest, I forget to lock the door half the time."

"Just thought you should know."

"Yeah, thanks. Were you able to get a few days off?"

"I have off until Brunswick's number one felon is put behind bars, as a matter of fact."

"Paid? For a small fee I'll keep driving north and never come back so that you have an infinite vacation."

"They better be paying me."

"You going to grab Star and head down to Beantown?"

"On my way now."

"Keep me in the loop." Langdon hung up the phone.

"I sense a little edginess," Chabal said. She reached out and squeezed his knee, and then trailed her fingers back down his inner thigh. "What did the Bart-man have to say?"

"Seems somebody has been storing stolen items in my basement." Langdon reached over and put his large hand on her leg and massaged gently. "I don't know why I'd be edgy. Maybe it's because I'm wanted for the murder of a good friend, and I've uncovered a school of pedophiles? And then, there seems to be a strange hand on my knee."

"Seriously, though, you'll be nice to Mrs. Peach? She likes me and

I'm sure we can ease something of value from her. Heck, I bet the woman knows every secret there is to know at MECI."

"Of course, I'll be nice." Langdon got off the second Waterville exit and took the left onto Route 104. "Then we got 4 by Four down in Boston being tested for AIDS? It seems like everything is falling apart."

"Some things are pretty fantastic." Chabal trickled her fingertips across his lap.

"We should probably talk about that sometime," Langdon said.

"I agree." Chabal slid her hand into the waistband of his khakis.

Langdon almost drove off the road. He attempted to focus on his driving, but it was a losing battle. So, when he saw a deserted building that looked like it had once been a gas station, he swerved into the parking lot and pulled the Lincoln behind the structure, the car crunching across the unplowed and glittering ice.

~ ~ ~ ~ ~

Richam had returned to his spot in the parking lot of the Admiral Perry House from which he could watch both the front of the building and the back parking lot. He'd called the hotel and asked for Eddie Jones' room, and when Fast Eddie had answered, Richam had hung up. At least he knew the man was there. He'd then walked around the parking lot and was willing to bet that the BMW with Massachusetts plates was Fast Eddie's.

After an hour he called Jewell to check in. He wasn't really worried about her, but knew she was likely unhappy at being left out of any direct involvement. Ever since the case at DownEast Power from a couple of years back when she'd been slugged by a man named Shakespeare, Jewell had been going to the firing range at least once a week. If her family were ever endangered again, she planned on shooting first and asking questions later. She had become fond of saying 'better judged by twelve than carried by six.' It was this attitude that worried Richam more than her safety.

"Hey love, what are you up to?" Richam asked when she answered.

"I'm about to go over to Amanda's. She couldn't find a babysitter so we're going to take Missouri down to Falmouth with our kids."

"Everything good?"

"Sure, other than being kept on the sidelines because I'm a woman."

It was at that moment that Fast Eddie came out the back door, walking fast. He was wearing a black Brooks Brothers overcoat and had a knit hat on his head with dark sunglasses, but Richam was certain it had to be him. As a matter of fact, if you discounted Jamal, Richam was willing to bet that he and Eddie were the only Black men within five miles of the Admiral Perry House. He did indeed go to the BMW and started it up before scraping the windows.

"I gotta go, love. Fast Eddie is on the move."

Fast Eddie drove recklessly fast to 295 South and then opened the Beamer up to a steady 80 on the highway. Richam hoped he wasn't leading him all the way back to Roxbury, but then the man exited onto Congress Street in Portland. There were two cars between them and Richam got clogged up turning right. By the time he got off the exit ramp, the BMW was nowhere to be seen. Richam's first guess was that Fast Eddie was going to the Cumberland County Jail down on the right, and this prediction proved accurate. As Richam pulled into the lot, Fast Eddie emerged from his car and walked briskly to the entrance.

Richam mentally kicked himself. They should have tried to talk to the remaining boy, what was his name? Maurice. This thing with Chabal had really put Langdon off the rails, because for him that was a rookie mistake, not interviewing a key player. It looked like Fast Eddie was beating them to the punch. He was probably telling the kid to keep his yap shut, maybe even offering his lawyers to represent them. What did they even know of Maurice? Richam thought he remembered hearing the boy was from California.

He dialed Langdon's number. When there was no answer, he called Chabal.

"Hello?" Chabal breathed heavily into the phone.

"Chabal? Is that you? Is everything okay?" Richam asked.

"Yeah, everything's good."

"Is Langdon right there?"

"Yeah."

"Ask him what the last name of Jamal's buddy is. The one who is in jail?"

There was a whispered conversation in the background, a rustle of clothing, and then Chabal was back. "Williams. Maurice Williams. Why?"

"I just followed Fast Eddie down to Cumberland County Jail. I'm thinking he's inside talking to Maurice Williams."

"Here, Langdon wants to talk to you."

"Richam? What's going on?" Langdon also seemed out of breath.

"Are you still driving?" Richam asked.

"We, uh, just pulled over to get something," Langdon said. Richam could hear Chabal snicker in the background. "What's Eddie doing at the jail?"

"I couldn't tell you for sure, but I'm betting he's offering legal counsel, maybe at Jamal's request."

"You have to go in and talk to him after Fast Eddie leaves."

"No chance. You have to set up an appointment to speak to an inmate at least a few days in advance."

"Not if you're working for him. Tell the clerk you're an investigator for, hold on, I got it here somewhere." There was about twenty seconds of silence. "Tell them you are an investigator for Drummond Peabody."

"That's the firm Fast Eddie retained?"

"The local one, anyway. I think they're affiliated with his firm down in Boston."

"What if they check?"

"Maybe they'll arrest you and put you in a cell with Maurice. Save your one phone call until after you talk to him."

Richam hung up on him.

Twenty minutes later Fast Eddie came out and got into his Beamer and drove off. Richam took a deep breath, got out of the car, and went into the entrance hall of the Cumberland County Jail. Nothing ventured, nothing gained, he told himself, and walked up to the jail clerk's reinforced window.

"I'm here to see Maurice Williams."

The clerk looked at his clipboard. "Williams already had his one visitor for the day."

"I'm doing investigative work for his legal counsel, Drummond Peabody. Pretty sure we're supposed to have reasonable access, no?" He smiled and raised his eyebrows.

The clerk stared at him. "I don't have any record of you coming in today."

"Last minute thing. Drummond Peabody was just retained to defend him, and they wanted me to get a jump-start on things. Call them if you want." Richam kept his face impassive and uncaring.

"No, that's fine. Give me your identification and your private investigator license and fill this out." The clerk handed him a clipboard with several papers on it.

Richam handed over his license. "I work for a private detective. I do the research and interviews. I'm not a private detective myself."

"Okay, okay, who do you work for?"

Richam only knew one private detective, and the man was currently wanted for murder. Then he remembered Langdon complaining about some sleazy detective over in Lewiston. "Richard Graham. Graham Associates. Lewiston, Maine." Richam said to the increasingly impatient clerk. A line of seven or eight people had built up behind him.

The clerk typed something into the computer. "Okay, fill out the papers and bring them back up. Next."

Fifteen minutes later Richam went and sat at a cafeteria-style table in a folding chair. A young Black man was brought in and led over and seated across from him. There were two guards in the room, but they stood far enough away to give them privacy.

"Hello, Maurice. My name is Rich. I work for the private detective agency hired by your counsel, Drummond Peabody, to investigate the details of your arrest."

Maurice broke into a broad smile. "Damn, man, that was fast. I just found out a half hour ago that I even *had* a lawyer, and now here you are turning over stones." Maurice was rail thin. He looked as if he'd grown too fast and not been able to add any pounds to his frame. On top of that, like he hadn't eaten very well recently.

"I need to clarify a few things with you, first," Richam said.

"Shoot, man, I got all the answers."

"Where'd you get the van?"

"It was provided for us by the same dude who set us up to rob the houses."

Richam's head buzzed. Why hadn't they talked to this young man before? "And who would that be?"

"This white dude from Brunswick. Goff Langdon is his name."

Chapter 25

A group of preteen boys stood by the corner of the deserted gas stations with sleds in hand as Langdon pulled the Lincoln back around the building and onto the road. He honked and waved as he passed them. A couple of them waved feebly back. Chabal was slumped against the passenger seat. She felt as if a tornado had just swept her up, whirled her around, and deposited her back in the car, such was the intense pleasure of their encounter, however brief.

"We really have to stop that," Langdon said.

"Especially as it feels so *terrible*," Chabal said sarcastically.

"Damn straight. Feels like I'm banging my head against a brick wall and sticking pins in my eyes at the same time."

"I feel like Dorothy in the *Wizard of Oz*."

"Does that make Coffee Dog Toto?"

"Not everybody has sexual chemistry. We can just say we gave it a shot, it didn't work, and go back to being friends." Chabal sat up and buttoned her blouse and twisted her pants straight on her bottom.

"Well, technically you work for me. We're not really friends." This earned Langdon a smack.

"I'm glad Richam didn't call a few minutes earlier," Chabal said.

"I'm surprised you found your phone."

"So, you promise to play nice with Mrs. Peach?"

"Of course. I might not play so nice with Peccance or Helot, and certainly not with Pious, but I think I can be cordial to an elderly lady."

"What is it we want to know, exactly?" Chabal asked.

"Well, I think you should start out with, 'I think it was Mrs. Peach in the study with the wrench', but that's just a guess."

"I think it much more likely that it was Mr. Pious in the gym with the basketball team."

"Ugh," Langdon replied, shaking his head. He could never outdo Chabal, probably because she had had a host of older brothers. By the time she was twelve, she'd seen and heard everything, and no amount of crudeness bothered her now.

"What if Jamal is lying about Pious?"

"No way."

"Why not?"

"No straight young man would ever lie about giving another man head. Jamal might be lying about some things, but not that."

"Okay, but let's play devil's advocate. What if he *is* lying?"

Langdon slowed down as they entered town, passing the hospital on the right, and then coming to the stoplight before crossing over the bridge. "That would mean that John Flanagan was lying as well about being forced out, house burned down, chased out of town? Maybe John and Jamal got together to discredit MECI just because they had some grudge? I can't even think what grievance against Peccance they might share."

"I believe it was Sherlock Holmes who said, when presented with many possibilities, eliminate all but one, and that one is your answer," Chabal said.

"I can't say I ever read even one Sir Arthur Conan Doyle mystery," Langdon said. "But it certainly seems logical."

"So, let's run it through."

"Jamal gets cut from the team, so he decides to get even, and concocts this whole story to destroy Pious' career. How does Flanagan fit into it? Why is he pointing the finger at Helot and Peccance?"

"I don't know." Chabal shrugged her shoulders. "I just want you to consider the possibility that they might be innocent before we get to the school, and you go blindly swinging punches with that god-awful Viking temper of yours."

"I don't feel as edgy as I did before our little stop."

"I was throwing you a bone."

"Mmm, and I you."

Chabal flipped him off.

"Are you suggesting we get a hotel room?" he asked.

"And face that abhorrent ordeal of pretending I'm enjoying myself again? No, thank you."

"Yeah, I was just offering to atone for my recent sinning ways. I thought some charity work might square my account."

"*Charity?*"

Langdon grinned. "How about you call the school and ask for Mrs. Peach? See if she'll meet us somewhere away from MECI."

Mrs. Peach was indeed working. She didn't think that she'd be able to get away from her desk until after five but agreed to meet them at the same restaurant she'd shared lunch with Chabal and Richam the previous week.

"Probably should've called before we drove up," Langdon said.

"She strikes me as being very lonely. I figured she'd jump at the chance to get out, especially if we're paying," Chabal said.

"We got almost two hours?"

"I don't think I can handle a hotel room."

"Me neither. How about we get a drink? See if we can't strike up some conversation with the locals?"

"Sounds good to me. The place we're eating at has a nice bar and is right on the river. As a matter fact, pull in here to the right." Chabal pointed into the narrow parking lot.

Five minutes later they were belly-up to the bar with margaritas in front of them. On the rocks for Langdon, frozen for Chabal.

Langdon's Motorola StarTAC vibrated in his pocket. "Hello."

"Hey, it's Richam. You are never going to believe what Maurice

Williams just told me."

"Did he tell you who put him up to the burglaries? That would be helpful as Bart tells me that I have a bunch of stolen shit in my basement," Langdon replied.

"Well, that goes hand in hand with what I heard, then."

"What's that?"

"Maurice said some white dude named Goff Langdon was behind the whole thing," Richam said.

Langdon sighed. "Of course he did. Right after Fast Eddie went to visit him, huh?"

"Yep."

"Sounds like Fast Eddie is setting me up."

"Yep."

"Can you see if you can pick him up again? Go back to the Admiral Perry House and keep an eye on him? I should be back into town late, after ten anyway, and I can take over and give you a break."

"Sure thing," Richam said. "But if you can get there close to ten, I'm sure Jewell will be much happier with both of us."

"I'll do what I can," Langdon said. "And Richam?"

"What?"

"Be careful. He might very well be the man that did Goldilocks."

"Got it." Richam hung up.

Langdon shared the latest information with Chabal, and they agreed that things were definitely pointing at Fast Eddie being the man setting Langdon up, which would seem to suggest that he was not only the mastermind, but quite possibly the killer as well. The only question was what role did MECI play in the whole mess?

It wasn't until the second drink that they broached the subject of their marriages. Chabal had her hand on her knee underneath the bar and Langdon reached over and squeezed it. "As soon as all this gets cleaned up, I'm going to tell Amanda that I want a divorce."

"That's a pretty major step," Chabal said. "Are you sure you're ready for that?"

"I've been ready for some time now. I just didn't realize it."

"And what made you aware all of a sudden?" Chabal was fighting back a smirk, caught between flirting and discussing a very serious matter.

"I met a girl."

"Yeah? Do you like this girl?"

"She's got these adorable cheeks and a caustic wit."

"That's a dangerous pairing," Chabal said. She'd always been a bit self-conscious of her rounded cheeks, but it made her warm inside for Langdon to say they were adorable.

"You don't know the half of it."

"You have no idea."

"So, you like this girl enough to walk away from the mother of your child?"

"I am getting divorced any way you look at it," Langdon said. "But I do hope that I can make things work with this girl."

"Yeah? Do you think you have a chance?"

"I don't know. She's married, you see."

"I also plan on asking my spouse for a divorce," Chabal said. "Once this is all over."

"Are you sure?"

"Yes."

"How do you think John will take it?"

"I think after our trip to San Diego together that he has a pretty good idea that it's coming."

"What about your kids?"

"I'll have to tread carefully, but when push comes to shove, John is a good man and a good father. He won't take them away from their mother."

"Won't you be lonely? Living all alone?"

Chabal pulled her hand free and pinched his arm. "I met a guy," she said.

"Yeah? Is he ruggedly handsome?"

Chabal wrinkled her nose. "Not so much, but he's funny and has a good personality."

Langdon squeezed her knee. "What if he goes away to prison?"

"I'll wait for him."

"Murder is a life sentence, I do believe."

"So is love, I'm afraid."

Chips and salsa appeared magically on the bar, goblets of tequila and lime-juice were consumed, all in a gentle, comforting rhythm.

"There you are, dears," Mrs. Peach said. "I was worried you might have left. Thought you might wait for me by the door." She sniffed.

Langdon stood up, knocking the bar stool over behind him with a crash. "Goff Langdon, ma'am."

"My, what a tall one you are. Sally Peach." She held out her hand.

"Hello, Sally," Chabal said. "We have a table right over there waiting for us."

Langdon picked up the stool and followed them over with his fresh margarita.

"And who is this tall glass of water?" Mrs. Peach whispered to Chabal as they sat down at the table.

Chabal winked at her. "A friend."

"Oh." Mrs. Peach covered her mouth and tittered. "That Black fellow you're married to is so stern looking. This gent looks more your type."

"Oh, he is. He's funny, and nice, and…" Chabal widened her eyes. "More than adequate, if you know what I mean."

Mrs. Peach giggled. It was fun to be naughty. "What are you drinking, dear?"

At that moment their waiter arrived, and they ordered another round, Mrs. Peach choosing the frozen version. Chabal and Mrs. Peach talked about this and that while they waited for their drinks. When the young man returned with them, they ordered food, Cobb salad for Chabal, citrus spinach salad for Mrs. Peach, and Langdon had a Cajun salmon sandwich.

Langdon waited until Mrs. Peach was on her second drink before he broached the real purpose of this dinner meeting. "Chabal told me an interesting story about a teacher that left here after his house burned down."

"You mean John?"

"Yes. John Flanagan. She was a little bit concerned about sending her son here if odd occurrences such as that are taking place."

"That certainly was strange." Mrs. Peach looked down at her placemat.

"So, because I have to go to San Diego once a month on business, I stopped in to see him and ask him about it."

"Where did you say you work, Goff?" Mrs. Peach now looked up directly into his eyes.

"The shipyard in Bath."

"BIW?"

"Yep."

"And did John tell you what happened?"

"He told me a very odd tale, to be perfectly frank, Sally."

Their food arrived at that moment, and they bent to the task of eating. Langdon didn't want to push too hard, but after several bites, Mrs. Peach spoke. "I heard about that," she said. "I didn't figure it was any of my business, is why I didn't tell you earlier, dear."

"I understand," Chabal said.

"You didn't think it was any of our business?" Langdon asked.

"Well, you know, my sister works for the insurance company that paid out on the house. There was an investigation and all, but they couldn't prove anything, so they cut the check and moved on." Mrs. Peach took another small bite and a sip of margarita.

"What did they suspect?" Langdon asked.

"That he burned it down, of course."

"Who?"

"Are you daft? John Flanagan."

"Why would John Flanagan burn down his own house?"

"Well, Belinda, that's his wife, she was always after him to move to a warmer climate, and with the housing market so poor, I guess he thought this was the best option. I never would have figured him for a criminal, but you can never know, can you?"

"That's not quite the story he told me," Langdon said. But it made sense. Flanagan burned down his own house and moved to a smaller home outside San Diego, and had enough left over to open a novelty shop.

"Whoops," Mrs. Peach giggled and covered her mouth. "I guess I spilled the beans, then. My sister swore me to secrecy. I wouldn't have said anything, but I thought you already knew. What *did* John tell you?"

"He told me about an incident he had with Jerry Peccance and Ed Helot."

"Ed? He is the nicest man. Jerry can be a little abrasive, but I'm sure his heart is in the right place."

"Did you ever hear about an issue between Flanagan and Peccance about some pictures?" Chabal asked.

"How do you know about that? I can't imagine John told you about that," Mrs. Peach said.

"What do you know about it?" Langdon asked.

Mrs. Peach leaned forward. She was one past her limit of one drink. "I've never told anybody this, well, that is, except for my sister, but she doesn't really count, you know."

"Told anybody what?"

"That wall between Jerry's office is pretty thin, and I've got good ears for an old biddy." Mrs. Peach laughed and then suddenly grew serious. "Anyway, Jerry called John into his office one day, and they were fighting over a photograph. It was of John with a girl and it sounded like they were pretty cozy, if you know what I mean."

"There was a picture of John Flanagan with a woman that was not his wife?" Langdon asked.

"Not a woman, a girl, one of the students. Monica, I think her name was, oops," she covered her mouth. "John argued that it was just friendly, and the camera had it out of context. I guess that was not the story she was telling her friends, and she was showing the picture around when Ed Helot took it away from her and brought it to Jerry's attention."

"Did Peccance suspend him? Open an investigation?"

"It didn't sound like he had any real proof, but he was going to pursue it, and he definitely told John that he was going to recommend to the board that they terminate his contract for bad moral character. Even if he had fought the charges, he would've been done at Meese."

"What happened then?" Chabal asked.

"Hmm, if I remember correctly, it was right after that that John's house burned down, and rather quickly, he moved to San Diego."

"And Monica?" Langdon asked.

"She was a PG, so I guess she graduated and went home. Somewhere in California, I think. She was a sweet young girl."

"So, John Flanagan may have been having a relationship with a student, Monica, and after they were discovered, they both moved to California?" Langdon asked.

"Oh, my! I hadn't even thought of that. You don't think…?"

Langdon knew that she was filing that juicy tidbit away to regale her sister. "Of course, we heard a completely different story from Flanagan," he said.

"We?" Mrs. Peach proved to be quite sharp yet.

"I mean, he told me, and I told Chabal."

"And what did John say?"

"He said he saw some pictures of naked boys on Jerry Peccance's desk and that he and Ed Helot were somehow in it together. At the very least, they were involved with each other." Langdon spoke gently, trying not to shock the older woman.

"Jerry and Ed?" Mrs. Peach clucked her tongue. "With each other?"

Chabal nodded, whether in a comforting or encouraging fashion, it was hard to tell.

"Jerry Peccance is very happily married to a woman I go to church with. The two of them dote on each other." Mrs. Peach again leaned forward over the table. "But Ed Helot is gay."

"Are you sure?"

"Oh, he doesn't try to hide it. I mean, up here in Skowhegan he doesn't exactly flaunt it, but he is very open about it with the people he knows," Mrs. Peach said. "He is an excellent administrator, great with the kids, and a very popular coach."

"He doesn't have a thing for young boys, does he?" Langdon asked.

"You're not one of those homophobes, are you?" Mrs. Peach asked. "Just because the man is gay doesn't mean he's a pervert."

Langdon blushed. Here he was treading water to not upset her sensibilities, and he'd gone and come across as biased. "I'm sorry, that's rude, but that is what John Flanagan led us to believe."

"Ed is a true gentleman. He loves children, not in some sick way, but in the best way possible. He has had a male friend for several years now. I believe he lives down in Portsmouth and they get together most weekends. Either there, here, or somewhere in between."

Of course, Langdon thought. That was why he'd seen Helot down in Bath, which was about halfway between Skowhegan and Portsmouth. They'd probably gone to a movie, or a show, and most likely got a room in a hotel for the night. Then, logically, it was not Ed Helot who killed Goldilocks, leaving Langdon back at square one for suspects. Unless Helot had mentioned to Pious that he'd been followed? That was unlikely.

"How about Rick Pious?" Langdon asked.

"Maybe you better tell me who you really are," Mrs. Peach replied.

Chapter 26

Jimmy 4 by Four was standing outside of Massachusetts General Hospital when Bart pulled up to the curb in his Caddie. He was wearing a New York Yankees baseball cap, which was not a good way to blend in in Red Sox–mad Boston. Star leaned out the passenger window.

"You know Strawberry is back on the white powder again, don't you?" he asked.

"Bullshit," 4 by Four said. "He's ready for a great rebound season and another world championship."

"Get in before somebody shoots you," Bart said.

"Be doing me a favor." 4 by Four climbed in the back. "Goldilocks is really dead?"

"Ugly scene," Bart said. "Somebody chopped him up good."

"Who?"

Bart pulled away from the curb. "I'm thinking it's this gangster Fast Eddie from down this way."

"Jamal's uncle?"

"Yeah, that's the connection."

Bart went on to catch 4 by Four up on what he'd missed, starting with Langdon having Goldilocks tail Ed Helot, the trip to San Diego and John Flanagan, the body of Goldilocks being found in the Town Commons, the blood and murder weapon found in Langdon's car, and most recently, the stolen items from the ice storm burglaries found in Langdon's basement. He omitted catching Langdon and Chabal in bed, figuring that was their business.

"Sounds like somebody is trying to stick it to Langdon good," 4 by Four said once Bart was done bringing him up to speed. "What's the plan?"

"We thought we might check out Latricia Jones," Bart said.

"Why?"

"Just a hunch, I guess. Langdon said she was sweet as pie with him, and then Fast Eddie showed up, and she went cold and nasty real fast."

"Isn't that just a normal woman?" 4 by Four asked, and the three bachelors all laughed.

"Go right up here." Starling had a map spread out across his lap.

"What's strange is the address she gave on the contract with Langdon is different than her business card." Bart said. "Some place on Warren Avenue."

"Probably her work address if it's a business card," 4 by Four said.

"Pretty odd business card for a banker," Starling said.

"What'd she say when she gave him the card?"

"He, uh, kind of picked it out of her purse." Starling reached the card back and gave it to 4 by Four.

"Queen Latricia? Is she some Voodoo priest or something?" Jimmy asked.

"Ah, maybe. We hadn't thought of that. Sort of like Marie Laveau, huh?" Starling said.

"This is Warren, go right," Starling said. "It should be just up here on the left. Number 15."

After about 100 yards, Bart eased the Caddie to the side of the road. "That's number 15," he said.

"That's a furniture store," Starling said.

"Ding, ding, we have a winner," Bart said.

"Do you think she works at a furniture store?" 4 by Four asked. "Why doesn't the card say *Fabienne's Furniture* on it? Why does it say Queen Latricia?"

"At least Star gave an answer," Bart said. "Fucking lawyers just create questions with no answers and then bill for them."

"Star is a lawyer, too." 4 by Four said.

"*Reformed* lawyer. He moved up a step on the human morality ladder and became a store clerk."

"How about we go ask that dude over on the corner?" 4 by Four asked.

The three of them looked at the man with no apparent place to be even though the chill of a winter night was descending upon the city. He had a hoodie pulled up over a baseball cap and a parka with feathers held back with bits of tape.

"Can't hurt," Bart agreed grudgingly. "You're up, Star."

"What? Why me? Why not all of us?"

"Because I got cop written all over me, and 4 by Four looks like the kind of yuppie fellows around here burn in trash barrels to keep warm. And you look like you just crawled out from under a bridge."

Starling started to argue, realized the man had a point, and got out. He leaned back in the open door. "How much money you guys got?"

"What for?"

"I've watched enough shows to know you gotta grease the palms if you want information in the city."

They came up with eighty dollars between them. Starling crossed over the street and walked up to the man. Bart and 4 by Four watched as he gestured this way and that, and finally reached into his pocket. A minute later, he was back.

"What'd you find out?" Bart asked. He was fairly certain the old fossil had just blown his last few dollars.

"The guy's name is Shakey," Starling said.

"What guy?" 4 by Four asked.

"The guy I was talking to," Starling said. "He told me that the Queen is up there on the fourth floor, that corner unit sticking out." He pointed above the furniture store. "The one with the two dormer things protruding out."

"He knew her?"

"Yep, called her just the Queen. Told me if I was visiting with her, why then, I could afford a few bucks for poor cold Shakey."

"Pretty fancy looking," Bart said. "Let's go check it out."

Shakey had taken his money and disappeared, probably to escape the cold shakes, and maybe develop other shakes. The outside door, down at the end of the furniture store window, had a buzzer system to get in. They elected 4 by Four to be the guy who caught the door when somebody exited, muttering that he was visiting Latricia under his breath, while Bart and Star lurked around the alcove. It took 4 by Four a half hour, and gained a suspicious stare, but he got inside, waited a minute, and then opened the door for them.

There was an elevator that took them up, opening across from the room they figured was the one Shakey had pointed out. When there was no answer, Bart pulled a small leather zippered case from his pocket and went to work. They all had latex gloves they'd pulled on in the elevator. Bart kept a box of them in the trunk of his car for crime scenes.

"Why is it that cops and criminals are the only people that know how to pick a lock?" 4 by Four asked ten minutes later when they'd gained entry and pulled the door shut behind them.

This was not the apartment of a single working mom struggling to put her only child through school, and it certainly was not a bank. The front hallway opened into the living room, which was elegantly, if sparsely, decorated. There was a small loveseat and two leather recliners with a small wooden table hand-carved with intricate designs. The wall had a single print, "The Kiss," by Gustav Klimt in an expensive frame. There was an entertainment stand with a Denon stereo and Mission speakers.

"Nice joint," Starling said.

"I didn't know Roxbury had fancy places like this," Bart said.

"Pretty diverse neighborhood, if three white men can walk down the street without getting the hairy eyeball." 4 by Four shrugged. He walked over and hit the power button on the stereo and classical music filled the room.

"What are we looking for?" Starling asked.

"Well, for starters, how about what Latricia Jones really does for a living," Bart said. "This ain't the home of a woman recently promoted from bank teller."

"Interesting taste in books." Starling was flipping through titles on the shelf. "She's got books on philosophy, poetry, biographies—all pretty highbrow stuff."

"Kind of like they were picked by an interior designer to impress?" 4 by Four said.

"Fridge is full of champagne." Bart came out of the kitchen holding a bottle and two glasses. He proceeded to pop the top and pour the frothing liquid into the glasses. "You still on the wagon?" he asked Starling.

"Yep."

"Maybe they got a glass of milk for you. I could warm it up?" Bart asked. "It's going to be obvious we were here, so we might as well enjoy. We should take the glasses when we leave, though."

"Wow, that's good stuff," 4 by Four said. "What is it?"

"Krug? Vintage Brut, 1988." Bart read from the bottle.

The three men shuffled down a short hall into the bedroom. A king-size bed dominated the room. Four posters rose up to a canopy draped with transparent white silk. Starling walked over and fingered a piece of fabric tied to the poster on the right headboard side.

"What's this?" he asked.

"I'd say that was a tie to slip around a wrist." 4 by Four slid his hand through the loop to demonstrate.

The closet was full of elegant evening gowns, exotic nightwear, and costumes. "French Maid, Disney Princess, Farm Girl," Bart was flipping through the various outfits.

The bureau held a variety of sexy undergarments, and the side table had condoms and lubricants, as well as the three remaining ties.

"I'd have to say the sweet-as-pie Latricia Jones is a prostitute," Star said.

"A high-end call girl," Bart agreed.

The next room was an office of sorts, with a recent model Mac on a desk. Starling booted the machine up, and in a drawer, found the password to get in.

"Look at the technical wizard," Bart said. "Anything good?"

"There's a file called expenses and another one entitled MECI."

4 by Four pulled a case of blank discs from a shelf. "How about you copy everything, and we can check it out later?"

"We should probably clear out," Bart said when the files had finally finished copying to the disc. He took a pillowcase from the bedroom and put the empty glasses in it, and as an afterthought, added another bottle of champagne. "Wasn't actually half-bad," he admitted. "Take this, would you?" Bart asked Starling, handing the sack over. "I've got to take a piss."

Once Bart had used the bathroom, 4 by Four cautiously opened the door and looked left and right. "Coast is clear," he said. He hit the elevator button, suddenly anxious to be clear of this place.

The elevator door slid open to reveal a Black man with an enormous Afro holding a pistol. He stepped out into the hall, the barrel pressed against 4 by Four's forehead. Two more men holding guns stepped out from behind him and spread to the left and right. The men were muscular and walked gently on the balls of their feet.

"Whatcha want with the Queen?" Afro asked.

4 by Four couldn't make his lips move.

"The Queen?" Bart asked.

"Yeah, Queen Latricia."

"You mean Latricia Jones? We had some questions for her," Bart said.

"She's not here. What was you doing in her place?"

"I'm a policeman."

"You do have that cop stink to you," Afro said.

"I'm going to reach my hand inside my jacket and grab my badge," Bart said.

"Put your hands up in the air," the man on the right with large sleepy eyes said.

"I'm just going to pull out my badge," Bart said.

"Freeze your goddamn hand motherfucker."

"This isn't *Pulp Fiction* and you're not Samuel Jackson," Bart said.

"I say we waste 'em," Sleepy Eyes said.

"We can't be killin' them right in the hallway in front of the Queen's Palace," Afro said. The six of them stood within five feet of each other in the confined space of the hallway. "Fast Eddie wouldn't like that at all."

"I'm going to shoot this motherfucker right now if he don't get his hands up," Sleepy Eyes said.

"Suppose we could shoot them, drag them inside, and figure out what to do with the bodies afterwards." Afro pressed the barrel of the pistol more firmly against 4 by Four's forehead.

"I've got AIDS," 4 by Four yelled.

The three thugs froze in indecision. *Could you get AIDS from blood splatter?* Afro wondered. Sleepy Eyes shifted his gaze to 4 by Four, and Bart pulled out his Glock 19 from his shoulder holster and shot the man in the chest.

At the same time, Starling swung the pillowcase with the glasses and full champagne bottle in a wide arc that crashed into the face of the man on the left.

Afro turned his pistol to aim at Bart and not the man with AIDS, but 4 by Four jostled his arm, and the bullet went wide. Bart stepped forward, the Glock tiny in his huge paw of a hand, and crashed the pistol down onto the bridge of Afro's nose, the man crumpling backwards so that he was half-in and half-out of the elevator.

4 by Four looked left and right, unable to believe that the three of them were unscathed while their assailants were flat on their backs. The only one moving was the man shot in the chest, and it did not look promising.

"Stairs," Bart said. "Come on."

Chapter 27

Fast Eddie went to the end of the hallway and checked the window that looked down over the side parking lot of the Admiral Perry House. The man was still there, sitting in his car, running the gasoline dry. What was his name again? Eddie sifted through the information in his mind. There had been a great deal of research done by his legal team and their investigators. Richam Denevieux. That was it. What kind of name was that? Eddie wondered.

He went back into the hotel room where his man, Carl, was keeping an eye on the kid. While he'd been leading his pursuer down to Cumberland County Jail a few hours earlier, Ray had taken Latricia to another hotel. When Jamal had gotten himself caught with those other two knuckleheads, Eddie's first thought was he better whack him, for he didn't trust the boy to keep his mouth shut one whit. But Latricia Jones was proving to be a financial windfall and pleasing asset, and he wasn't quite ready to give that up. And Jamal was his nephew, after all.

"What do you tell that private detective? Langdon. One more time," Fast Eddie said to Jamal.

"I tell him that you want to have a sit-down with him. You don't want to hurt anybody, but you needed to get his attention, so you grabbed his buddy, just so you can talk to him, private like. I will bring him out to the farmhouse you showed me at exactly noon." Jamal's cheek was puffy and eyes scared, and the words came out in a nervous tumble.

"What time?"

"Noon tomorrow."

"What happens if you tell him the truth?"

"My mom dies."

"What happens if you can't convince him to show?"

"My mom dies."

"What happens if we get a whiff of cops?"

"My mom dies."

"Call him at eight sharp in the morning, you hear?"

Jamal mumbled something.

"What's that?" Fast Eddie asked. He nodded at Carl, who dragged the boy to his feet. "You're not going to get anywhere in life being a mumbler. Speak up."

"Yes, sir."

"You give me twenty minutes to clear the tail out of here, and then you move the boy to the other place we talked about," Fast Eddie said to Carl.

"Got it, boss."

Fast Eddie walked briskly down the stairs. The plan was coming together. He'd come up here to this godforsaken backwoods hovel of a town to personally fix things, and the first day he arrived, that bartender fellow named Goldilocks had spotted him and followed him from the Greenlander Motel. How he ever got on to him that quickly, Fast Eddie had no idea. He'd had fun carving the man up, though, and then planting the evidence pointing the finger at Langdon. Damn cops up here were useless, though, and they let the man slip away. Now, he had to take matters into his own hands. Again.

The night air met him with a blast when he opened the door, and he tugged his black winter hat further over his shaven skull and triangular ears. He'd been back from the jail for about four hours now, the man Richam having reappeared about an hour afterwards. The window to his Beemer was starting to ice up, but Fast Eddie jumped in without scraping it and pulled the car out of the space. Then he stopped just past where Richam was parked to get out and scrape the windows and allow the engine to warm up. He snuck glances at Richam who had buried his face in a map, Fast Eddie thought with disdain, like he was planning a trip, for chrissakes.

Fast Eddie drove fast, trusting that Richam wouldn't get a chance to call anybody as they raced up Maine Street and past Bowdoin College. Hopefully this entire ordeal would be over by this time tomorrow. Richam would be dead like Goldilocks. The deaths of both bartenders would be blamed on Langdon. Fast Eddie idly wondered if it said something about the man's character that Langdon was a friend with a variety of bartenders, and if he himself would be given a tabloid nickname of some sort such as the *barkeep tapster* or the *mixologist liquidator*.

The roads were icy and the night dark. Fast Eddie had to slow as he turned onto Woodside. If the man behind him went in the ditch, everything would become much more complicated. He turned down a long driveway and hoped that the man following him would be as dumb as the blond idiot. He pulled up to the house and sat in his car with the engine idling. It was a long farmhouse, the old attached woodshed converted to extra rooms. There was a barn about fifty yards to the right they had been using to store the stolen items. Fast Eddie was rewarded when his two men pulled up next to him with Richam.

The man said nothing as he got out of the car, his eyes wide, and a tremor in his hand.

Once inside, Fast Eddie took the man's phone to ensure he'd made no recent calls. He had not. Time to have some fun.

~ ~ ~ ~ ~

"Shoot," Langdon said. "Where's Richam's car?" He dialed Richam's number for the third time.

"I don't see a Beemer with Massachusetts plates anywhere," Chabal said. They had circled through the parking lot twice.

"So, Richam must be following Fast Eddie? Why hasn't he called?"

"Maybe he just hasn't had a chance to check in. I'm sure he'll call as soon as he's able," Chabal said. "What time is it?"

"Ten minutes past ten. I told him I'd do my best to get here by ten so he could go home."

"I'm betting he just followed Fast Eddie up to the grocery store or something like that, and he'll be back soon."

"You'd get less of an earful than me calling Jewell and seeing if he checked in with her," Langdon said.

Chabal stared at him. It was true, and she knew it. She took a chance to figure out what she'd say, and then called to see if he was there. When Jewell told her no, she just told her the truth. The plan had been to get back from Skowhegan, have Chabal jump in with Richam, then Langdon was going to resume keeping an eye on the man and his car, as the other two went back to the Denevieux house for the night.

Langdon had been debating the necessity of spending a frigid night in a parking lot when 4 by Four had called with the news of what they had discovered in Latricia's apartment, her apparent other life as Queen Latricia, high-end escort. That coupled with the fact that they'd had a run-in with three goons, and that Bart might have killed one of them, or even Starling, as a full bottle of champagne in a pillowcase was a formidable weapon, all added up to Langdon spending the night in the car. But, now, neither Richam nor Fast Eddie was here.

After another thirty minutes, Langdon sent Chabal inside to find out what the front desk phone number was, and then called, asking for Eddie Jones' room. He was told that Eddie Jones had checked out a couple of hours ago. With nothing else to do, Langdon and Chabal drove to the Denevieux house to be with Jewell.

Chapter 28

Chabal and Langdon arrived at the Denevieuxs to find Amanda keeping Jewell company. "What do you mean you don't know where he is?" Jewell voice was chilled with anger.

"He was keeping an eye on Fast Eddie, Latricia, and Jamal at the Admiral Perry House," Langdon repeated. "I told him I'd spell him at ten. When we got there, he was gone."

"So, let's go shake some information from those damn people from Roxbury."

"They checked out."

"Of the hotel? You mean they're up and gone?"

"Without a trace."

"And my man is not answering his phone." Jewell had opened the door holding the 1970 Smith & Wesson that she'd carried across the border a few years back when Richam and she had crossed into America before eventually finding their way to Maine.

"For all we know he is sitting in some bar and left it in the car," Langdon said.

"Did you call the police?"

"Can't do that. I'm wanted by the police for the murder of Goldilocks."

"But I can call them," Jewell said.

"Bart is almost back from Boston and on his way here," Chabal said. She knew better than to physically comfort Jewell when she was caught up in this mix of anger and fear. "How about we wait until he gets here. He should have some ideas."

"And until then we sit here and do nothing?"

"What can we do?"

At that moment the landline rang. Jewell rushed to the kitchen to answer it. It could be nobody else at this time of night.

"Is this Jewell Denevieux?" It was not Richam.

"Yes. Who is this?"

"That doesn't matter right now. What does matter is who is standing right next to me. Say hello to your wife, Richie."

"Hi, honey, I'm fine. Don't worry about me," Richam said, the tremor in his voice belying the words he spoke.

"What's going on?" Jewell had turned ashen at her husband strained words.

"I just wanted to make sure you understood who is in charge here, Jewell," the voice said.

"What do you want?"

"Several things, actually. But only two right now. Jewell, my dear, can you hear me clearly?"

"I hear you."

"One, do not call the police or your husband dies. Two, make sure that Langdon is at your house. We will be in contact in the morning." The phone went dead.

"They have Richam." Jewell hung up the phone and sat down heavily.

"Who?" Amanda asked.

"I don't know."

"Eddie Jones," Langdon said. "What did he want?"

"Only that I don't contact the police."

"We could call Jackson Brooks," Amanda said. "I spoke with him earlier, and he seemed willing to help out."

"The man said no police," Jewell said.

"He can be discreet," Amanda said.

"I heard that about him," Langdon said.

"Better than others," Amanda said, casting a look at Chabal.

"Who cares who is fucking who?" Jewell asked. "What are we going to do about Richam?"

There was a long and uncomfortable silence.

"We wait for a phone call," Langdon said. "That's all we can do."

"How about Amanda touches base with Jackson and asks if she can see him tomorrow?" Chabal asked. "That way, if we need him…" she trailed off.

"He's an early riser," Amanda said. "I'll call him at six and let him know we have a very delicate situation down here."

"Yeah, that makes sense," Langdon said. "Why don't you see if he'll meet you for coffee somewhere. Tell him what's going on, but don't give him the Jones' names or tell him where I am, only that Richam has been kidnapped, and it's somehow related to Goldilocks being killed."

"Okay, then," Amanda said.

There was the sound of a car crackling down the icy dirt driveway. Langdon went to the window and peeked out. "Looks like Bart's Caddie. Maybe we can figure some things out."

~ ~ ~ ~ ~

Fast Eddie hung up the phone as the first twenty-six-foot rental truck pulled into the driveway. There had been five teams of people preying upon the ice storm victims, and only Jamal's had run into difficulty. This was because they'd been stupid. How hard was it to break into a vacant house that had no electricity and load a van with valuables and then drive to an empty barn and unload it?

For some reason, Jamal and his two buddies had gone completely off the rails and began trashing the homes, delaying their in and out time. The boy had been unable to tell him where the idiotic notion of racist and homophobic graffiti, and the wanton vandalism, had come from. Fast Eddie had some ideas on that score.

It was essential that he get the stolen items out of the barn, out of Brunswick, and out of Maine, but the five truckloads would, he estimated, have been too hot right after the arrest, so Fast Eddie had waited until that night. They'd load up and disappear from the area like they'd never been there, and if that kid Maurice wanted to run his mouth, what did he really know anyway? As for Jamal, he had certain guarantees that the boy would keep his mouth shut.

Of course, his well-thought out plan and patience had run into a hiccup when he had been tailed back from the Greenlander Motel by that curly-haired blond bartender. Fast Eddie had immediately picked up the car behind him. The man had even followed him into the convenience store parking lot while he went inside for a pack of smokes and then pulled back onto the road right behind him. Should he have killed the man? Maybe it hadn't been strictly necessary, but he couldn't be dealing with a prisoner until it was time to move, and there was something about the man that had irked him.

Once the deed was done, it was a short step in his mind to framing that damn Langdon for the crime. The man seemed like this humble-bumble redneck, but he kept sniffing around. An hour ago, there was a phone call saying that Latricia's apartment in Roxbury had been tossed and that three of his men were in the hospital, one of them in critical condition with gunshot wounds. Was that just random? Fast Eddie didn't believe in coincidences. This had to be related to Langdon.

Fast Eddie had begun setting up Langdon while the man was off in California running down red herrings on MECI. He'd sent two of his men to drop Goldilocks' body in the woods by Langdon's house in a spot he would be found, and then to deposit stolen goods in Langdon's basement. Fast Eddie had thought to collect a Tupperware container full of Goldilocks' blood before finishing him off. He'd decided to wait for Langdon's car to return instead of leaving it in the basement, which had worked out perfectly. Fast Eddie had personally used a spatula to spread the coagulated blood in Langdon's car, and had hidden the murder weapon in the trunk, before calling the police with an anonymous tip. Somehow the man had escaped, and worst of all, had showed up to converse with Jamal like they were old pals.

The nail in Langdon's coffin was when he had asked Eddie if he'd killed Goldilocks. That was hitting a little too close to home. Now this Langdon character had to die. Once Langdon was dead, with all evidence pointing to the fact that he'd killed Goldilocks and then died in a shootout with Richam, it would be case closed. Who would be left to point the finger? The ex-wife who hated the goofy screw-up? The little chipmunk-faced employee he was hot for? Or maybe the fat cop? Certainly not the sick lawyer, or the alcoholic dude with a face like a road map. No, Eddie thought, by tomorrow afternoon he would be home-free.

~ ~ ~ ~ ~

Jewell had inserted the disc in the computer and was now scrolling through the files taken from Queen Latricia's computer. 4 by Four shared with the others the description of the apartment, and the assumption that Latricia Jones was most likely a prostitute. As he delved into the incident with the three men in the hallway outside the elevator, Bart cut him off and took over the discussion. 4 by Four was well known for embellishing such things, usually bragging on his own self.

"We pulled around the corner just as the first police car arrived at the scene," Bart finished up. "Then we drove straight here."

"Did anybody see you?" Langdon asked.

"When we first got there, we asked some guy named Shakes or something if he knew where we could find Queen Latricia," Starling said. "But I don't think that fellow will be popping up to converse with the police."

"When I slipped into the apartment, the guy I passed gave me a look, but it was pretty dark." 4 by Four shrugged. "I can't imagine he saw much."

"I'm sure there were people looking out the windows as we crossed the street to my car," Bart said. "But outside was clear. People in Roxbury know enough to burrow down when they hear gunfire, not like some places."

"So, you doubt anybody got your license plate number?" Chabal asked.

"Wouldn't think so. Not in the dark and far away. I guess I'll know soon enough." Bart smiled.

"This looks like something," Jewell said. The group crowded around behind her. "It looks like Latricia took a loan from somebody named Larry Ciampi about a year ago."

"The Fish," Langdon said.

"What's that?" Jewell asked.

"Ciampi is Larry the Fish. The guy who Jamal claimed set him up on this whole robbing spree, and conveniently enough drowned two nights ago."

Chabal smirked.

"Well, it was for 20K with a 25% interest rate," Jewell said. "She made the payments for about two months and then a month goes by with no payment."

"I wonder what that was all about?" Langdon asked.

"Well, either way, in August of last year she's again making the payment, with an additional expense simply called Apple Jacks."

"Apple Jacks?"

"That's what it says. Looks like Apple Jacks are running her anywhere from a 100 to 500 a month."

"What's in the MECI file?" Bart asked.

"Looks just like an acceptance letter and a bill for 20K," Jewell said.

"Dated a year ago?" Langdon asked.

"Yep."

"So, Jamal gets accepted to MECI, Latricia borrows from some loan shark to pay the tuition, something happens to prevent her from being able to make payments, and then payments resume a month later along with a bill for Apple Jacks." Langdon walked around the room as he spoke, trying to grab the picture in his head.

"What would make her stop making payments, or more accurately, what would affect her cash flow so that she couldn't make payments?" Chabal asked.

"Lost her job," 4 by Four said.

"Medical problems?" Starling asked.

"Drug problem?" Bart asked.

"Let's go with lost her job for now," Langdon said. "Let's say she really did work at a bank, got laid off, couldn't pay the vig, and—"

"What the heck is the vig?" Starling asked.

"You need to get a television," Langdon said.

"The interest on the loan," Bart said.

"So, she can't pay the vig to Larry the Fish and starts hooking to pay the money back," Langdon said.

"Hooking is the wrong term. That's for poor people. I believe she was an escort," 4 by Four said.

"Sex for money," Bart said. "Same thing, different income bracket."

"What are Apple Jacks?" Jewell asked.

"Cereal," Chabal said.

"Expensive cereal," Starling said.

"I can look it up on the internet," Chabal said.

"Let's summarize what we do know," Langdon said, trying to keep the discussion on topic. "Jamal has said that Larry the Fish is the one that put him up to thieving, and that Rick Pious sexually molested him. Do we think these things are true, and if so, is there any connection?"

"What reason would he have to lie?" Chabal asked.

"To cover something else up," Bart said.

"Such as the real reason why he was robbing houses," 4 by Four said.

"Yeah, I think Larry the Fish was a patsy. He may have hired Jamal, but it was pretty clearly at the direction of Fast Eddie," Langdon said.

"Maybe Jackson Brooks can help us out with what criminal activities the man is actually into?" He looked at Amanda.

"I'll talk to him in the morning," she said. "How involved do you want him?"

"Let's keep him at arm's length for now," Langdon replied. "We don't want a bunch of staties showing up and scaring Fast Eddie into—"

"We get it." Chabal interrupted with her eyes cast warningly at Jewell.

"What do we do now?" Jewell asked.

"We wait for the phone call."

Jewell and Chabal were at the computer scrolling through, trying to find any dirt on Fast Eddie. Bart, Starling, and 4 by Four had slipped into the guest room and empty kids' rooms to grab a few hours of sleep.

Langdon found himself on the sofa with Amanda.

"Missouri is down in Falmouth with Richam's cousin?" he asked her.

"Yes. Jewell and I took her earlier today. She was excited to see Will and Tangerine."

"How is she holding up?"

"She seems okay."

"Does she know what is going on?"

"Hard to say with her. You think she's totally oblivious to everything around her, and then three weeks later she'll recite word for word a conversation you didn't even know she'd heard." Amanda sighed, closed her eyes, and leaned her head on the back cushion.

"Sharp as a tack, that kid of ours," Langdon said.

"We've done okay there, haven't we?" Amanda opened her eyes and looked sleepily at Langdon.

"She's a rip corker."

"We wouldn't want to mess that up, would we?"

"She has to come first," Langdon said.

"What does that mean in regard to us?"

"Us?"

"We're not exactly working out our marital differences, are we?" Langdon sighed.

"Don't get me wrong," Amanda said. "I messed up and sent the whole ball of mess rolling downhill."

"Chabal and I slept together," Langdon said.

"I know. It's like a neon sign on your faces."

"I'm sorry."

"No, that's what I'm saying. It's not my fault or your fault, it just is." Langdon nodded. "We had our good times."

"Yeah, we sure did." Amanda tilted her head to rest on Langdon's shoulder. "And we got one helluva little girl out of the deal."

The phone ringing woke Langdon up. Jewell had already answered it before he was able to stand. By the time he got to the kitchen, she was holding the receiver out for him to take.

"This is Langdon."

"Yo, Langdon, this is Jamal." But the voice did not support the confidence of the words.

"What's the deal, Jamal?"

"You know that building they're using for a library in town?"

"Yeah, the old high school."

"Yeah, that's the one. Pick me up there in half an hour. No police, man, not even Bart. You come alone. Got it?"

Chapter 29

Langdon was ten minutes early. He pulled into the parking spaces alongside of the back of the building with a view of the door of the library. This building had, for many years, been the Brunswick High School, but a new one had been built a few years back. Now, and with a huge renovation taking place at the Curtis Memorial Library, this old brick building had become the temporary library.

Somehow, with little to no sleep, his mind was clear and functioning well. It was obvious that Fast Eddie was the mastermind behind the local burglaries, and it was probably worth looking into if his ring extended throughout more of Maine than just Brunswick. Latricia Jones was a prostitute, most likely forced into it by her debt to Fast Eddie, which meant that he was also involved in prostitution. So, Fast Eddie was a thief and a pimp.

Langdon would be willing to bet the man was also into illegal gambling and drugs. The recent shake-up of the various gangster factions in Boston had created an opening for a rising star, and Fast Eddie meant to be just that. Langdon kicked himself for not investigating Fast Eddie more thoroughly earlier, but everything had happened so quickly, and the red herrings had been abundant.

MECI had proved to be a false direction. Larry the Fish was exactly what his name suggested. And Fast Eddie proved to be charming and glib. He never would have guessed that Latricia was whoring, even if it was forced. And what about Jamal?

Jamal seemed like a good kid, but was he really? After all, this had all begun with him getting arrested for vandalism and burglary. He'd then pointed his finger at a dead man to distract Langdon from the real culprit, and to add to that, made up some story of being sexually molested at MECI.

Langdon's thoughts were interrupted by Jamal coming out the front door of the library and trudging through the cold towards the Lincoln that Langdon had again borrowed from Jewell. The boy walked with a long gangling stride, his head lurching from side to side with every step. He had on an old army surplus jacket and dark glasses. His attire was street tough, but his walk was adolescent. Jamal opened the door and tumbled into the passenger seat, seemingly nothing more than a collection of elbows, arms, knees, and legs.

"Man, it's cold out there," he said.

Langdon did not reply.

"Can we drive?" Jamal asked.

Langdon put the car in gear just as Coffee Dog snatched Jamal's skullcap from his head. The boy yelled in fear and ducked, certain that he was being ambushed.

"It's only Coffee Dog." Langdon pulled the car onto the road.

"Yeah, right, I know that." He straightened up and ignored the dog. Coffee Dog started jabbing him in the back of the head with the hat clenched in his teeth. It was a good sign that the canine liked the boy.

"Drop it, Coffee," Langdon said. Any such command as this was almost always ignored, but the dog sensed the edge in his tone and immediately dropped the hat on the seat-back and began looking around for the danger he now sensed.

Jamal snatched his hat back and opted against putting it back on. "Look, I want to do the right thing here," he said.

"Why don't we start with the truth, then."

"Okay, here's the real skinny," Jamal said. "All that stuff I said about Coach Pious?"

"Yeah." *This was the part where he admitted his lie*, Langdon thought.

"Well, that's the truth. Every bit of it."

"Let's say I believe you." Langdon turned left on Church thinking he might take the coastal loop back through Freeport. "Does it have anything to do with what happened?"

"It does and it doesn't." Jamal stared out the window at the glittering landscape. "I think it may have happened to Stanley as well, not that we ever talked about it. That's why he killed himself. That's why we went overboard with the graffiti and breaking shit."

Langdon nodded. That had the ring of possible truth. "But it was your Uncle Eddie that sent you robbing houses?"

"My mom took a loan from him to pay for me to go to Meese. He's a loan shark—no, he's the guy behind the loan shark, the money man, or I guess you could call him The Bank."

"Larry the Fish?"

"He was the one who came by to collect the payments."

"Did Fast Eddie kill him?"

"I don't know. When Eddie showed up here, he instructed me to give you the name. I never even met the guy."

"Did your mom work at a bank?"

"Yeah, man, she was there forever, but they had to tighten things down last spring, and they let her go. That's when she started missing the payments, I guess. She didn't tell me about this until later. Didn't even tell me she lost her job. Didn't tell me she had a loan out from The Bank. I guess she couldn't even get a loan from the actual bank she'd worked at for so long, so she didn't have much choice. She didn't tell me a lot of shit, man."

"So, your mom has a loan from a gangster to pay for you to go to school, and then loses her job?"

"Yeah, man. I knew she was in a bind. She was just able to pay the interest in July but none of the principal. I told her I was going to skip going to Meese. That it was no big deal. I could figure out another way. I could go to UMass. We could get a refund and pay The Bank back."

"What happened?"

"We fought for days. I knew what it meant if I did go, and she knew what it meant if I didn't." A lone tear was running down Jamal's cheek.

Langdon could imagine the scene. It was a battle of wills between a mother and son, and in that scenario, there was only one possible outcome. There was little as selfless in this world as a mother, and less as selfish as a teenage boy.

"I pretended I didn't know, but I knew," Jamal continued. "So I went off to school knowing my mother was up shit creek with a scumbag. The second I walked onto that campus I forgot all about her and money troubles. I made friends who didn't come from the ghetto. Guys that had two parents. Teachers who cared about me. The girls loved me." Jamal closed his eyes and sighed.

"And Coach Pious?"

"Oh, he treated me like a hero for a bit, at least until the real practices began. I had about six weeks where I was on top of the world. My mom was lying to me on the phone that everything was fine, and I was enjoying myself too much to read between her words and know what was really going on."

"And then Pious started in on you?"

"Yeah, all of a sudden, I couldn't do anything right, and the more he attacked me, the worse I played. I went home for Thanksgiving break. My mom told me some lies about working from home and paying the bills, and I told her some lies about how well basketball was going. We both pretended to believe the other." The face of an adolescent boy had replaced the hard ghetto mask of Jamal.

There wasn't a damned thing Langdon could do that would help, so he just drove the car and listened.

"I went back to school like I'd been sentenced to hell." Jamal wiped his hand across his face. "After a few weeks back, I couldn't take it anymore and jumped a bus home. Break wasn't for another week, but I felt like I was going to bust. I needed to tell my mom everything. I couldn't keep it secret anymore. I was fucked up, totally fucked up."

Langdon had circled back around and now pulled the car into the lot next to the boat access at Maquoit Bay. The frozen ocean was as stark as the ice-crusted trees on the peninsula of Mere Point behind, both matching the flatness of the gray sky.

"Fast Eddie was in my home. My mom was crying. She was messed up on drugs. I started to go after the dude, but my mom grabbed me and wouldn't let go. That rat-fucker sneered at me, walked to the door, and then turned and told my mother that the trick the following night wanted her dressed like Cinderella. Fucking Cinderella."

Tears were now coursing down Jamal's cheeks, futilely trying to douse the anguish that burned in his soul.

"You can stop if you need to." Langdon put a hand on the boy's shoulder.

"I can't. I got to tell you or I'm gonna do the same thing Stanley did. And how is that going to help my mom?"

"Take your time."

"That bastard made my mom a whore. I got it out of her finally. That was how she was paying the vig. It was that, or Eddie threatened he'd kill me. I'll tell you; I was ready to offer myself up just about. The past few months my mom had been fucking strange men, not just sex, but perverted fantasies and whatnot." Jamal opened the car door, leaned out, and vomited. He spit several times, wiped his hand across his mouth, and pulled the door shut.

Luckily, it was Jewell's car with tissues in the glove box, and Langdon handed him the entire box. "Apple Jacks?" he asked.

"Street slang for crack, man. Yeah, Eddie, he got her hooked on that. I guess it was the only way she was able to do what she did. And this was all so I could go to some fancy school with a bunch of white kids."

"It's not your fault," Langdon said, hearing the lameness in his own words.

"I went a little bit crazy and stormed out. There was a guy I knew who hooked me up with a piece, and I went to the Glitter Club to confront Eddie."

On cue, a glittering sliver of ice spit from the sky and bounced off the windshield. This was followed by more, the tiny pieces of hail clattering on the roof, enclosing them in a box of metal assailed by the overwhelming power of life.

Jamal barged into Eddie's office, but when he went to pull the pistol from his pocket, he found his arms pinned behind him by Carl, who was never far from Fast Eddie's side.

"You come into my domain and threaten me?" Fast Eddie rose from his desk and came around to stand in front of Jamal. He slammed the palm of his hand up and into his chin, bright blood creasing the suddenly broken lips.

"Fuck you, man." Jamal futilely struggled to get loose until Carl pulled the pistol from his hand and threw him to the floor.

"You bring a gun to my house?" Eddie's eyes were wild in his head, and spittle spurted from his lips. "You leave me little choice."

"Go ahead, kill me, I don't care."

"Kill you? Not at first, my boy. First, I'm going to have you watch as I fuck your mother like the slut she is. Did I tell you I was the first? It's always a good idea to sample the merchandise before you start selling it, don't you think? And she is a mighty fine slice of cake."

Jamal lunged at him, but Carl kicked him in the side and sent him spinning to the floor.

"Then you can watch me kill her real slow-like. It will be too bad to lose the money she brings in, and the occasional services she provides me, but you leave me no other choice." Eddie walked over and kicked Jamal in the face. "Then, if you're lucky, I'll kill you."

Jamal hiccupped and contorted his face trying to contain the anguish and revulsion. "He went into... more detail... of what he was going to do to my mom. And what she would be forced to do to him.

He said he would tell her that if she satisfied him that he would spare my life, and that I would see one helluva show. I guess he hit me a few more times in there as well. Then he looked me dead in the eye as if he'd had some grand inspiration and said that maybe we could find a solution."

"Robbing houses for him," Langdon said. "So, he wouldn't rape and kill your mother, and then you."

"At first he had me delivering packages. That very night. That very moment. I was his lap dog through Christmas, and then I returned to Meese for basketball. We had a tournament over break. I'd made up some story about my mother being ill, so I wasn't expelled or kicked off the team or anything. I was in Purgatory, you know, that waiting place prior to Hell, but in my case, both sides were Hell. Eddie said it was okay for me to go back, but that I still owed him. I worried what he was going to do with to my mom. I had nobody to talk to. I thought maybe I could talk to Coach Pious, you know?"

"And that's when Coach Pious forced you to… engage in… to…" Langdon drifted off uncomfortably.

"I barely played in the four games of the tournament, and when I got in, I was horrible. After it was over, I went to see Coach Pious and told him everything, and that's when he said I was being kicked off the team. That would have ruined my chances of getting a scholarship anywhere. With no scholarship, I wasn't going to college, and without college I had nothing. I'd turned my mom into a whore for no reason."

"It's not your fault," Langdon said.

"So, when he gave me the option, I took it, I went down on him." Jamal said. "To get into Meese, I turned my mom into a whore. To keep her alive, I became a criminal. To stay on the team, I gave head. My life story in three easy sentences. They can put that on my gravestone."

Chapter 30

"What do we do now?" Langdon asked. The sleet had stopped falling and the sun was beginning to peek out overhead.

"Fast Eddie has your friend Richam," Jamal said.

"I know."

"He plans on killing him and you."

"I figured as much."

"You both treated me fair enough."

"What's supposed to happen, Jamal?"

"I'm supposed to convince you that Fast Eddie wants to make a deal, one that you can't refuse, and then he'll let you and Richam walk. At noon he's going to call and tell you where to go, and I'm to go with you, but nobody else."

"But that's not the plan?"

"Nah, I overheard him talking with Carl. They're gonna kill you both and make it look like you were fighting. Something about Richam finding you with Goldilocks' wallet and having it out with you like you killed the man. I didn't get it all, but it ended with you both dead, and you as Goldilocks' murderer and the one running the burglary ring."

"Is Fast Eddie your real uncle?" Langdon asked.

"Yeah, he's my dad's brother. To think I used to look up to him? That stuff about my mom banning me from seeing him when I was younger was straight up. I used to sneak off to see him anyway. The man had money flowing out of his pores. He wore thousand-dollar suits and always had some broad on his arm."

"Where is the farmhouse where they're holding Richam?"

"That's the thing. They got my mom, too."

"At the farmhouse?"

"No, they got her somewhere else. If I don't deliver you in a nicely wrapped package, or if the police show up, or anything at all goes wrong, they're going to kill her. Fast Eddie says I got until noon to bring you out there or she is dead."

Langdon got out of the car and walked down the boat ramp. His head was spinning. The vileness of Fast Eddie, coupled with the shattered innocence of Jamal and Latricia Jones, made the bile rise in his own mouth. Somehow, though, he had to shake all of that away and concentrate on the matter at hand.

There seemed to be three parts. He had to save Richam and not die in the process. He had to salvage the damaged lives of this mother and son from Roxbury. And, he had to do this without further endangering his friends. This was supposed to have been a simple burglary case, and now it had morphed into something he couldn't even wrap his head around.

Jamal came out and stood next to him. He'd put his hat back on, dog slobber and all. He also brought the Coffee Dog with him. "We need to get my mom to safety, and then I will tell you where Richam is, but not until," he said.

"And you don't know where she is?"

"No, but I heard Fast Eddie telling Ray to take her to a hotel somewhere nearby."

"Okay. We'll see if we can find her, but if we can't?"

"Find my mom, man, and make her safe. You're the private detective."

Langdon called Amanda, hoping that she answered her phone and that she was still having coffee with Jackson Brooks. She did, and was, and put the state policeman on the line.

"Jackson?"

"Yes."

"Do you know who this is?" Langdon asked.

"I don't want to know, especially if this someone happens to be a fugitive from the police."

"Fair enough. I've got a missing person that needs to be found."

"Richam Denevieux."

"No, not Richam. It would be a problem if the police were to find him, especially for the person I'm talking about." Langdon still sat at the boat access in the car with Jamal. He was not very comfortable talking while driving.

"Okay, then, fill me in."

"Not much I can tell you. This woman is being held hostage by a thug who works for the man responsible for the ice storm robberies and the murder of Robert Southie."

"Goldilocks?"

"Yes."

"And why is he holding her hostage?"

"It's complicated, but I am asking you—begging you—to find her and get her to safety before noon today."

"What happens at noon?"

"I can't tell you that, and I don't think you want to hear it anyway."

"Tell me about the woman," Jackson Brooks said, so Langdon did.

The second call was to Danny T. If there was a person more suited for finding Latricia Jones than the state police, it was this man. Blackballed from fishing boats at an early age, this high school dropout spent his days either working at Cumberland Farms or hanging out around Rosie's Diner. Langdon found him at the latter. Danny T. was like the phone operator of olden times who knew everybody's business as well as they knew it themselves.

"Yeah?" The surly voice of Danny T. came over the line.

"This is Langdon. I need your help."

"Seems like the only time I talk to you is when you need something." Danny T. was huffing and out of breath from the walk from stool to phone.

"You want to come over Sunday and watch the Super Bowl?"

"You making chili?" Sports and food were Danny T.'s only hobbies.

"Sure, but I need you to do me a favor."

"You taking the Broncos?"

"Yes, and I will give you odds, but I need an urgent favor right now."

"Sure then, as long as it's five to one I'll do whatever you want."

"I need to find a woman."

"Shit, me too, Langdon, but ain't ya married?"

"This woman is a Black woman in her late thirties. Quite a looker. Long black hair, tall, built like a brick shithouse. She's with a Black man the size of Paul Bunyan. They should've checked into a hotel in the greater Brunswick area yesterday late afternoon. Her name is Latricia Jones and his name is Ray, but the room might be under Eddie Jones. Got it?"

"You just need to know where she is?"

"Yes."

"Why?"

Langdon understood he not only had to take the underdog in the game *and* give odds, he had to share some gossip, which was the barter upon which Danny T. lived. "The guy that murdered Goldilocks has Richam, and I can't help him until I locate this woman."

"Everybody that knows anything knows that you didn't go and kill Goldilocks," Danny T. said.

"Thanks."

"But, while the cops are chasing you around for the killing, I want to know, who is looking for the real murderer?"

"I'm in a rush here, Danny T."

"Okay, okay. When do you need to know by?"

"Yesterday, Danny T., yesterday."

Langdon hung up the phone and checked the time. It was 9:12 a.m. They had less than three hours to locate Latricia and get her to safety, come up with a plan to free Richam, that is, if he were even still alive. He backed the car out and headed back to the Denevieux house.

"I need to know where Richam is being held," he said to Jamal.

"I told you, not until my mom is free."

"I am doing everything I can. Now tell me."

Jamal was silent.

"What happens if the police show up wherever Richam is being held?"

"They call and have my mom killed."

"What if we have already saved your mom? Will they just surrender, or will they kill Richam?"

"I don't know."

"This is what I think. I think Fast Eddie has enough evidence against me planted out there to convince Maine to institute the death penalty. Him and his posse will claim they just showed up and found the body, and then the police will be looking for me again. This plan has some holes in it, but I can't take the chance of that, because the end result is Richam murdered. Even if I get off, and Fast Eddie takes the fall, it's too late for my friend. So I need you to tell me where he is?"

"When my mom is safe."

"I need to come up with a plan to save Richam, and to do that, I need to know where he is being held."

Jamal was quiet.

"What happens if I tell Fast Eddie you squealed on him, and the police are on the way?" Langdon asked the boy.

"Why would you do that?"

"I need to know where Richam is being held."

Jamal bit his lip and looked out the window.

Langdon pulled into the Denevieux driveway. "This is Richam's house," he said. "We're going inside to rally the troops to save your mom and Richam. I'll let you tell Jewell, his wife, that you don't want to help us out."

"How do I know I can trust you?"

"You don't. But I've never yet lied to you."

"Okay, okay, man, I'll tell you. But you better be saving my mom. The fuckin' house, we practically drove past it earlier about five minutes after you picked me up."

"Where's my husband?" Jewell asked Jamal as they walked in the door.

"We know where," Langdon said. "But we have to take care of a few things first."

"Like, what do we need to do before going and collecting my man?"

Langdon walked past her and sat down in the living room. Jewell followed. Bart, 4 by Four, Starling, and Chabal were all sitting there waiting.

"Fast Eddie has Richam at a farmhouse off Woodside."

"And why aren't we getting him back right now?" Jewell asked.

"He said if anybody other than me shows up, he's going to kill him. That includes the police. Supposedly, he has arranged it to point the finger at me being the killer."

"Why does he need you to show up at all, then?" Bart asked.

"I suppose to tidy things up." Langdon shrugged his shoulders. "One neat and tidy package for the police."

"Or he looks forward to killing you," 4 by Four said. "If he's the one who killed Goldilocks, then he is one sick fuck."

Chabal blanched. "You can't be thinking of going in there?"

"If I don't show up at noontime, he kills Richam."

"And if you *do* show up, he kills both of you," she said.

"We go early and surprise him?" Bart asked.

"Can't." Langdon looked over at Jamal who was standing in the doorway. "Fast Eddie has Jamal's mom, Latricia, stashed away in hiding somewhere. If anything goes wrong, she dies."

"Goddammit." Jewell went and sat next to Chabal.

"What's the plan?" Starling asked.

"I've got Jackson Brooks and Danny T. looking for her," Langdon said.

"So, you're telling me the plan rests upon the pretty boy and the chubby midget?" Bart asked.

"Pretty much," Langdon said.

"What happens if they fail?" Jewell asked.

Langdon again looked at Jamal. "They won't. Once Latricia is located, Jackson Brooks and the state police will go bang on the door. The flunky there, some guy named Ray, isn't going to kill her with the staties outside. No way he's going to add a murder charge to what, at worst, is kidnapping. Hell, he can probably even get it down to a lesser plea if he rats out Fast Eddie."

4 by Four nodded. "Any decent lawyer would get it dropped to a Class B offense. The most he would serve would be ten years, probably a lot less if he talks."

"Once word comes that Latricia is safe, we're going to go in and get Richam," Langdon said.

"I suppose you have a plan?" Chabal asked.

"We're going to need your guns, Bart," Langdon said. "All of them."

"They're in my trunk already. I packed them up for the trip to Boston just in case." Bart went to the kitchen and returned with a beer.

"And we need three snowmobiles," Langdon said. "Anybody got any ideas?"

Chapter 31

"I don't really want you to get killed," Chabal said.

Bart, 4 by Four, and Starling had gone off to collect three Arctic Cats from a man Richam knew from the bar. Jewell was certain that he would be accommodating, and he was. The man allowed the use of his truck and trailer as well. Apparently, he liked to frequent the bar at the Wretched Lobster with a woman that was not his wife.

"I don't really want to get killed, either," Langdon said. "If you have a better plan, let's hear it."

Amanda had returned, and she, on the landline, and Jewell, on her cell phone, were calling hotels in the greater Brunswick area and asking for Eddie Jones, hoping that they would find the hideout for Latricia. Jamal was using Chabal's cell phone for the same purpose, but off in a corner by himself. They thought it best to keep Langdon and Amanda's phone lines clear for any calls from Danny T. and Jackson Brooks.

"I don't think they'll kill Richam if the police come down the driveway," Chabal said. "There's no way they're going to be able to pin the charges on you once Latricia is freed. With her and Jamal's testimony? Plus being discovered with the body?"

"Fast Eddie, the gentleman you found so charming in Boston on Sunday, had probably just arrived from hacking up Goldilocks. Yet, he had time to chat with us, flirt with you, and try to send us down the wrong path."

"Yeah, so what are you saying?"

"I'm saying the man is a twisted puppy who doesn't know right from wrong and lives in his own reality, is what I'm saying. You never know which way a dude like that is going to go. He might kill Richam just for spite."

"Langdon, it's 11:15," Jamal called across the room.

"We'll find her, just sit tight."

"Dude, we got to be at the farmhouse at noon or my mom is dead."

"Patience, Jamal, patience."

"I don't want to lose you," Chabal said. "Now that I have you. Do I have you?"

Langdon looked at her. "It's not going to be easy."

Chabal was about to ask whether he meant their relationship or the rescue operation but never got the chance.

The phone rang.

"Hello," Langdon said.

"Langdon, this is Danny T."

"What do you got? Give it to me?"

"You said the Brunswick area."

"Did you find her or not?"

"And they are not using the name Latricia Jones or Eddie Jones."

Langdon didn't have time for the normal foreplay required by Danny T. when exchanging gossip, especially information as exciting as this. "Tell me in the next two seconds or I'm going to come find you and shoot you."

"Okay, okay, I'm just saying, okay," Danny T. said. "I can't be certain because the names don't match, but I heard that a couple fitting your description checked into the Motel Six down in Portland. You know, off Exit 8 on Riverside by the strip club?"

"Yeah, okay, I can find it. You know what name they're using?"

"My buddy hooks me up with a room down there once in awhile, you know, when I'm, uh, attending business?"

"You got a name?"

"He said that a real classy black lady and this huge man came in. Sam, he thought the guy must be a professional football player or something."

"Danny T."

"Ray Johnson. Room 22."

"Thank you." Langdon hung up.

"Your buddy found my mom?" Jamal asked.

"Think so," Langdon said. He called Jackson Brooks with the information.

"It's 11:35," Jewell said.

"Okay, let's get on the road," Langdon said. "We'll meet with the boys at the trail by Crystal Springs around the corner from the farmhouse. That way, we'll be only a couple of minutes out when we get the phone call that Latricia is safe."

Langdon and Jamal went in the Lincoln. Chabal and Jewell rode in Amanda's Subaru wagon. It was about a ten-minute ride. They left Coffee Dog behind.

"Is my mom going to be okay?" Jamal asked.

"Jackson Brooks is a professional. She'll be fine," Langdon said.

"What happens if Fast Eddie escapes?"

"What do you mean?"

"He believes in that whole 'eye for an eye' thing. He'll come after her. He'll come after us."

"The police will get him. Amanda shared the whole case with Jackson Brooks, and they're out looking for him right now. As soon as we walk in the door of the farmhouse, Amanda is going to call him and tell him where we are. He isn't going to get away."

"You think Fast Eddie would really kill Richam if the police showed up?"

"It doesn't matter now, because he's going to kill him in fifteen minutes if we don't get over there." Langdon took the left onto

Pleasant Hill Road.

"We don't have to wait for word that my mom is safe. We can go in on time, just to be sure," Jamal said.

"Okay."

"Man, I really fucked everything up. Everything. My mom, college, basketball—poof! All gone."

Langdon looked at the boy, who was clearly coming undone. "Are you willing to testify against Rick Pious?" The words were spoken so softly Jamal had to lean forward to hear them.

"Yes," he said, just as quietly.

"I'm sure the school would have to suspend him pending a trial. Would you still play for Coach Helot?"

"I don't know."

"The world is full of second chances, Jamal. Let's take care of this business, and then we'll figure out your life."

Langdon pulled into the small cutout at the side of the road. There was a large Ford truck parked there hooked to a trailer. Three lime green snowmobiles with flames splashed across them purred gently at the entrance to the trail.

Langdon climbed out of the car. Before he could say anything, his phone rang. It was brief. All eyes were on Langdon as he put the phone back in the holster on his belt.

"Latricia is safe," he said to the group. "Everybody set with the plan?"

Chapter 32

Chabal nestled the Colt M4 carbine under her chin and sited down the barrel at the farmhouse below. Bart had handed her the shorter automatic weapon back at the truck with a grim look. The farmhouse was only about a half mile through the woods, just off a trail used by snowmobilers and cross-country skiers.

She looked to Bart on her right who was settling his bulk into the snow with a Remington hunting rifle, and then to her left, where Amanda had a .22—she had never fired a weapon before in her life. The three of them had settled themselves into a copse of trees facing the driveway, then the farmhouse, with the barn to the right. The driveway led off to the left, several hundred yards to the road.

A car idled partway down the driveway. It was Amanda's job to keep that car from coming to the aid of the occupants in the house. Chabal was supposed to shoot high, blasting the second floor more as intimidation than anything else. After all, Langdon, Richam, and Jamal were going to be inside as well. Bart was going to be aiming for people. There was a large plate glass window facing them, and shadowy figures could be seen moving behind it.

Over a small rise to the right, behind the barn, the three Arctic Cats idled. Jewell, 4 by Four, and Starling manned these beasts. Their job was to wait for gunfire, and then come in for the evacuation like choppers in a Vietnam War movie. Jewell had brought her own Smith & Wesson 1970 model pistol, and Bart had given his Glock and Sig Sauer to 4 by Four and Starling with a warning not to lose them.

Since Chabal had grown up with four brothers and was, second to Bart, the one most familiar with weapons in the group. She'd been to the firing range with Bart several times, and it was for this reason he'd entrusted her with the automatic weapon. She'd hunted in her younger years, and shot four deer and various birds, but never had she fired at a human being. She hoped she wouldn't have to today.

At the same time, if it came down to Richam or Langdon versus some gangster from Boston, she was fully set and ready to fire to kill. Or Jamal for that matter, as the kid seemed to be decent enough, even if he had dragged them all into this mess with his burglaries and lies. It seemed that there had been weighty forces shoving him towards the wrong path, though she, like the others, sensed that under it all was a vulnerable kid who just needed a loving family.

Partway down the slope, Chabal saw a snowy owl perched in a pine. He blended in well with the ice-sheathed tree, and she wouldn't have seen him except he turned his head. She realized that the bird had heard Langdon's car in the driveway. She watched as the Lincoln pulled up next to the waiting car, and paused, before continuing down to the house. Langdon and Jamal got out and walked to the house. The door was visible to Chabal as she watched it open to reveal Fast Eddie, who gestured Langdon and Jamal to enter. And then the door shut behind them.

"We're seriously not packing any heat?" Jamal asked.

They had waited five minutes to give the others time to go set up the covering and rescue operation and were now pulling back onto the road to go to the farmhouse.

"Just the pistol Bart taped under the front bumper," Langdon said.

"We're gonna just walk in there rent-a-cop style?"

"What's that mean?"

"Unarmed, man, with no piece, no way to protect ourselves."

"Well, yeah, I guess the answer would be yes. The first thing these guys are going to do is search us. They're not amateurs."

"They're not gonna search me," Jamal said. "They think I'm one of them."

"What if they do?"

"I just say I picked it up to protect me from you, is what I say, man."

Langdon considered this, but then he was turning into the driveway and there was a car, dark and ominous, idling about fifty feet down on the left. It wasn't a bad idea, but it was too late now. He pulled up next to the black Oldsmobile and rolled down the window.

"You Langdon?"

"Yeah."

"And that's Jamal Jones?"

"Yeah."

"You get any stupid ideas?"

"No."

The man stared at them as if his will alone could cause them to admit their deceit. "Okay, pull on down and park in front of the barn. Go to the front door. They're waiting for you."

As Langdon pulled forward, the man pulled the Oldsmobile sideways blocking the driveway from further entry. "We got to make sure that we lay eyes on Richam," he said.

"That won't be no problem. Fast Eddie, he wants you to know what's coming. He sure does talk angry about you, man. I don't know what you did that pissed him off so much, but it was when he was trashing you, I realized you were my best bet."

"Good," Langdon said. "Angry men make mistakes."

"You still haven't told me what the play is, man."

"Guess I won't know until I see the lay of the land."

The barn was a weather-beaten red, the paint wearing away to expose the boards underneath. The farmhouse was the old style, with an extension to one side of the kitchen originally for firewood and now probably transformed into a bedroom. The dining room was on the other side, flowing into a living room, with another extension built more recently, perhaps for a study. There was a second floor over the original part with a Cape roof. In the not too distant past a large picture window had been inserted into the front wall of the living room.

Langdon and Jamal got out of the car and went to the door, studiously not looking up into the trees on the right to see if their friends were there. Before they could knock, Fast Eddie opened the door. Off to his side was a surly Black man with large eyes and a hard face with a Heckler & Koch USP45, the ugly pistol pointing directly at Langdon's head.

"Come in, come in," Fast Eddie said. "Don't you worry about Carl. Jamal can tell you he's meek as a lamb."

Jamal's face belied these comforting words. They entered the kitchen, and a third man stepped forward to frisk both of them. The man had virtually no neck, his thick head disappearing directly into his barrel-shaped body. As far as Langdon could tell, there were only the three of them.

"Where's Richam?" he asked.

"In the living room," Fast Eddie said. "Right this way." He gestured toward the doorway leading within.

The living room was a long, narrow, and sprawling space. It was perfectly designed for a large family—or a gang of thieves. Richam was in the far corner tied to a support beam that ran across the ceiling. The rope went around his neck and stretched him upward so that he had to stand on his toes to prevent choking. Gray duct tape was wrapped around his mouth. A cinder block was suspended from each hand making it even more difficult for him to stand on his toes just to keep breathing. His white shirt was torn and dirty and had a series of circles hand-drawn on it surrounded by red splotches.

Langdon went to cross the room but was restrained by Fast Eddie. He turned to see Carl pointing the ominous Heckler & Koch at his face. No-Neck picked up a sub-machine gun with a drum magazine similar to ones Langdon had seen in old gangster movies and took up position at the large plate glass window looking down the driveway. It seemed that Fast Eddie had a bit of nostalgia to him.

"Patience, Mr. Langdon," Fast Eddie said. "You will soon get an opportunity to better check the welfare of your friend."

"I thought we were just meeting to come to an agreement," Langdon said, playing the game as established by Jamal.

"In any negotiation, having the upper hand is a crucial element, wouldn't you agree, Mr. Langdon?"

"What do you want?"

Fast Eddie smiled maliciously. "First, I would like to welcome you. It is truly an honor to be in the presence of Brunswick's number one villain."

"As it is good to be here." Langdon forced a broad smile upon his face for the man who had killed his mentor, framed him for murder, and currently had his good friend strung up in the corner. "Should I call you Fast Eddie or Uncle Eddie?"

"Fast Eddie is fine, seeing as you are too white to be my nephew."

"I think perhaps I will just call you Eddie Munster."

Fast Eddie's smile dried up quicker than dew in the desert. "If you knew what was good for you, you'd be on your knees calling me Master Eddie."

"You are the spitting image of Eddie Munster, now that I think about it," Langdon said. "Look, you got that same triangular cow lick pointing at your nose, the big old buck teeth, and the pointy ears."

Carl went and picked up a machete leaning against the wall by Richam. He pressed the blade against the man's throat and looked at Fast Eddie for guidance. Richam's legs were quivering under the exertion and sweat ran in rivulets down his face.

"What did you have in mind?" Langdon asked.

"Death," Fast Eddie said.

"How about you let Richam go and you can kill me instead?"

"But I already have both of you. What's in it for me?"

"I will sign a confession that I was behind the burglaries and that it was me who killed Goldilocks."

"But your friend Richam will be running around telling another story," Fast Eddie said. "I can't have that. What we have here is a dilemma."

"So, what is it you have in mind?"

"Are you a sporting man, Mr. Langdon?"

"Sure."

"Perhaps we could have a game of skill to determine the outcome of our dilemma."

"What do you propose?"

"Darts, Mr. Langdon. The ancient game first played 700 years ago by bored soldiers using spears and wine casks."

"Sure," Langdon said. After all, he was quite proficient at the game, having been taught by none other than Goldilocks when he was just a youngster.

Fast Eddie clapped his hands in delight. "The dartboard and choice of weapons, please," he said.

No-Neck set his gun down and picked up a thin piece of cardboard with a crude dartboard drawn upon it. It had a string taped to the top in a loop, and he took this and hung it around Richam's neck, carefully pressing the tape back into place when done.

"Don't look so alarmed, Mr. Langdon," Fast Eddie said. "At first we weren't going to use a board other than the man's shirt, but it seems you really have to hurl those tiny javelins so they stick into the flesh, and I worried that he might not live through the game."

"You are a sick fuck," Langdon said.

Fast Eddie shrugged. "It shouldn't be much worse than a bee sting by the time it gets through the cardboard."

No-Neck brought over the darts, long sleek missiles with razor-sharp points. Langdon took the set with the purple barrel and shaft, while the feathers of the flight were yellow, subconsciously choosing the Viking's team colors. This gave Fast Eddie the red and black.

Langdon looked around the room. Carl was sitting in a chair facing them in the corner opposite Richam, probably only ten feet away in the narrow living room. He had his Heckler & Koch held across his lap. No-Neck had gone back to his post by the window with the Thompson pointing straight up in the air. Richam stood straining to keep from choking, his nostrils flared in fear, his eyes almost as wide as the room. Fast Eddie approached a strip of duct tape on the hardwood floor in front of Richam.

"Carl said eight feet is standard, but I believe he was thinking soft tip. These steel tips should be thrown from a distance of seven feet nine and a quarter inch. How about we play 501?" Fast Eddie was enjoying himself immensely. 501 was the most common darts game in which both players start with 501 points and subtracted their points as they went until they reached zero.

Langdon's glazed eyes took in the hopeless scene, hearing but not comprehending the words.

"Let's shoot for honors," Fast Eddie said. He threw the dart forcefully, its tip piercing the cardboard and lodging in Richam's stomach about a quarter inch outside the bullseye. "Beat that," he said, clapping his hands again.

Langdon stepped up, eyed the board, his friend, and tossed the dart, which hit the cardboard and clattered to the floor.

"Out of play." Eddie clapped his hands. He went forward and pulled his dart from Richam's flesh, and then retrieved Langdon's from the floor. "I go first," he said, handing Langdon his dart.

Langdon looked at Jamal and shifted his eyes to No-Neck by the window. Eddie threw his first dart. "Double 20," he said. He added another 20 and an 18 to the score. "58," he said to Carl. "What's that?"

"443, boss," Carl replied.

"Your turn," Fast Eddie said, turning back to Langdon. His pinstriped jacket flapped open to reveal a shoulder holster.

Langdon's first dart hit the board and hung on. The second hit the bullseye, but both darts fell to the floor. He threw the next one with more oomph and scored a triple 20.

"Very impressive, Mr. Langdon. I believe that is 60 for you. What's that make it, Carl?"

Carl licked his lips nervously, whether because adding was difficult or because the score might anger Fast Eddie. "The private dick has 441, boss, and you got 443."

"I didn't think you'd have, what is the word you Mainers like to use, moxie? I seriously doubted you'd have the moxie to drive the tips into your friend's body like that. Perhaps I have underestimated you, Mr. Langdon?"

Langdon grunted and went to retrieve his darts. He pulled the one from the board, mouthing the words *be ready* to Richam. He risked a look over his shoulder where Fast Eddie was waiting impatiently. No-Neck stood looking out the window, but Jamal had gotten the hint and had moved over closer to him. Carl was smiling to himself at some private joke.

With a deep breath, Langdon leaned over, scooping one of the darts in his hand and came up with a side-arm delivery. Carl did not even have time to blink as the dart buried itself in his eye with a sucking-popping noise, his eyelid trying desperately to close but prevented by the shaft, the point into and through the retina. Carl screamed a high-pitched wail, surprising for such a large man.

Langdon took two steps towards the machete and away from Richam, aware that the man with the Tommy Gun was bringing the weapon to bear on him. He grasped the long blade and swiveled around as Jamal shoved No-Neck hard, the rattle of bullets redirected into the floor. The inertia of the man's 300 pounds barely staggered, and he was bringing the weapon back up and in line as Langdon swung the machete overhead.

Fast Eddie had also produced a pistol and was yelling something when the heavens exploded. Upon hearing the gunshots inside Bart had pulled the trigger, his first shot piercing No-Neck, who was framed in the window, in the shoulder, as Chabal unleashed thirty rounds into the mid-section of the house in the snap of a finger. Fast Eddie dove behind the couch as Langdon severed the rope holding Richam, and then went about sawing the ropes attached to the cinder blocks.

"Look out!" Jamal yelled.

Langdon turned to see the kid tackling Fast Eddie, his legs driving through the blow in a hit that would have had the MECI football coach recruit him the following year if they got it on tape.

Carl stood up, his Heckler & Koch wavering in his hand as he tried to aim with only one eye. Langdon managed to cut through the second rope, and then turned and threw the machete at the man's hard face, the weapon smacking flat against Carl's forehead as he pulled the trigger, the bullet grazing Richam's bicep.

Fast Eddie had lost his gun in the struggle and was circling warily with Jamal. Langdon stepped forward and kicked Carl in the private parts, doubling the man over in further agony. As Richam toppled to the floor, Langdon scooped up the machete and turned to face Fast Eddie just as he picked up his pistol.

"Now you die!" Fast Eddie said.

Richam rolled over and into Fast Eddie's legs sending the bullet whizzing past Langdon's cheek. Fast Eddie regained his balance and brought the weapon to bear again, but Jamal crashed a cinder block over his head, driving him to his knees.

"Fuck you, man," Jamal said.

The back of his head a gooey mess, Fast Eddie somehow raised his head, a glazed look on his face. He struggled to raise his hand, which still held the gun. Langdon took two steps forward and buried the machete into the side of his neck just above the collarbone.

Langdon thought this was a good time to make their escape. "C'mon, let's get out of here," he yelled, half-dragging Richam along, as his friend's limbs were yet far from cooperating. Jamal turned and followed them. They charged for the kitchen door as No-Neck brought the tommy gun to bear just as his head tilted forward, and the rear of his skull went flying past them.

Carl took three shots at them as they dove through the opening that had so recently been the large plate glass window past the body of No-Neck who hadn't yet fallen to the ground, even though he was already dead.

"Get to the back of the barn." Langdon dragged Richam to his feet.

Before they could get there, the whistle of lead past his ear made him dive behind the car they'd arrived in. The guard in the driveway had attempted to get to the house when the shooting started, but Amanda had managed to hit the windshield with one of her shots, urging the man to exit the vehicle. He was now firing over his open door.

Langdon pulled the pistol loose from the duct tape under the bumper. It was a Walther P99, a blunt ugly weapon. "Can you run fifty feet?" he asked Richam.

"I can help him," Jamal gasped.

Carl had moved to the kitchen window and was shooting at the car they hid behind, trying his best to stay out of sight of the shooters in the copse of trees facing the farmhouse. Over the sound of this gunfire they could hear the high whine of the Arctic Cats coming over the hill behind the barn.

"Okay, when Chabal opens fire again. Now that we're out of the house, she won't have to shoot high."

As if on cue, the angry clangor of the Colt M4 began belching, laying waste to the façade of the farmhouse. "Go!" Langdon came to one knee over the hood of the Lincoln and aimed at the car in the driveway, sending five shots screaming into the metal. He then turned and followed Jamal and Richam, scrambling towards the corner of the barn. As he dove around to safety, Jewell, Starling, and 4 by Four came skidding to a halt on the brightly-colored snowmobiles.

As Langdon got on behind Starling, he could hear the sound of sirens in the distance, and then nothing but the shriek of the engines as they revved and went hurtling over the hill to safety.

Five Years Later

The noise was deafening. And the game had not even started yet. The crowd was on its feet yelling, stamping their feet, and going altogether crazy. Chabal had never been to an event like this before. They were at the Fleet Center in Boston for Game Six of the opening round of the playoffs.

She held tightly to Langdon's hand so as to not get lost. Her kids were running down the cement steps ahead with Missouri who was just a couple of years from becoming a teenager. The four of them were still very much children, relishing the excitement of the moment. The kids were held up by security, but Langdon held their tickets aloft, catching the guard's eye, and they were waved through to the floor seats underneath the basket. Second row. Jewell and Richam were already in their seats, sitting next to Latricia Jones.

As they took their seats, Langdon squeezed Chabal's hand and looked out onto the gleaming court. The immediate reason for the crowd's frenzy was the face on the Jumbotron over center court, also the reason they were here, for that face was none other than Jamal Jones, whose spectacular play had almost certainly cemented the star status he'd so far shown in the series. Langdon's gaze came to rest on Richam, and the events of that cataclysmic winter afternoon five years earlier came hurtling back.

After the shootout at the farmhouse they'd taken Richam directly to the hospital, where he was treated and released with no serious physical injuries other than strained muscles and flesh wounds from the darts, though as for the psychological damage, only time would tell.

Bart, Amanda, and Chabal had kept the two surviving goons pinned down until the police arrived. Fast Eddie was quite dead. No-Neck was also dead. Carl was screaming in agony as the adrenalin of the moment had given way to the pain of a pierced eyeball. The man in the driveway came away unscathed. In subsequent weeks, Fast Eddie had been revealed as the kingpin of an organization that dealt in burglary, gambling, and prostitution. He was posthumously convicted of criminal threatening and terrorizing, kidnapping, aggravated assault, and for the murder of Robert Southie, aka Goldilocks. The charges against Jamal and Latricia were dropped in exchange for their testimony.

The ensuing publicity had been another boon for the mystery bookshop and private detective businesses. Langdon and Chabal had both gotten divorced, one more amicably than the other, and three years later had gotten married in a raucous celebration in their backyard.

"Wow, how did we get such great seats?" Richam asked.

"Connections," Langdon said.

"Fantastic," Jewell said.

Latricia Jones gave Langdon a tight hug and whispered into his ear, "Thank you."

"For seats like these, I might offer my services as a dartboard more often," Richam said.

"For seats like these," Jewell said, "I might rent you out as a dartboard more often."

"Bart! Jimmy! Star! Over here!" Chabal was hollering and jumping to gain the attention of the hulking cop, the diminutive lawyer, and the ex-alcoholic.

The test results for 4 by Four had come back negative for HIV, a sigh of relief for all of them over the false alarm. Bart had earned a slap on the wrist from the police department for his involvement helping a wanted man prove his innocence. This hadn't bothered him at all, as he was used to his tactics being frowned upon by the top brass.

Jamal scored the first basket of the game with a soft floater in the lane, and the crowd went berserk.

Rick Pious had been arrested and convicted of rape. Jerry Peccance had been fired as headmaster, and while it hadn't been proven that he had knowledge of what was going on, his reputation was in tatters. Ed Helot had taken over the head coaching position and had welcomed Jamal back to the team. While the season had been largely wasted, Jamal had gotten the SAT scores necessary to get into Boston College, where he had played spectacularly. He was currently being considered a top contender for the NBA's Rookie of the Year.

Jamal hit a jumper from thirty feet, and the group from Brunswick came to their feet screaming.

At halftime, Jamal came over and hugged his mother and high-fived everybody. His body was glistening with sweat, and his eyes were glowing with the joy of being a man allowed to do what he loved most in life. Of course, 30,000 fans chanting your name can have that effect as well.

Langdon pulled the young man into an embrace. "Once you're done winning this game—Chabal, Bart, and I want a rematch."

"You're on," Jamal said.

The beer continued to flow freely in the stands.

The game resumed intensely on the court.

Friends cheered and groaned together. For the living, life went on.

About the Author:

Matt Cost aka Matthew Langdon Cost

Over the years, Cost has owned a video store, a mystery bookstore, and a gym. He has also taught history and coached just about every sport imaginable.

During those years—since age eight, actually—his true passion has been writing. *I Am Cuba: Fidel Castro and the Cuban Revolution* (Encircle Publications, March, 2020) was his first traditionally published novel.

Mainely Power is the first of the Mainely Mysteries trilogy featuring private detective Goff Langdon, followed, of course, by *Mainely Fear*. *Mainely Money*, book three in the series, will be released in March of 2021.

Cost now lives in Brunswick, Maine, with his wife, Harper. There are four grown children: Brittany, Pearson, Miranda, and Ryan. A chocolate Lab and a basset hound round out the mix. He now spends his days at the computer, writing.

CPSIA information can be obtained
at www.ICGtesting.com
Printed in the USA
BVHW050615240722
642291BV00001B/17